SPIRIT OF THE FALLEN

WHITE HAVEN HUNTERS BOOK ONE

TJ GREEN

Spirit of the Fallen

Mountolive Publishing

©2020 TJ Green

ISBN 978-1-99-004705-3

ISBN Paperback: 978-1990047060

ISBN Hardback: 978-1-991313-11-9

Cover Design by Fiona Jayde Media

Editing by Missed Period Editing

www.tjgreenauthor.com

Contents

One

Shadow watched Gabe roll his shoulders and square up, ready to attack again. He held the sword easily, like it weighed nothing, and she assessed his stance, deciding how he would strike this time.

If she was honest, it didn't really matter; she was pretty confident she'd best him, despite his strength. She had agility on her side. She raised an eyebrow at him, and the corner of her mouth turned up as he narrowed his eyes at her.

"Feeling pleased with yourself, aren't you?"

She shrugged. "Why wouldn't I? I've beaten you twice this morning."

"Just to remind you, I haven't fought with a sword for a long time."

"Well then, this is the perfect way for you to learn!"

He prowled around the perimeter of the barn where they had set up their practice area, and she mirrored his actions. The barn was rustic and basic, but it was solid, giving them adequate protection from the rain and the winds that blew in across the moor above White Haven. The ground was made of beaten earth and it was covered in sawdust and straw, providing a reasonably soft landing when they tumbled and rolled.

Gabe struck quickly, covering the space between them in a split-second, and she parried, reminding herself that his lightning-quick reflexes were similar to her own.

"You know, I'm still recovering from my encounter with the Empusa," she reminded him as she retaliated.

He continued to attack, and responded in between swings of his sword. "Well, if you involve yourself with the affairs of the White Haven witches, what do you expect?"

"They needed my help!"

He laughed. "And you saw a way to help yourself!"

"That is not true!" She glared at him, furious, and rolled under his legs, swinging aggressively at his calf, and he dived over her, on the attack immediately.

She regained her footing and circled him again. The Nephilim's size still impressed her. He was a good deal taller than she was, and muscular. Over the last couple of months since she had first met him, his dark brown, almost black hair had grown a few inches, and he wore it swept back, showing his hard-edged jaw. He smirked at her. He'd caught her off balance and they both knew it.

"I hit a nerve," he told her. "It distracted you."

"I like the witches. You make me sound like a mercenary."

"I thought that's exactly what you are."

"Sometimes I've had to be, but not always by choice."

She struck at him, whirling across the room like a dervish, and they traded blow for blow, up close and personal. She tried to press her advantage, pinning him against the wall in a dusty corner of the barn. He let her draw closer, watching her with a gleam in his eye.

"And now?" he asked.

"Now I need to make a life. I'm about to earn a lot of money."

"You think. If Beckett doesn't short-change you." He was referring to Harlan Beckett, the American man who worked for the Orphic Guild, the mysterious organisation that obtained occult and arcane objects for private buyers.

"If he does, I won't sell!"

They were inches apart, her sword under his chin, the cold blade against his neck.

"You're good, Shadow, but you need to be careful. Your overconfidence may cost you one day."

She smirked and dropped her weapon, backing away from him. "It hasn't yet."

"Hasn't it? You're stuck here, aren't you? If you hadn't forced your way past the coven's perimeter circle on Samhain, you'd be back in the Otherworld by now." He held his sword loosely, stepping close to her again, his dark eyes holding her gaze. "I'm serious. You should be more careful."

Shadow fell silent for a moment, knowing he was right. She had been reckless that night. The energy of the Wild Hunt had heated her blood and made her act rashly, but in her defence, she really hadn't thought anyone would stop Herne. The Cornwall Coven witches may not have fey magic, but their magic was strong, and they commanded it well. She refused to let Gabe intimidate her. "I'm fey. I'm faster than any human. And you."

He grinned. "You might be faster, but you're not stronger, and one day I'll beat you at sword fighting, too." He headed to the hook on the wall and pulled a towel free, wiping the sweat from his face. It may have been cold out, but they had both become hot while they fought. "Have you heard from Beckett?"

He always called Harlan by his surname, and Shadow detected a brooding resentment behind his words. "I'm expecting his call any minute. The last time I spoke to him, he said he'd found a buyer and was negotiating a price." She grabbed her own towel, putting her sword in her scabbard while she dried off.

"Where have you put the Empusa's sword?"

"Somewhere safe, don't you worry."

"I'm not about to steal it! Are you sure you wouldn't be better off keeping it?"

She shook her head. "I've examined it carefully, on my own and with El, and we can't find any special qualities or hidden powers, other than its age and skilled forging and design. It's unique, and the pair of them together would sell for a small fortune, but El is refusing to sell hers." She was referring to Elspeth, one of the White Haven witches who owned The Silver Bough jewellery shop, and who was particularly adept with metalwork. She continued, "We've even tested them together, and still can't detect anything unusually magical—you know, enhanced abilities when used at the same time."

It had been over two weeks since Shadow and the White Haven witches had fought and defeated Caitlin, and retrieved The Callanish Ring. Caitlin had turned into the Empusa in the campgrounds of the Crossroads Circus, and fortunately they had been helped by the Raven King and the Green Man. Shadow was sure they wouldn't have defeated her without them. The Raven King had taken her and her relatives to the Underworld to face justice. The Empusa had carried two swords that had made the fight particularly difficult, and Shadow had to reluctantly admit that she had met her match.

That night, when she had escorted Harlan away from the wild forest that had sprung up under the command of the Green Man, they had talked for quite a while about how they could help each other. He had promised to discuss their meeting with the director of the London branch, and said he knew of several potential customers for the sword.

Gabe flung his towel on a long bench that ran across one side of the barn and pulled on a sweatshirt. "I can't believe El won't sell it."

"She loves weaponry, and besides, I think she's still testing hers." Shadow was pulling on her jacket when the phone in her pocket rang, and she answered it, aware that Gabe was watching her. "Harlan, we were just discussing you."

His voice was low. "Only good things, I hope! You'll be pleased to know that one of my clients wishes to make you an offer." He named an impressive sum. "Obviously we'll be taking a commission, but be assured this is the best possible price—for both of us." He paused, and then added, as if he sensed some reluctance from her, "I haggled hard, and I'm excellent at it."

Shadow grinned. She and Gabe had discussed how much to accept, and although they had never negotiated arcane objects before in this world, Shadow had done it plenty of times in the Otherworld. She'd learnt to quadruple any price offered, and knew collectors would pay. But, if Harlan was taking a commission, it was in his best interest to get the highest price, too.

"You know what, Harlan, I bet I could make it go higher, but as this is the start of our beautiful friendship, I'll accept that. Just tell him that I won't be so generous next time. And that's in both our interests."

Harlan's tone hardened. "You know that he'll pay much more for the pair."

"But the other is not for sale, so let it drop," she said sharply. Of all the witches, El was her favourite. She called her 'sister' for a reason. She was similar in height to her, and her love of gems, weapons, metalwork, and forging made her interests comparable to her own. In a world where she was finding her feet, her friendship with El had been unexpected. There was an edge to her that she liked, and Shadow was not about to betray her.

He sighed. "Fine. I have your account, so I'll organise the deposit straight away, but I need to get the sword before we complete the transaction. How do you fancy a trip to our headquarters?"

"In London?" Shadow asked, staring wide-eyed at Gabe.

"Yes. I'll introduce you to the director, too. You've intrigued him."

"Hold on." Shadow thought quickly. She was sure she could handle this on her own, but she'd like backup, just in case. She'd be on their ground, not hers, and that would put her at a disadvantage with an organisation she knew nothing about. She covered the phone and said to Gabe, "I need to take the sword to London. Will you come?"

He nodded straight away. "Sure, I'll get Nahum to take over at Caspian's warehouse."

Harlan hadn't met Gabe, and Shadow wasn't sure if this would be an issue, but she pressed the phone back to her ear. "No problem, but I'm bringing Gabe. He's my partner, after all."

There was a slight pause before he answered. "Okay, I'm confident I can make the director agree."

A wave of suspicion washed over her. "Why wouldn't he?"

"He's just wary about people he doesn't know coming into our branch," Harlan said smoothly. "We tend to restrict visitors, and he knows about you, but not Gabe."

"Tell him we work together, and if you want the sword, he'd better say yes."

"He will. Shall we say Friday at one? That should give you time to get here."

"Sure, send me your address."

"I'll text it. See you soon," he said, and rang off.

Shadow realised she'd been holding herself tensely, and she took a deep breath of relief. She raised an eyebrow at Gabe, who was still leaning against the wall, watching her. "We're on."

He nodded. "Good. We'll take the train in—it will be easier than driving."

Shadow had never travelled by train before, and had only just got used to cars and bikes. There was nothing like them in the Otherworld, but they made getting around much simpler. She couldn't decide whether that was a good thing or not. "London is big. Do you know where we're going?"

"No, but that's what maps and taxis are for. We'll be fine." He pushed away from the wall and headed to the door. "I'll go and speak to Nahum, and then I'm heading to the shower. What are you up to?"

Shadow still had a lot of nervous energy, especially after the phone call, and she needed peace and quiet. "I need to ride. I think I'll head to Ravens' Wood." The ancient forest that had grown in a matter of moments was the place she felt most at home now, and she spent long periods of time there.

Gabe held the barn door open for her and then headed to the house, calling over his shoulder, "Sure, I'll see you later."

Within ten minutes, Shadow had saddled her horse, Kailen, and was riding across the moors towards the wood that bordered White Haven Castle. It was early March, and spring flowers were starting to appear. Hedgerows were buzzing with life, and the birds were busy making nests and preparing for their small broods. She paused on a rise along the downs and inhaled deeply, smiling at the scent. She could feel new life all around her and it settled in her blood, making her even more restless. At the foot of the hills she could see White Haven nestling in the folds of the valley, the jumble of buildings heading down to the harbour. She couldn't see it all from here, but her mind filled in what was obstructed, and she thought of her friends in their shops and businesses. It was mid-afternoon, and the sea was a brittle blue, the waves choppy with the brisk wind that cut through her jacket.

This was home now, and she considered herself lucky. Despite her less than auspicious arrival, she had been welcomed, albeit cautiously, and she had to admit that she liked it here. White Haven's charm was infectious, more so if you embraced magic. The land rustled with it, especially since Imbolc and the appearance of the Green Man. It made her feel closer to the Otherworld, the place she'd most likely never see again. And she could see beings here that she knew no one else could.

She was distracted by one of them now, a small, wizened figure that popped up out of nowhere. It was a tiny pixie with brown and green skin, skinny limbs, and an angular face. Her heart swelled, and she laughed and waved, but it didn't reciprocate. They were grumpy creatures, and it scowled at her and then disappeared with a *pop*. She had been surprised when she had first seen them; she hadn't thought that any creature from the Otherworld would be here, and they gave her hope that she'd find others. Admittedly, they weren't like the pixies in the Otherworld, which were taller, brawnier, and vicious fighters. These were their smaller cousins, and their size helped them remain unseen. And they were also stuck here, like she was.

Kailen stamped his feet, eager to be off, and she turned him towards Ravens' Wood and let him race, crouching low against him. It was exhilarating, and it was with reluctance that she slowed down to cross the lane and enter the leafy shadows of the old forest.

Silence fell like a cloak, and she slipped from Kailen's back, leading him along the ancient paths. It felt warmer in here, and bright green leaves were already unfurling around her. She meandered for a while before she spotted a familiar figure kneeling in the undergrowth. It was Briar, the earth witch, and she must have heard her, because she looked up and smiled.

"Shadow! I was just thinking about you. How are you?"

"I'm well, thank you. You look full of spring." It was an odd thing to say, but it was true. Briar's eyes gleamed with old magic, and her dark hair fell thick and wild down her back. She was wearing a heavy jumper and one of her long skirts, and she'd taken her boots off, so her bare feet could wriggle into the earth.

Briar stood up, brushing grass off her clothing. She'd been gathering roots and herbs, and an overflowing basket sat to the side. "This spring I feel more acutely than any other. My blood sings with it! And look at my hair!" She dragged her fingers through it. "It resists all attempts to comb it. It's nuts."

"That's the Green Man for you. He's wild, and he's a part of you now." Shadow frowned. "I must have lost my touch. Normally, no one can hear me coming, but you did."

"The earth told me." She gestured around her. "This place feels you, you must know that. It feels me, too. I can't work out whether I feel wilder here, or more at peace. It's so weird. Hunter likes it, too."

"Your wolf-shifter? That doesn't surprise me. I told you he had a sort of fey blood."

For once, Briar didn't deny their relationship, and she laughed. "I told him that, and I think he quite liked it. And what about you? Did you hear from Harlan?"

Shadow nodded as she stroked Kailen's side. "Yes, he's found a buyer for the sword and offered me a lot of money. We're going to London on Friday to complete the deal."

"That's great," Briar said, nodding. "It will help you establish yourself here." A note of caution entered her voice. "But don't go alone. London is big and confusing, and I know you're not stupid, but it's very different from here."

"I'm going with Gabe. I thought it was important to have support." She hesitated as she recalled their earlier conversation, and she wondered what Briar would think. "He tells me I'm too headstrong."

Briar frowned. "You are, but you know that. And I know you've told Harlan that you're fey, but you really shouldn't tell anyone else. You need to be careful about who you trust with that knowledge. Gabe doesn't tell anybody about what he is, and we don't reveal that we're witches, other than to our close friends."

Shadow felt a ripple of unease pass through her, but she shrugged it off. "I'm fey. Anyone with any sense should take that as a warning not to mess with me."

"And it also makes you a target. Some people are devious. You must have fey like that in your world."

"Of course we do. I'm not a child. I'm years older than any of you, and have been in some interesting situations in my lifetime, and dealt with fey who are considerably more dangerous than most humans."

Briar just regarded her quietly, her dark eyes solemn. "I know, but you're new to our world, and it's important that you understand its dangers. Many people hate things that are different. It scares them—or makes them greedy. Be careful."

Shadow's annoyance increased, but as she felt Briar's magic roll off her, she sensed the wisdom in her words, which was strange from someone so young. In her race's years, Briar was like a new-born, but she was uncanny. She drew her strength from the earth, and that in itself imparted wisdom beyond normal years. And besides, she meant well.

Shadow softened her stance and smiled. "Thanks, I'll try. Anyway, you're busy, so I'll leave you to it." She turned, ready to head deeper into the forest. "Say hi to the others."

Briar nodded. "I will."

But as Shadow walked away, she felt Briar's calm regard like a weight between her shoulder blades, and she shrugged, eager to dismiss her concerns.

Friday would be fine, and it would open her up a whole new world.

Two

The headquarters of the Orphic Guild was located in an impressive building made of pale grey stone in a very exclusive area of London.

Gabe watched it from across the street, Shadow next to him. They had arrived slightly early in order to stake it out, but so far no one had gone in or out. His eyes roved over the exterior, noting the discrete cameras and alarm system, the brass plaque that announced its name, the shiny black front door, and its general air of smart respectability that made it seem impressively expensive. He hated places like this. They made his skin crawl. It reminded him of all the rich people he'd ever dealt with, and most of them were completely selfish and egocentric. No matter that it was over 2,000 years later than his previous life, the entitlement of the affluent never changed.

Shadow stirred. "We're not going to see anything from here today."

He kept his eyes on the building, but said, "You're probably right. I'm sure it will have a back entrance anyway for anyone who needs discretion."

"Don't we?" she asked.

He turned to her, needing to look down to meet her stare. "No. We're not the rich buyers who want to keep their anonymity. We're the workforce, never forget that. You can be damn sure they won't."

"You know they might have spotted us?"

"Probably, but we're not hiding. Are you ready?"

Shadow firmly gripped the sturdy black case that contained the Empusa's sword, and fire lurked behind her eyes. "In a minute," she said, distracted by the busy street, and she frowned as she studied the comings and goings. Her stance looked easy, but it wasn't, and Gabe knew she'd leap into action if something untoward happened.

Gabe admired her attitude. She had been completely separated from her kind, but that hadn't slowed her down. If anything, it had spurred her on to make a life for herself in this strange world that was full of technology, so different from her own. He knew he'd made the right decision all those weeks ago when he offered her a place to stay. He'd watched her pacing in the iron cage and recognised her fire as being similar to his own. He respected that. And he'd wanted to keep an eye on her. She was like a firecracker that was liable to go off at any point, and he didn't want her bringing disaster to their doors.

Besides, he and Shadow had lots in common. Awakening in this world had been hard for the Nephilim too, he reflected, but like Shadow they knew they were stuck here and were determined to make it work on their terms as much as possible. That meant acclimatising to modern culture. They'd arrived naked, and with no money, and had stolen clothes and cash, bought fake identification, and rented the old farmhouse that was well out of the way from anyone else.

Gabe was a warrior, and had also been an occasional mercenary with flexible morals. He and his kind had been revered and feared equally, and most of the time he had displayed his huge wings as a symbol of his difference and power. Here it was impossible, and he kept them hidden. While Shadow had revealed who she was to some people, Gabe hadn't. The witches and Newton were the only ones who knew what they were, and he aimed to keep it that way. He'd told Shadow not to divulge what they were to Harlan, and he hoped she'd honour that.

Shadow looked up at him, her violet eyes bright with the anticipated meeting. "Okay, I'm ready." She crossed the street, and Gabe's gaze lingered on her shapely figure, before quickly focusing on the job at hand. There were added benefits to her living with them, too.

Shadow rang the doorbell, and they heard a corresponding chime from deep within the building. In a few moments, the door was opened by a man in his thirties wearing a sharp dark grey suit, and a suspicious frown. He looked them up and down imperiously. "You must be Shadow." He stared at Gabe, and he had to look up to meet his eyes. "Were we expecting *you*?"

Gabe smiled coolly. "Yes, you were. Gabe Malouf." He held out his hand and gripped the other man's in his own tightly before releasing it.

"Ah yes, I do remember your name being mentioned."

He didn't introduce himself, but instead led the way into the large reception hall, which had an elaborately tiled floor, a sweeping stairway, and doors on either side, and then turned into the room on the right, which was decorated with expensive furnishings, many antique. "Take a seat, and I will let Mr Becket know you're here."

He left them alone, and Gabe grinned. "He's an ass."

"I think you intimidated him."

"I think he was trying to intimidate me. He failed." Gabe paced around, a wry smile on his face. "I think this room is meant to intimidate, too. Is it working?"

Shadow shook her head, amusement in her eyes. "No. I'm intrigued as to how much money this place makes. I may not know much about this world, but expensive stuff is the same everywhere." She frowned. "There's nothing here that looks remotely occult, though."

Gabe heard footsteps, and a voice interrupted them. "No, you won't find anything like that in this part of the building."

A tall man was in the doorway. His dark grey hair was swept back from his face, and he had a trace of stubble across a square jaw. He was dressed informally in jeans and t-shirt, and his blue eyes focussed on Shadow first as he stepped forward to shake her hand. "Hey Shadow, welcome to the Orphic Guild. I'm glad you could make it."

"Harlan. Good to see you, too. This is Gabe," she said, introducing him.

Both men eyed each other suspiciously, and Gabe was acutely aware that he was being assessed as to how much of a threat he was. That was okay. He was used to it. Again he was given a cool but firm handshake. "Hi, sorry we didn't meet last time."

Gabe smiled. "Me, too. This is quite some place!"

Harlan looked pleased. "It is, isn't it? The owner has very defined tastes, and is responsible for how it looks, even though he's not here that often. Our director, Mason Jacobs, oversees the branch, and ensures everything remains pristine." He nodded at the case in Shadow's hand. "Is that the sword?"

"It is. Want to see it again?"

"Not here. I'll take you to Mason's office, upstairs." As he led them out of the room and up the grand, sweeping staircase, he said, "The ground floor rooms are for administrative staff. The next floor is where the offices for the collectors and the director are."

Gabe's gaze travelled over the expensive artwork and antique furniture, which was mixed with modern, sleek design elements. He didn't know much about modern design, but he was certainly beginning to know what it looked like. He'd done his homework before coming here, and he also knew that Eaton Place was one of the most exclusive addresses in London. He idly wondered who the director was, and was about to ask more about him when Harlan stopped in front of a polished wooden door.

Harlan knocked as he told them, "This is Mason's office."

A voice called, "Come in."

Harlan opened the door and ushered them through.

This room was as impressive as the rest of the building, but the colours were muted and the furnishings modern, except for the huge antique desk and Persian rug on the floor. A man who Gabe estimated to be in his fifties rose from his seat behind the desk and walked around it to greet them. He had a short beard, grey hair, and a slim build. His suit was immaculate and clearly tailored, and Gabe realised that, like everything in this place, it was designed to impress. And there was something about him that Gabe didn't like.

Harlan made the introductions, and Mason offered them seats in the tan leather chairs that clustered around a table. "Please sit, the coffee will be here shortly. You do drink coffee, I hope?" His voice was clipped and assured, without any discernible accent, other than English.

"Of course," Shadow said, sitting nonchalantly and placing the case on the floor. "As long as it's good."

Mason looked slightly affronted. "I can assure you, it's excellent."

Gabe took his seat and noticed Harlan suppressing a smile. That was good. He liked Shadow, he could tell, but he was pretty sure Mason saw them as merely commodities.

Mason continued in his smooth voice, "I'm glad to finally meet you. Harlan has kept me apprised of the negotiations. You came by the sword in a very unusual way."

"You managed to get the Ring of Callanish in a very unusual way, too," she countered, amused. "Are all of your acquisitions obtained in such a manner?"

Mason looked slightly put out to be answered with a question. "We deal with arcane and occult objects, and as such they often come from unusual and sometimes dangerous places. Our collectors consequently have special skills," he nodded towards Harlan, "and we use contractors, too. That's what I would like to discuss with you today, once I have seen the sword."

He held her gaze in his own steely one, and Gabe realised he hadn't looked at him once since their first greeting. Amusing. Maybe he thought he was more bodyguard than partner.

A knock at the door broke their conversation, and the man who had let them in to the building entered with a tray containing an antique coffee pot, cups, and a platter of tiny cakes and pastries. He wordlessly put the tray on the table and left.

"Excellent, thank you, Robert," Mason murmured. "Harlan, would you be so kind?"

Harlan was already rising to pour coffee and offer the refreshments, and Gabe realised this was a longstanding ritual. He took a cup from Harlan and sipped his coffee, recognising an Arabic brew. Mason was right. It was excellent.

Shadow asked, "Would you like to see the sword now?"

"Yes, please," Mason said, sipping his coffee.

Shadow unpacked it from the case and placed it on the table, and Mason's eyes fired with excitement. He placed his cup down, pulled a pair of glasses from his pocket, and lifted the curved blade.

"Magnificent." He examined it carefully, almost reverentially, and then looked up at Shadow. "It has some slight marks, and what looks like a nick along the edge, so it's not pristine."

Shadow raised an eyebrow. "It's an ancient weapon that belonged to Hecate's servant. I think you'll find she used it often. And of course, we had quite a heated battle. My own sword is made from one of the strongest metals ever forged. The clash of our blades rang across the forest that night."

She was using her fey glamour, Gabe could tell. There was a swell of power around her that was subtle, but to his eye it was unmistakable. He was pretty sure, however, that Mason wouldn't know that. He'd just feel overwhelmed. Shadow continued, a trifle smugly, "You should thank me. I've added to its provenance."

Mason's carefully manufactured expression glazed as he placed the sword back on the table. "Ah yes, I heard you defeated a mysterious creature to get it."

She nodded. "With help. The Empusa had arrived straight from the Underworld, so it was a tricky fight."

"I've certainly heard of her," he confessed. A gleam entered his eyes. "You couldn't capture her?"

"That would be like trying to catch the wind," Shadow said sharply.

Gabe stared at Mason and spoke for the first time, a dangerous edge to his voice. "Why would you want to capture the Empusa?"

Mason looked at him properly, his eyes narrowing, and for a second didn't answer, his discomfort apparent. "I just thought it would be interesting to see such a creature up close, that's all." He sipped his coffee casually, trying to make it look as if his comment was nothing.

Shadow lowered her voice. "I saw it 'up close.' It would have killed you in a second." Her gaze ran over him dismissively. "You're too soft, too weak. She would have broken you like a doll."

Gabe winced inwardly. Ouch.

Mason didn't respond, instead turning back to Gabe. "Sorry, I didn't catch your name earlier. Are you a friend of Shadow's?"

"I'm her business partner."

"Oh! Yes, of course, Harlan told me." Mason glanced between the two of them, no doubt weighing their relationship up. "You didn't mention that though, Shadow."

She shrugged and smiled. "It doesn't matter to you, does it? Now, are you happy with the sword? I would like to finalise our deal. I have other things to do today."

They didn't really, other than a celebratory pub lunch. Both Gabe and Shadow had embraced the English pub culture.

Mason nodded, still trying to control the conversation. "Of course. The client who is buying this will be very happy with it. As you say, it has provenance, particularly its unexpected arrival in this world." He looked slightly awkward as he asked, "What about its sister sword?"

"It's not for sale, and never will be," Shadow told him.

"Just checking," he replied. "Harlan tells me you might be interested in more work in the future?"

"Yes, both of us are, actually, as long as we can fit it into our schedule."

"Of course." He rose to his feet as he brought the meeting to a close. "Excellent. We look forward to working with you again." Mason nodded at Harlan. "Please transfer the money."

There was a flurry of handshakes before they exited the room. Gabe was the last one out and he turned, catching Mason staring at him with a frown. Gabe smiled and closed the door.

𝙭 𝙭 𝙭

As soon as Harlan had dealt with Shadow and Gabe, he returned to Mason's office, knocking softly before he entered.

Mason was standing with his back to the room, looking out of the window onto Eaton Place below, and he turned, a cut glass crystal tumbler in his hand with a healthy measure of amber liquid. Whiskey, no doubt. It was his favourite drink.

"Is she what you expected?" Harlan asked as he joined him.

"No, not at all." Mason headed to the cabinet where he kept a small bar. "Whiskey? I think you should join my celebration."

Harlan knew better than to refuse. His charming boss was also ruthless, and these celebratory drinks didn't happen often, so that meant he must be impressed by Shadow.

"Of course, thank you."

Harlan waited patiently while Mason poured a couple of fingers of whiskey and passed him the glass, raising his own in salute. "Well done. She was a good find."

"She was, but I have no idea of what to really make of her, or her partner."

Mason returned to the window, watching the pedestrians and the cars coming and going on the street below.

"I saw them walk towards the Palace," Mason noted. He meant Buckingham Palace, which was a short stroll away. "I wonder how they met. I especially wonder about her. Did you say she's fey? She doesn't seem any different." He levelled a narrow, accusatory glare at Harlan.

"She may not, but I can assure you she is. She uses glamour to disguise herself. But I detected her energy—well, her magic really, while I was investigating in White Haven. There's a lot of magic in that town, but hers feels unique. It's why you employ me." Harlan had been doing his job for a long time, and he'd honed his skills in the paranormal world, often at great risk to his life.

"How did you say you found her?"

"I followed her when she left Happenstance Books, Avery Hamilton's book store. She knew I was behind her and confronted me, so over a drink in the closest pub, I explained what I wanted. It was clear from the start that we had mutual interests."

"And she took you to the castle?"

"Yes, when it was obvious that Avery wouldn't help, Shadow was my next option." Harlan sipped his whiskey, recalling the night the ancient forest grew in White Haven. He'd dreamt about it time and time again, until the event itself seemed like a dream. "I met her at an agreed rendezvous along the lane, and she took me to the edge of the field and left me with her horse, another Otherworldly animal. I saw it all happen—it was extraordinary. The rush of magic and power was unlike anything I've experienced before, and as you know, I've seen my fair share." He'd been gazing into his drink, but he looked at Mason now, and was taken aback by the fervent gleam in his eyes, but Harlan hid his surprise well. "When she came for me, with the witch called Reuben, her magic was obvious, and I could see the fey in her. She'd unleashed it for a while, and her Otherness glowed within her."

"You admire her," Mason said, watching him carefully.

"Yes. She's very honest—well, with the witches and me at least. She was stranded here after the witches defeated the Wild Hunt on Samhain."

Mason's hand tightened on his glass for a brief second, his face becoming taut. "You didn't tell me that."

"Sorry, didn't I? I guess we've been too busy finding the right buyer and arranging the sale. It's earned us a good commission."

"And her partner, he's not fey?"

Harlan shook his head. "No." He didn't like to admit that he knew nothing about Gabe. He was very reserved. All he knew was that he ran a security firm that employed a handful of men, and Shadow lived with them.

Mason fell silent, looking out of the window again, but his gaze was distant. Harlan had to remind himself that no matter how useful Mason's contacts were, and no matter how efficiently he ran the London office, he wasn't as good at detecting magic and the Otherworldly like Harlan and the other collectors. It's why Mason had moved from being a collector to becoming the director at such a young age. That put Harlan at a distinct advantage, not that he ever showed that.

Mason finally looked at him. "I can't think of a job we need her for at the moment. Can you?"

Harlan ran through their current workload. They had a number of regular clients, and they also had some who approached them for single commissions. The Guild's role was to source suitable objects by keeping an eye on auction houses, both legitimate and those of a more private nature, and advising them accordingly. Or it could be that the client would identify an object and employ them to get it. As an organisation, they were flexible. Whatever the client wanted they would find, within reason. At present they were working a few contracts, but nothing they couldn't handle. But Mason would know that more than anyone. He had oversight of everything.

"No. She has a select set of skills. I suggest we use her carefully."

Mason gave one of his most calculating smiles. "I agree. In the meantime, try and find out a little more about Mr Malouf. We employed a fey once before, but it was long before my role here. He was tricky, I know that much. Did you see her fight the Empusa?"

"No, I was too busy watching the meteoric rise of the ancient forest, and hoping I wasn't about to end up dead."

"Shame. I'd like to know how good she is." Mason returned to his desk, and pulled his phone towards him, a distinctly calculating look on his face. He had a mobile phone, but Mason was old-fashioned and hardly ever used it. "Thanks, Harlan. If you have no other business, take the rest of the afternoon off. You've earned it."

Harlan drained his glass and headed for the door. It was Friday, and he had plans for the weekend, so he wasn't about to hang around. "Thanks. You too." As he exited the room, he wondered just who Mason might be calling, but if he had any thought of eavesdropping, it was quickly dispelled when he saw Robert coming towards him, treading as softly as a cat. He was Mason's private secretary, and as slippery as a mongoose.

"Business concluded?" Robert asked sharply.

"Like clockwork," Harlan answered, refusing to bite back. He grinned broadly. "Have a nice weekend." He added asshole silently to himself, and as he headed to the stairs, shrugged off the trickle of concern Mason's fervid gleam had given him.

Three

Gabe joined Shadow at the table and placed her beer in front of her. They sat in the corner of a busy pub, both with their backs to the wall so they could watch the patrons' activities. Shadow was still full of nervous energy, and she picked up her pint and took a long drink. When she finally put it down, she sighed. "That's better."

"The meeting went well. Pleased?"

"Very. I'm not sure if I like Mason, though. Something about him made me uncomfortable."

"Me too," he agreed, nodding thoughtfully. "But we don't know him. He could treat everyone like that. At least he looked at you most of the time. He ignored me completely."

"That's because I'm prettier."

"Pretty annoying," he shot back.

"Pretty useful, actually. Have you seen our account?" She pulled her phone out of her pocket, brought up the app for their bank, and then passed it to him.

Gabe grinned, animating his normally serious face. He had a good sense of humour, but didn't often show it. "That's a solid start," he said, settling himself against the back of his seat.

"Do you think you'll eventually stop the security work?"

"Maybe. But for now we're contracted to Caspian, and I'll honour that. Besides, the discipline of daily work is good." He referred to Caspian Faversham, who was the director of Kernow Industries, and was a powerful witch from an old magical family. Gabe had secured a contract to provide security at Caspian's main warehouse in Harecombe, the town next to White Haven.

Shadow watched him over the rim of her glass. He was cagey about his history, but his physique and bearing betrayed his warrior past, and dictated his future, to an extent. All the Nephilim were close, despite the fact that they weren't all from the same region—they'd told her that much. Other than Gabe and Nahum, who had the same Angel father, the others had different fathers, and that might mean some of their powers differed too; but again, that was pure speculation on her part.

"You seem to know what your life will be here."

Gabe laughed. "Do I? What makes you say that?"

"You seem confident, not worried about change or this strange world we live in."

"Change is inevitable—it's how we deal with it that's important. And this world is no different to how it was in my time, not really. There's just more technology."

She wasn't sure what her future would be, and she mused aloud, "At least I'll have the money to pursue trying to find my way back home."

He frowned. "You should listen to the witches. They're right. You're stuck here. Isn't that what the Raven King said, too?"

"I refuse to accept that. There are portals between this world and ours, but they're well hidden. However, I'm creative and good at finding things."

"So, now what?"

"Now I make a list of the most probable places and start there. Dan has already helped me with this."

"Dan from Avery's shop? You're nuts. That could take forever."

"I've got a long time." As she said it, she felt a weight settle within her. She did have a long time, and the prospect of endlessly trying to get home and trailing around a whole list of mystical places suddenly didn't seem that exciting. What was she thinking? She pushed her doubts aside. She had to try.

As if he'd read her mind, Gabe said softly, "We are as long-lived as you, probably. We need to think smartly about what we do with our lives. No social media, no showy lifestyles. We need to blend in, like the witches. And we'll have to move at some point, pretend to die, and reinvent ourselves."

"But I like White Haven, and I like Ravens' Wood."

"I don't mean now, but we will in the future."

Shadow had a vision of her life as a fugitive, and she wasn't sure if that excited her or depressed her, but Gabe had said 'we.' She liked that. It made her feel less lonely. She finished her pint. "Have we got time for another?"

"I think so. Your round," he said, pushing his glass towards her.

𝔎 𝔎 𝔎

When they arrived back at the farmhouse that night, it was late. Three of the Nephilim were at home, all playing on one of the games consoles in their large living room at the side of the house, overlooking the moors.

When they first moved in, the place was bare, and Gabe hadn't wanted to spend their earnings on luxuries, but as they'd made more money and secured better jobs, they pooled their cash and bought more goods. Most of the Nephilim were from the ancient Middle East and the Mediterranean, except for Barak, who was from Ethiopia. Their decorations reflected those styles. Various tables were dotted around, and lamps lit dim corners. As well as a couple of long low sofas, there were also huge cushions and thick rugs spread across the wooden floor. Nahum still liked to smoke a hookah, and one stood to the side of the fireplace. That was the other thing they all agreed on—a fire that blazed pretty much all day if they were in. They all liked the warmth, and even though they could tolerate the cold easily, they didn't like to.

Tonight, the only light came from the fire and the large TV mounted on the wall, and Nahum, Ash, and Zee lounged in front of it, yelling at each other, surrounded by half-full bowls of crisps and discarded beer bottles. The Nephilim loved war and action games, and competed furiously. They thrived on physical combat, and consequently picked up the occasional injury. That was okay; they healed fast, a gift from their fathers. However, new technology meant they had found other ways to fight, and this was safer. Gabe watched the screen, still amazed at the quality of the picture. He would never have imagined that this would be the future of mankind, and he couldn't decide if it was good or bad. At least these games were better than actual war, and they'd all had their far share of that.

Shadow was as competitive as any of them, and she hustled Zee along on the couch, grabbing a controller. "I want in!"

"Too late," Ash told her, distracted. "I'm about to kick Nahum's butt."

"No way!" Nahum objected. His fingers punched the controller aggressively before groaning loudly as his character experienced a grisly death.

Ash grinned. "Told you!"

"You must have cheated."

"Yeah, right," Ash said, standing and stretching. Ash, short for Asher, hadn't cut his hair like some of the other Nephilim, and it fell below his shoulders. He wore a short beard under intense hazel eyes. "It must be time for another beer."

Zee was already setting up the next game, but shouted, "For me, too!" Zee had a new scar on his cheek from his encounter with the Wild Hunt. He looked around at Gabe. "How did business go?"

"Successfully. We closed our first deal! I like Harlan, but not Mason Jacobs," he told them as he thought back over their meeting. "There's something slippery about him, but there is also potential for future work."

"There's still more going on in that place than we know, though," Shadow said. Her violet eyes shone with fey light. She eased her glamour when she was around them, and her Otherness was more obvious.

"Of course there is," Gabe admitted. "We'll probably never know half of it."

Zee frowned. "That doesn't matter though, does it, as long as they pay us?"

"True, and we were paid well today," Gabe said. "But I like to have the full picture. I'm a strategist." He sat on the end of the sofa and reached absently for some crisps, pondering the best way to find out more about the Orphic Guild. He could ask Newton, the DI and head of paranormal investigations for the Cornwall and Devon police, but he was wary of involving him in their business. However, they had skills, too.

He looked at Nahum, who looked back at him warily. He was physically similar to Gabe, but while Gabe had brown eyes, Nahum's were blue. Otherwise, they both had thick dark hair, and were square-jawed and olive-skinned. Back in their old life, they had worked together all the time; Nahum was his right-hand man, and all the others knew it.

Nahum put the game controller down. "Why do I get the impression you have a job for me?"

"Beckett and Jacobs know me, but they have no idea about the rest of us. How would you like to hang around in London for a while and check out their place?"

Nahum's eyes gleamed with intrigue. "Sounds good. What exactly am I looking for?"

"Visitors, unusual behaviour..." Gabe shrugged. "I don't know exactly, but I just want to find out more about them. They have lots of money, and I want to know how legitimate it is."

Shadow sat cross-legged, watching him. "You think they're lying?"

"I don't know, but that's the trouble. You might find nothing significant, Nahum, and that's okay. Just hang around and watch. We've got enough cash to put you up in a decent hotel."

"When do you want me to go?"

"In a couple of days, maybe even tomorrow if we can get a room booked quickly. Is there much happening at the warehouse?"

Nahum spent most of his time there, splitting his shifts mainly with Othniel and Barak, but the other Nephilim took their turns, too. Caspian had originally planned to fire his regular security team, but in the end on Gabe's advice had kept them on, and the Nephilim were in charge of them, allowing them time to pursue other avenues of business.

Nahum shrugged. "No. Everything is going smoothly, although Caspian is away at the moment, and I'm dealing with Estelle on everyday matters. There's a big shipment expected in tonight, though, so that's why Barak and Niel are there. She insisted on needing two of us." Estelle was Caspian's sister, and she was as mean as a snake.

Gabe groaned. "She makes life so awkward."

"I like her," Nahum said, a wicked grin on his face. "Awkward is fun."

"You're so weird," Shadow told him.

Nahum just laughed as Ash came back into the room with a handful of bottled beers, and handed them out. "Nahum has always had a thing for feisty females."

Feisty was one word for her, but Gabe had better ones. "It's unlike Caspian to be away for so long."

"Just business, I guess," Nahum speculated.

Shadow laughed. "You men know nothing. Avery has broken his heart, and he headed off to clear his head."

Gabe grunted in surprise. "Caspian likes Avery? I thought he hated the White Haven witches."

Shadow looked at him in disbelief. "You're such an idiot sometimes. Don't you notice anything? That last business with the Empusa had him and Alex almost at each other's throats over her. It's only the fact that Alex is Mr Cool that he didn't punch him."

"Interesting," Gabe said thoughtfully. "Avery is a little too quiet for my liking. I don't get it."

Zee just grinned. "You're as bad as Nahum. You like women with a temper." He slid his gaze toward Shadow, who was too busy setting the game up to notice.

Gabe did not dignify his dig with a response. "I presume Eli is out tonight with another woman?" Eli was proving popular with the ladies in White Haven, and working at Briar's Charming Balms Apothecary meant he met lots of them.

Ash reached for a controller as he answered. "You presume correctly. He must be exhausted."

"The best kind of exhaustion, right?" Nahum said, smirking.

Gabe rolled his eyes. "Let's hope he doesn't catch something."

"That's the beauty of being us though, isn't it?" Nahum replied. "We don't get diseases! Anyway, Gabe, what's my plan?"

"I'll sort the hotel out tomorrow, and get you a train ticket. The Orphic Guild is in an exclusive part of London, so I'll book you a room as close as we can afford. If you find out anything and think you need help, we'll send backup."

"No, don't bother with a train," Nahum said with a grimace. "I hate public transport. I'll drive. Find me a hotel with parking."

"Fair enough. But call me every day with updates."

"And now can we stop talking business?" Shadow asked. "I want to fight one of you, and I'm going to win."

"Game on," Zee said, picking up the spare controller and settling himself in front of the TV.

Gabe popped the cap off his bottle, leaned back in his seat, and settled in to watch the fun.

文 文 文

The next morning, Shadow had a last-minute panic attack after selling the Empusa's sword, despite the fact that they'd tested it extensively, and she phoned El to arrange to meet her for another check on the remaining weapon. El had suggested that they meet at the smithy that she used to make her bigger pieces of metalwork, such as her daggers and swords.

The blacksmith was situated just out of town, in a hamlet called Polkirt. Shadow had never been there before, and she was looking forward to going. Because it was located in such a small place, it was easy to ride to, and she raced across the fields on Kailen. There was a cool wind blowing, and by the time she arrived at the forge, her cheeks were flushed from the journey.

She dismounted, tying Kailen to a fence surrounding the courtyard. El's Land Rover was already there, next to a black van, and on the building was a sign that read, Dante's Forge. She headed to the open door of the old stone building, and as soon as she stepped inside, the heat of the furnace hit her, as did the resounding clang of metal on metal. She squinted to see into the dark interior. The windows were small and grubby with long-accumulated dirt, and mostly blocked with shelving and a random assortment of objects that were stacked on the counter that ran along walls. A fire dominated one end of the room, and a well-built man was hammering out a long piece of hot metal on the anvil. At his side, watching him closely, was El.

As usual, El was an arresting sight. Her long, white-blonde hair was cascading down her back, and she wore black jeans tucked into leather biker boots, and a blood red leather jacket that matched her scarlet lipstick. Her rings, necklaces, and piercings glinted in the low light. The man next to her had dreadlocks pulled back from his face with a bandana, and sweat beaded his brow. As Shadow approached, El turned and saw her, and headed to her side, hugging her tightly.

"Shadow! Good to see you, I'm so glad you could meet me here. It's my second favourite place on Earth!"

The noise stopped as the man halted his work and looked around. He laughed. "Is it?"

"You know it is!" She threw her arms wide. "All this stuff! I love it. And of course, you're here too, I guess that helps."

"Oh, thanks," he said dryly, but he was obviously joking, and it was clear they had a good friendship. He dunked the long piece of metal into a water butt, where it hissed and steamed, and then slipped his thick leather gloves off and shook Shadow's hand with a strong grip. "I'm Dante. Welcome to my smithy." He wore a grubby t-shirt, jeans, and work boots, with a heavy apron protecting his chest, and when he smiled, he revealed white, even teeth that looked even whiter against his black skin. But it was his eyes that were so arresting; they were a pale sea green, lively with intelligence, and there was something about him that radiated trust.

"Thanks. This is a very interesting place. And it's hot!"

He laughed. "My family is from Jamaica; we're used to the heat. That's partly why I opened this place, so I don't freeze to death in English winters."

Shadow frowned, trying to place where Jamaica was. She'd been studying maps and reading all sorts of books as she tried to figure out how this world worked. She was familiar with England and Europe, and Gabe and the other Nephilim had taught her about the Middle East and the Mediterranean, but Jamaica? And then it struck her. It was a Caribbean Island and the birthplace of reggae. Zee had made her listen to Bob Marley, and she loved it.

"I love Bob Marley," she told him. "I should visit there one day."

"Everyone loves Bob Marley," he said, winking. "If they don't, there's something wrong with them."

"Too right," El agreed. She pulled the Empusa's curved bronze sword out of her bag and placed it on a wooden table laden with objects. "So why are you worried about the swords, Shadow? We've tested them to death!"

She shrugged. "I wouldn't say worried, but I sold mine yesterday, and then had a last-minute fear that we missed something." She was cautious about what she said, as she wasn't sure how much Dante knew about El and the events a few weeks ago with the Empusa.

El's eyes widened. "You've sold it already? Wow. Who to?"

"There were a few interested parties, from what I could gather. Harlan wasn't exactly forthcoming on the details."

"Neither of those things surprises me." She looked at Dante. "This bronze sword has a twin."

He folded his arms across his chest. "You were holding out on me! I thought that thing was unique!"

"It is, well, they are. They came from the same place."

"Say no more. The less I know, the better."

An impish grin appeared on El's face. "Trust me. There's nothing dodgy about how we got them, it's just unusual."

"I'm used to your unusual, remember?"

"This was more unusual than most." El turned to Shadow. "He may look rough and ready, but his skills go far beyond smithy work. He knows metal and weapons manufacturing and their history really well. Dante was the one who told me about the sword's worth."

He frowned at her, but he was teasing. "What do you mean by rough and ready?"

"You know exactly what I mean. He has a degree in art history," El said, "so he's very good at dating things."

"Some things," Dante explained. "I worked in a museum a long time ago, and I specialised in weapons and war, but working in a museum bored the crap out of me, so now I work for myself. But," he tapped his head, "it's still up here, and I still keep myself up to date with research and auction prices." He picked up the blade, examining it. "This is called a Sickle Sword, and they are commonly associated with power. It was believed they were the swords that Gods carried."

The myths were right. It was surprising how much of the truth trickled through time. Shadow nodded. "A Sickle Sword? Yes, that makes sense, but we have a different name for them—the Crescent Moon Sword."

Dante frowned. "I've never heard of that before. Where are you from?"

El interrupted, "A long way from here. How old is it?"

Dante was still frowning at Shadow, but he said, "Typically 2500 BCE onwards. Often they're badly damaged, so won't fetch a huge amount, a few thousand at the most, but this one is incredibly well-preserved, with a high level of detail. Depending on the provenance, that would affect the price."

Shadow thought about the money currently sitting in their account. "I sold mine for more than a few thousand, so obviously the provenance mattered to them."

El smiled. "Excellent. I keep this on my wall at home. It looks amazing. And I'm still not selling."

"Fair enough, but we needed the money, and it starts off our relationship with the Guild." Shadow eyed the sword speculatively. "So, other than its unusual background, there's definitely nothing to worry about otherwise?"

"No," El reassured her. "We've examined it here extensively, and Dante didn't notice anything particularly worrying."

Dante nodded in agreement as he leant back against a heavy wooden table scarred by years of work, still holding the sword. He ran his hand across the surface admiringly. "It's skilfully made, and as I said, well-preserved, but I couldn't see anything different about its manufacture."

"Did you work in London?" Shadow asked.

"Sure, twenty or so years ago. It's where the best museums are, and the only place to find the big auction houses."

"Have you ever heard of a place called the Orphic Guild? It's not an auction house, as such..."

He narrowed his eyes as he thought for a moment, and then shook his head. "I don't think so. Where is it based?"

"Eaton Place."

Dante whistled. "Wow. That's an expensive address. They must do well. Who runs it?"

"Mason Jacobs. He's an older man, grey hair, smart suit, very slick. But he doesn't own it. Someone else does, but I don't know his name."

"It still doesn't ring any bells, sorry."

Shadow smiled. "It's fine. I'm just curious about them."

Dante shrugged. "If they got you over a few thousand for the sword, then they clearly know what they're doing."

Shadow looked at the objects stacked around the room. "What do you make?"

"Garden stuff, mainly. I work with wrought iron. I make fencing and hanging baskets, but also gates, decorative things, and swords and daggers on occasion—like today."

Shadow shivered at the mention of iron, but Dante didn't notice, as he'd already given the sword back to El and was heading to the fire. He poked it, and the flames roared back to life. "Now, I need to get on with it. You're welcome to stay and watch. I'm showing El some tips and tricks."

El nudged her. "Come on. You'll enjoy it. He's the best. I'll take you for a pub lunch later. I'm meeting Reuben—you can tell us about your deal."

Reuben, El's partner, was a keen surfer and water witch with a dry sense of humour she wasn't always sure how to take, but he was fun to be around. "All right. You're on," she said as she followed El to Dante's side.

Four

Harlan was at lunch with William Chadwick, one of his most demanding clients, and more than most people, had the ability to annoy the crap out of him. He tried not to show it.

It was Monday, and his weekend had been busy. He'd gone out for dinner with a very attractive American woman who worked at one of the smaller auction houses, and they exchanged news over items that would benefit them both. Occasionally, these meetings became something more than business, but not this weekend. He'd headed home slightly drunk on expensive wine, and slept late on Sunday. To clear his head, he'd gone out on his Moto Guzzi motorbike, enjoying its speed and power, and then he spent the rest of the day relaxing.

Chadwick frowned. "What do you mean you can't find it?"

"Just what I said. All trace of it has disappeared."

"But it's an ancient document rumoured to have been written in the fifteenth century and stored for years in the library of Thomas Norton. There was a lot of buzz around it! It can't just have disappeared."

Harlan took a deep breath and counted to ten. Well, tried to. He made it to five when Chadwick said, "Harlan! Are you deaf?"

Do not punch him, you'll be fired. "No. I know exactly what it was rumoured to be, and believe me, I've been following those rumours for weeks, but now the chatter has stopped. It's gone!" He stared at his client to reinforce his words. Chadwick was an ugly man with pockmarked, sallow skin and beady eyes that even his silk shirt and Italian suit couldn't improve. "I can only presume that someone has already bought it."

"I want to put in a better offer."

"And if I ever find out who bought it, I'll make sure to make that offer, but for now, I don't even know who to approach."

Chadwick's eyes blazed and he snorted like a pig. "I bet it's Cavendish."

"Perhaps. I can contact him if you wish, but as you know, I can't guarantee anything. Or it may have been stolen, although potentially that would make waves."

Chadwick leaned back in his seat and fell silent, and Harlan could practically see his brain cells whizzing around as he thought through his options. Harlan also leaned back and sipped his wine, hoping to ease the tension. Chadwick was an old and valued client, part of a group of very rich and obsessive collectors of alchemical documents. However, he was not a member of the Order of the Midnight Sun, and consequently loathed them. Cavendish was a member of the Order, hence the accusation. And Chadwick could well be right. Competition for such manuscripts was intense. Especially between practising magicians, which they all were. Even those who belonged to the Order were competitive with each other, but others who were not members actively sought to deprive them of any opportunity to obtain ancient texts.

This business was cutthroat. Many of them may have had worldly aspirations, but it didn't stop them from being mean. The thing was, the Orphic Guild also did work for the Order; they worked for anyone who hired them, but as far as Harlan knew, they had not had anything to do with this particular document.

Chadwick stirred out of his long, thoughtful silence. "No, leave it for now. Rumours may resurface. They sometimes do if you wait long enough."

Harlan nodded, relieved. "Of course, but I will continue to listen for any news, as always."

"Good. Let's move on to my other issue." He shuffled forward and lowered his voice, pushing his empty plate out of the way as he did so. "I have found the ancient tomb of a man I have been researching my whole life! I need to get in there for the grave goods, but I can only get so far. I want help."

Harlan had leant forward as well to better hear him, and for a moment thought he'd misheard. "You mean you've already broken into it?"

"Yes! But I believe I've only reached a false outer tomb. The real one is there, but hidden by a veil of magic." He widened his eyes as he said the final word, uttering it almost as a whisper. "I need you to help me get in."

"Forgive me for seeming dense, but you are a magician and alchemist. You deal with the magical all the time. Why can't you handle this?"

Chadwick narrowed his eyes in annoyance. "Because my magic is bound with ritual and research. This is beyond my ken. It's wilder—different."

Interesting. Chadwick had pretty much admitted where his magic ended. "You think it's mystical in nature?"

"Isn't that what I said?"

"I need more details. What is it, and where is it?"

"You can help then? Because I've never asked for this type of assistance before."

Harlan eased back, eager to be further than inches away from this annoying little man. "We have many contacts in the occult and arcane community, as you well know. I am sure that once I have the full details, I can find someone to help you."

"I trust the information will be kept a secret? To the best of my knowledge, I am the only one who knows about this."

"Have I ever been less than discrete?" A note of annoyance crept into Harlan's voice; he simply couldn't help it. "I recently successfully negotiated the Empusa's sword for you, and ensured that you won the bid!"

"I just had to be certain. The sword is magnificent, by the way." A feral glint entered Chadwick's eyes.

"I hope you appreciate how hard that was to come by," Harlan told him. "The Empusa met an unpleasant end, and not by my hand. Now, give me some more details!"

Chadwick flinched and smiled tightly. "Fair enough. As I said, I have been investigating an ancient shaman and Druid for many years. He was reputed to have strange powers. I recently found his burial site. It's close to Belas Knap."

"Sorry, I'm not sure I know what that is."

"Belas Knap is a chambered long barrow, from the Neolithic times. It's in Gloucestershire, and particularly well-preserved."

Harlan had already pulled out his phone, and he typed the name in, waiting impatiently for the information to load while Chadwick talked.

"I found a reference to his tomb in an obscure text, and initially thought it was referring to the existing barrows, as there are a few in that area. But then I realised it was another one, as yet unfound."

Harlan looked at his screen and then at Chadwick with disbelief. "Are you nuts? Belas Knap is well known and heavily researched, and is owned by English Heritage. The surrounding area has been farmed for years. There can't possibly be anything close by."

"Wrong. Belas Knap is set in the corner of a field on a rise, only accessible by a public footpath called the Cotswold Way, and yes, part of the surroundings are farmlands, but it is also next to a small wood that has been undisturbed for ages. That's where I found the tomb."

Harlan folded his arms and stared at Chadwick. "You're proposing an archaeological dig?"

"No! Aren't you listening? I have been in it already! I dug out the entrance myself, and once inside, the place is accessible, but..." He paused as he tried to articulate his experience and then repeated his earlier assumption. "There's something there that stops me from progressing further, and I think it's magic."

Harlan reassessed Chadwick in the light of this news. He hadn't thought he had it in him to do grubby field research, which meant that whatever he hoped was there, must be worth it. "I take it you have disguised the entrance again?"

"Of course, but I have the GPS coordinates, and am prepared to give them to you, if you have someone who can break through the magic at the site."

"I have a very good idea who we could use, but I would have to check first."

Chadwick smiled. "Excellent. If your contact agrees, we will organise the contract. I would like to act as soon as possible."

"What are you prepared to pay?"

"The usual hourly rate, all expenses, plus your cut. And I want to be there, too."

Harlan winced. He was going to ask Shadow, obviously, but he wasn't sure she'd agree to a witness. "I'll see what I can do."

Gabe leaned against the corner of Caspian's warehouse, situated on the outskirts of Harecombe, watching the unloading of the containers that had been delivered from the quay. There were half a dozen men milling around, and despite his relaxed demeanour, Gabe watched them like a hawk.

This shipment had been delayed for a variety of reasons, and Estelle was anxious. She emerged from the inner office, striding purposefully to his side with a scowl on her face. Her long, dark hair was swept up into a chic chignon, and she wore an expensive outfit. Unfortunately, the hard hat and fluorescent jacket she also wore covered them both up, but Gabe knew Estelle well enough now to know her vanity was more bound up with her magic than her appearance, although she always looked immaculate.

Watching the unloading, she asked, "Any issues?"

"None. The manifest matches up so far. We should be finished in a few minutes." He checked his watch. It was nearly three in the afternoon, and he was finishing soon. Barak was due to arrive to cover the evening shift, and Gabe was looking forward to contacting Nahum and hearing his update on the Orphic Guild.

Estelle's expression relaxed. "Good. Our buyers are getting impatient. I see you've brought Shadow today?"

She nodded to where Shadow stood talking to the driver. She was an arresting sight in her black fatigues, even with the fluorescent jacket and obligatory hard hat. She'd complained bitterly about wearing them, but in the end hadn't had a choice.

He nodded. "She has some free time right now, so she's doing some shifts this week. Barak and Niel need a break. I must admit I didn't think she'd agree, but she's easily bored, and curious."

Estelle raised an eyebrow. "A dangerous combination."

"And then some."

Estelle watched her for a while, and then said, "Caspian likes her, actually, and he's hard to please. Although if I'm honest, I think his judgement is waning at the moment."

Gabe twitched his lips with amusement. She could only be referring to the fact that he now liked and worked with the White Haven witches. "Oh, I don't know. He employed me." He winked at Estelle, and she looked at him coolly, but he heard her heart rate rise and her pupils dilated slightly. Okay, that was interesting. Does Estelle like him?

However, before she could speak, Shadow joined them.

"There are some strange items in that delivery," she noted. "Bound for a private address in London."

Estelle's tone was sharp. "It is not your job to pry about the inventory. You just make sure it matches."

Shadow stared at Estelle, who stared back. "I am merely commenting. You can't check something off without reading it."

Gabe saw Shadow's hand move to the small knife she kept strapped to her thigh, hidden by glamour to most people. He intervened swiftly. "Of course not, Shadow, but best to keep such information to yourself. We have to pretend we haven't read it, if you know what I mean."

Her violet eyes turned to him now. "I'm not about to blab it at the pub."

"I know. If I didn't trust you, you wouldn't be here," he said softly.

"Lucky me."

"Lucky both of you," Estelle said. "I'm the one who's paying you."

"I think you mean Caspian is," Shadow shot back.

Estelle's hand balled at her side, and Gabe felt a faint spark of magic before she clearly thought better of it. She glared at Gabe instead. "Keep her on a leash, or I won't let her back in." She turned her back on them and headed to the office. In seconds, the door slammed behind her.

Gabe looked at Shadow with impatience. "Could you stop being a smart mouth just once?"

"She's the smart mouth, not me," she said, bristling. "Anyway, you like my smart mouth."

"I like it sometimes, but Estelle doesn't, and that's who is important right now. I'm trying to cultivate a relationship with her."

"Really? I think you'll find she's incapable. She certainly hates women. And she has what is commonly called a Resting Bitch Face."

Shadow looked very pleased with herself, and Gabe couldn't help laughing.

"Where on Earth did you hear that? Oh wait, El?"

She grinned. "Of course. All the witches hate her."

"Well, you need to get over it. Today, she's your boss." He looked away as the last of the shipment was wheeled into the warehouse behind them. "Anyway, we're done here for now. Barak will be here soon." He steered her up the stairs towards the mezzanine floor and the office they used next to the manager's room. It was small, containing a couple of chairs, a desk and computer. Half a dozen additional monitors displayed what was filmed in various places around the grounds, and a window looked out on the warehouse floor. He headed to the corner and turned the kettle on to boil, getting mugs ready at the same time.

Shadow leaned against the wall, and said, "I heard from Harlan earlier. He's offered me another job."

"Us, I think you mean!"

She wrinkled her nose. "Yes, us. It sounds intriguing. We have to go to a place called Gloucestershire and find a Druid burial site."

"That is intriguing. Who for?" he asked, turning around to face her.

"He didn't say. I said I'd discuss it with you first, once he emailed me some more details."

Gabe almost dropped the cup he was holding. "You actually said you'd consult me?"

Shadow looked offended. "Yes! We are partners!"

"Have you had a recent head injury?"

"No! Was that wrong?"

There was hope for her, yet. "No, it was very right. Well done!"

"Thank you, Mr Patronising. Shall I show you the job?"

"Please do!"

She pulled her phone from her pocket and started scrolling, just as Barak walked in. He nodded as he entered. "Coffee for me too, Gabe."

Barak was as big and muscular as the rest of them, but where some of the Nephilim were lean with muscle, Barak was heavier set, with huge biceps and thighs. He was from Africa originally, and his skin was a deep mahogany colour. He kept his hair clipped short and he was clean-shaven, showing off his strong jaw and generous mouth, but his eyes were gentle and humorous, and of all of them, he was the joker.

He grinned at Shadow. "Finally getting some work out of you, then?"

"Your cheek will get you nowhere! I have a new job, thank you!"

"We do!" he said, reiterating Gabe's early comment. "Do you need my help?"

"No, thank you," she answered primly. And then she frowned. "I don't think so, anyway. Here, you can both look at what Harlan has sent through."

Gabe took the phone from her, and scrolled through the short message and the images of Belas Knap and the woods. "Sounds straightforward, but what do you think?" He passed the phone to Barak for his opinion.

Barak scanned the message and shrugged. "Agreed. It's hidden, and easy to do at night with little local risks. But I'd take a couple of us to keep watch." He looked at Shadow. "It all comes down to the magic that's there, though. Can you handle it?"

"It really depends on what's going on. I should be able to see through a glamour, but it's hard to say until I'm there."

That was enough for Gabe. He was anxious to get more work utilising their unique talents. Security was fine, but they could do more, and he didn't want the team getting restless and doing anything rash. "Sounds good. Tell Harlan that you accept the job. We'll plan for the middle of the week."

"There's one more thing," Shadow said hesitantly. "The man who's hiring us wants to be there, too."

"Why?"

"I guess he wants to ensure we don't mess up or steal whatever it is we find."

That would undoubtedly make life harder. If they needed to use their special abilities, he didn't want outsiders to see. He frowned. "Can you say no?"

"I don't think so."

"Bollocks. We'll just have to put up with him, then."

Five

G abe drove his SUV onto the small car park at the base of the walk to Belas Knap, and looked at Shadow and Niel. "Ready?"

"Always," Niel said, already halfway out of the passenger door. "I need to stretch."

It had taken them almost four hours to get to the site, and it was now early afternoon. The skies were grey and Gabe felt a chill wind slice through him. He headed to the boot and pulled out his thick coat, and next to him, Shadow grabbed hers.

"Just one other car," she noted, looking around the lot.

"Good, let's hope it's quiet at the site, too," Gabe said. It was a fifteen-minute walk from the car park to the site, but it was part of a long, popular walking track called the Cotswolds Way. With luck, the weather would keep people away.

Niel pulled his jacket on and looked up at the sky. "I think it might rain. That will make it very unpleasant tonight."

"We can't help that," Gabe told him. He shut the boot and locked up, asking Shadow, "Did you tell Beckett we're arriving early?"

She shook her head, a mischievous glint in her eye. "No, I just said we would meet him later."

"Good. I don't like people hanging over my shoulder when I investigate."

Gabe headed to the sign that said, *Belas Knap Long Barrow, Ancient Monument*, and set a good pace up the path. The walk featured a mixture of fields and woodland, but rather than try to find the GPS coordinates he had been given to the hidden tomb, he headed straight for the burial site.

It was a steep climb in some places, but the view at the top was spectacular, and Gabe looked around appreciatively. "What a place to be buried!" They were surrounded by fields, and the land fell away below them, brooding under a cloudy sky. A small wood was next to the chamber, but Gabe could see other wooded areas not too far away.

"It's so quiet," Shadow observed. "I like it."

Gabe knew what she meant. The isolated location, devoid of modern buildings and technology meant the land spoke to them, and he knew Shadow felt that more than he did. Niel was already exploring the site, heading past the false entrance, and they followed him as he ducked into one of the stone chambers. Gabe had to bend almost double to get in, but as soon as he entered the tiny space he heard muted voices, as if someone was whispering in his ear.

"Niel, do you hear that?"

Niel nodded, his eyes wide. "The voices of the dead. They're restless."

"The dead?" Shadow said, her voice rising. "You hear the dead?"

"Not all of the time," Gabe confessed, "but in certain places, yes. It's a sign of a place's power."

"Can you tell what they're saying?" she asked.

Gabe paused, listening intently, the hairs on his arms lifting as the voices swirled around him. "Snatches of words, pleas to the Gods, but they're too quiet."

Niel shuffled past him, heading back outside, and they followed, Gabe straightening with relief.

Niel laughed dryly. "This place is almost as old as we are. I like it. In fact, I like this land. It has layers of civilisations here." Niel was a big blond man, who looked as if he'd been hewn from rock. A beard and sideburns adorned his face, and his hair was swept back from his head into a small ponytail.

Shadows hands were on her hips and she stared at both of them. "Can you all hear the dead?"

"To a degree," Gabe told her. "A gift from our fathers, along with other things."

"Can you ever understand them?"

"Sometimes, depending on what they need to tell us, or how agitated they were at death." He shrugged, wondering how to explain what was to him something he had experienced all his life.

"Can you hear them in White Haven, too?"

"No. The place is too busy."

"I did once," Niel said, "up at Old Haven Church when the witch was doing blood magic. The dead didn't like it."

Gabe hadn't known that and he looked at Niel, surprised. "You never said."

"I presumed you'd heard them, too. But I was patrolling the wood all the time, at the boundary of the cemetery. Maybe that's why."

"Can you speak to them?" Shadow asked.

Gabe shook his head. "They are echoes really, not sentient. They're trapped in repeated cycles. But we can't see them," he added, suspecting he knew what Shadow would ask next.

Shadow shuddered. "I'm glad I just hear the earth. I certainly don't want to listen to what's buried beneath it." She looked around, her eyes bright with curiosity. "I've been reading about this place. It's aligned north to south, which is unusual, apparently. Many think the design of the tomb echoes the shape of a woman kneeling down."

"Do you?"

She narrowed her eyes as she stepped back and looked at the tomb. "Perhaps."

"A celebration of a Goddess, then?" Gabe asked. "Mother Earth, possibly. We had such beliefs."

"I thought your God was the only God?" Shadow said scathingly, as she walked up the turfed sides of the tomb to stand on the top.

He walked next to her, trying to keep the disdain from his voice. "So my father would have me believe, but it's not true. There are too many Gods to count, and they all covet worship."

She paused on the rise and looked at the lay of the land, but her eyes were concentrating on something else. "Your angel father?"

He tried not to sound impatient. "Yes, that one. And no, he's not a sylph."

She ignored his jibe. "Is he still alive? If you're superhuman, it would suggest he had immortality."

Gabe found it a strangely painful subject, but he answered her honestly. "He was alive, not that I saw him often, and then the flood came, a punishment to me and my kind for our perceived heresies, and I have no idea what happened to him, because I don't feel him now."

"What about when you were in the Underworld with the other spirits? Did you not hear whispers about them?"

"No. That place was crowded and tormented, and we were there for millennia. I look back to my time before the flood as if it was a dream. A sometimes bloody, battle-filled dream, but a dream nonetheless." Gabe wasn't quite sure why he was having this conversation now, on an ancient burial chamber, with the dead whispering beneath his feet, but maybe just being here was the reason. He had talked to the other Nephilim about it on occasion, but he sensed that it was a topic they would rather bury, along with their past. The betrayal of their fathers burned deep.

She looked at him, her violet eyes bright with intelligence. "You're part of myth and legend. Giants, according to some stories. I've read about you."

He smiled. "I know. I see all of your books lying around."

"Don't you want to read them?"

"Someday. The other guys have looked at them, and have told me enough. There are truths in there, but plenty of lies, too. Of more interest to me is what happened after the flood."

"Why?"

Gabe shrugged. "Unfinished business, I suppose."

"You should tell me what you were really like all those years ago. I could correct the stories," she teased.

"Some things should live beneath veils of illusion," Gabe said, "the better to protect us now. It's a strange world we walk in, and not all dangers are as obvious as we expect."

His voice was soft, and standing so close to Shadow he saw her vulnerability up close, something she normally hid so well. But he was starting to see the real Shadow now, and he liked it, more than he cared to admit.

She stared at him for a moment more, and in the silence he heard the soft thumping of her heart as they were both caught in stillness. And then she looked away, down the bank towards the dry stone wall and the wood beyond.

"Let's head into the wood and find the hidden burial site so we can go and eat. I'm starving." With that declaration she walked away, and after a moment's pause to look around once more, he followed.

It was gloomy beneath the trees, and Shadow led the way, following the directions programmed into her phone. The signal was spotty up here, but she forged ahead into the undergrowth, virtually disappearing at times. Gabe blinked as if to clear his vision, and there she was again, a perfect blend of light and shadow. He laughed to himself. She was certainly well named.

Gabe and Niel were right beyond her, and despite their bulk, they moved quietly. Unfortunately, they weren't alone. There were paths through the woodland, and every now and again, they heard the distant bark of a dog and a raised voice, and Niel muttered, "Bloody dogs."

Shadow stepped unerringly forward, pushing through a thick stand of trees and bushes, slipping through their tangled branches with ease as if they parted for her. As he followed, Gabe noted a few broken branches and some disturbed ground in places, and realised it was probably where their mysterious employer had come through, because Shadow didn't disturb a thing. They followed her up a steep rise and into a small space surrounded by dense bushes on all sides, which protected them from casual onlookers. There was still a heavy canopy of branches overhead, just starting to bud with leaves. Shadow pointed to the mound of rocks against the bank that was smothered in torn ivy and other ground-covering plants. "It's under there."

Niel looked at it sceptically. "Really? Because it looks like a pile of crap to me!"

"Can't you feel it?" Her eyes gleamed. "There's something on the other side."

"Good or bad?" Gabe asked.

"I'm not sure yet."

"That's what worries me," Gabe said.

Niel grunted. "Too late to be having second thoughts now."

"No, it's not. We can pull out anytime we want—not that I'm suggesting we do," Gabe said reassuringly. "I just like to know the odds." He looked at Shadow. "Is it fey magic?"

"I can't tell. Shall we look?"

He shook his head. "We'll wait for tonight; best not to upset the client. Let's just check the area before we go, and then we'll pick the keys up for the cottage and find a pub for lunch. What time are we meeting Harlan later?"

"About seven," Shadow told him.

"Excellent," Niel said, pushing his way back through the bushes. "There's nothing like a pint before a night of grave robbing."

Six

H arlan met Chadwick in the bar of the hotel they had both booked into for their arranged meeting. He hadn't really wanted to be at the same place as his client, but it was the easiest thing to do, and besides, Mason had sort of insisted on it.

Chadwick was as well groomed as always, and he had a glass of white wine in front of him, which for some inexplicable reason annoyed Harlan. *Why couldn't he just order a pint?* Harlan almost defiantly ordered the local beer and sat opposite him.

"Are you looking forward to tonight?"

"I am! I've been searching for this burial site for a long time."

"Perhaps you'd like to share exactly why that is? You've been very coy." *And perhaps that was the reason for his nervousness*, Harlan reflected. He was usually well prepared for these events, but Chadwick had refused to reveal any details. "You should know by now that you can trust us."

"I do trust you," Chadwick said smoothly, "but I'm also suspicious. I wouldn't like to think that someone else would beat me to it when I'm so close." He leaned forward, his eyes filled with a maniacal gleam. "That's why I have to be there."

"Why?"

"Why don't I wait and tell you all together? What time are we meeting your hunters?"

"They'll be here at any moment. In fact," he looked around, hearing the door swing open and voices behind him, "I think they're here."

Shadow was standing next to Gabe and another man that Harlan hadn't met before who looked like a marauding Viking, and they stood to meet them. Shadow smiled, and her eyes darted to Chadwick, before resting on Harlan. "Harlan, fancy meeting you so soon!"

"Aren't I lucky?" he said, amused. "This is William Chadwick, our client. Chadwick, this is Shadow, Gabe, and—"

"Niel," the large blond man supplied, shaking his hand and then Chadwick's.

"Three of you?" Chadwick said, sitting again after greeting them. "I'm not sure you'll all be needed."

"Oh, trust me, we will," Gabe replied, smiling charmingly while flashing his perfect teeth. "Seeing as we've been told very little, I like to be prepared."

Harlan looked at him, impressed. "Me, too. Chadwick has been worried about security, but is obviously ready to tell us now."

Chadwick glanced down at his glass as they settled themselves at the table. "I believe I have found the burial place of a Druid and bard called Kian. He should have his ritual objects buried with him, and I want them."

"Have they any particular significance?" Harlan asked.

"Not really, but the fact that they have been masked with some sort of magic may suggest otherwise."

Harlan started to get an uneasy feeling. "Is it something that could cause danger?"

"I thought you liked danger, Harlan?"

"I don't mind it, but I'd rather know what we're facing."

"And seeing as I'm the one who'll be breaking through the magic, I'd really like to know more," Shadow said, a dangerous edge to her voice.

Chadwick sipped his drink, unperturbed. "Well, as I said, he's a Druid, and therefore whatever went with him to his grave would have been his personal objects. A window into his world."

"Surely most things would have rotted away?" Niel asked, sipping the pint he'd brought with him to the table.

"Perhaps, but I have to see anyway."

Gabe leaned forward, his curiosity piqued. "There must be something of value?"

Chadwick just looked at him. "It is *all* of value. A powerful Druid who wielded magic and served the old Gods. That must be what protects his grave, even now."

Harlan hated it when his clients became fervid about the old Gods. It almost always caused trouble. Like the Callanish Ring did. *Which reminded him...* "Shadow, Chadwick is the man who brought the Empusa's sword."

Shadow turned to him, frowning. "Oh! And what are you doing with it?"

"Nothing. It is displayed on my wall. Harlan hasn't exactly said how you came to own it, but I'm very grateful you did. "

"I had help," Shadow said, cagily. "Let's hope tonight is not so tricky."

Niel nudged her. "It's just some grave robbing, Shadow."

"And what skills do you two bring tonight?" Chadwick asked, looking at Gabe and Niel.

"Just security," Gabe said nonchalantly. "Hanging about in woods at night could have consequences. What else can you tell us about this Druid?"

Chadwick spread his hands wide. "Nothing. He was the Druid for a powerful tribe, and travelled between here and Breton, and well, did what Druids do! Protected his people and pacified the Gods. But they were revered for their knowledge. Surely you know that?"

"But why him?" Gabe insisted.

"Not many names make it through history. Most are lost in time. His name is found in documents written much later, and his deeds were impressive. But he was overshadowed by one of his contemporaries—or near contemporaries, at least—Merlin."

"Merlin!" Harlan exclaimed.

"But no one's heard of Kian, which is good for me," Chadwick said brightly.

Gabe pushed his chair back. "Fine. In that case, we'll meet you there at midnight, at Belas Knap. I trust you'll be wearing something more suitable?"

"Of course." Chadwick looked slightly affronted.

"Good. Wouldn't want you to damage your nice suit," Gabe told him, and he nodded at Harlan as he left the table.

"Until tonight then," Shadow said, all smiles as she and Niel followed Gabe out of the room.

Harlan watched them leave and then looked back at Chadwick. "Well, that was short and sweet."

If Chadwick was perturbed, he didn't show it. "Excellent. To tonight." And he raised his glass, downed his drink, and ordered another.

Shadow stood on top of Belas Knap again and gazed across the dark fields, enjoying the cool night air on her skin. There was a pale crescent moon rising, and it gave off a faint light that silvered the fields.

She could see well in the dark—better than most humans, she'd realised—but maybe not as well as Gabe and Niel, who seemed as comfortable at night as in the day. Gabe stood silently next to her, but Niel stood below them, by the path, while they waited for Harlan to arrive.

They'd come back early, and once again had walked around the ancient site and along the edge of the woods, making sure no one was there.

"This place has more power at night," Gabe observed, stirring out of his silence.

She nodded. "I know. I feel the weight of its years. Can you hear the dead?"

"Faintly. Remember to keep your powers as secret as possible, Shadow. Be careful tonight. I'm not sure I trust Chadwick."

"I'm not sure I do either, but it's unlikely he'll put us in danger. He wants his Druid objects very badly."

Earlier that evening, when they had returned to the cottage they'd rented for the night, they had tried to find out more about the Druid Kian, but had failed miserably. They would need to do proper research to discover anything significant, and even then Shadow suspected they would require more unusual resources than they had access to at the moment.

Gabe pointed to the path where dark shapes were coming into view. "They're here. Good. I want to get this done."

Harlan was in his sturdy leather boots, jeans, and a jacket, but Chadwick was in hiking clothes and he didn't waste time on pleasantries. He nodded at them and simply said, "I'll lead."

He brought them over the break in the dry stone wall and into the foliage, leading them confidently to the burial site. It was dark under the trees, and Chadwick's torch flashed along the ground. Shadow was behind him, and the rest followed closely, Gabe at the rear. When they reached the covered cairn of stones against the slope, Gabe stepped into the enclosed area with them, but said to Niel, "Just patrol around the edges."

Niel gave a short jerk of his head, and then disappeared silently into the trees.

"How do you want to play this?" Harlan asked Chadwick, who was already pulling on sturdy leather gloves.

"Help me clear the entrance," Chadwick grunted as he started work. "And someone keep the torch on it."

Gabe pulled gloves out of his pocket and started to move the rocks, while Shadow stood next to Harlan, who kept his torch trained on the spot, and watched. Within a few minutes they had cleared the ivy and pulled the stones away, revealing a small hole in the side of the bank. Chadwick stopped and took out his own torch out, shining it inside.

Shadow shuddered, feeling a strange, unrecognisable power drift out of the opening and swirl around them. Interesting. This was a type of fey magic, but it felt darker somehow. Only Gabe caught her movement, as Chadwick was too busy peering into the tomb.

Concerned, he asked, "Are you okay?"

"It feels odd. Do you sense it?"

"I'm afraid not."

Harlan looked between them, worried. "What is it?"

"I'm doing what you hired me to do," Shadow told him. "I sense a strange sort of power, stronger now that the tomb is open."

Chadwick grinned, a gleam of excitement in his eyes. "You feel it? Good. Beyond this entrance is a short passageway, but you'll have to crouch. At the end is a square, stone-walled tomb, but I feel I'm not seeing everything properly."

They seemed to be making a lot of noise, but around them was silence, and Shadow was glad that Niel was out there, somewhere. Chadwick continued to clear the stones, and with Gabe's help they moved quickly until the entire entrance was revealed.

Chadwick stepped back, inviting her forward, and Shadow stared down the passage. Chadwick's torchlight showed nothing but an earth floor and rock walls that were crumbling in places. Tree roots had thrust through the walls, and debris and stones were scattered across the ground. She glanced up at Gabe's worried face, and placed her hand on the knives sheathed against her thigh.

Chadwick cleared his throat behind her. "I'll go first."

"No, you won't," she said, turning quickly and throwing a hand out to stop him. "It's too small, and you'll get in my way."

"No, I have to see," he said, his voice rising with annoyance.

"And you will, when I've finished."

Gabe put in, "It's going to be a tight squeeze if I come, too."

"No one is coming, including you," Shadow said to Harlan as he looked as if he might protest. If she had to do anything odd, she certainly didn't want Harlan or Chadwick seeing it. She turned back to Gabe. "If there's room further down I'll call for you, but only you!" She shot a warning glance at Chadwick to emphasise her point.

Shadow pulled her knife out and edged down the low passageway, ducking her head and stooping. In her left hand she held her torch, knowing it would look too odd to Chadwick not to use it. The passageway led downwards and then turned left, and she picked her way slowly, careful not to trip and twist her ankle. It was musty, the strong earthy smell of decay almost overpowering. Dust rose around her, and she lifted her jacket across her mouth. She felt as if the roof might collapse at any moment, and it was with relief when the passage opened into a small square room as Chadwick had said.

A low rock shelf had pottery objects on it, and a stone coffin lay on the left. The top had been pushed open and bones were inside it. Shadow wondered why Chadwick would think there was more to this tomb, but she turned her torch off and let her eyes adjust to the dark. The prickle of power was stronger here, and it seemed to be coming from the back wall. Chadwick was a ritual magician, which was probably why he could feel it, too.

Gabe called from behind, his voice low. "Shadow, are you okay?"

"I'm fine. Come on through." There was enough room for both of them, just about. *Damn tombs.* They were damp and cold, and she remembered why she'd stopped doing this kind of thing in the Otherworld.

She heard a short, sharp whistle, and then within seconds Gabe was next to her, his shoulders covered in dust, still ducking due to the low ceiling. "Sorry, I called Niel to guard the entrance. I didn't entirely trust Chadwick not to follow us. What have you found?"

"This wall at the back is either enhanced or constructed with fey magic." She placed her hand on the cold stone, pushing her energy out of her fingers and into the rock. "It's odd. The power that's protecting whatever's beyond here is strong. But who did this?"

Gabe stood next to her and felt the wall, too. "Maybe it's like you said before. Years ago, the boundaries between worlds were weaker. Perhaps your magic was shared."

She handed her blade to Gabe. "Let me try something." She placed her hands on the wall again, closed her eyes, and concentrated on the feeling beneath her fingers. It felt as if her palms were sinking into the rock, and she pushed harder. "It's working!" Gabe cried. "It's shimmering!"

Shadow hadn't had the occasion to use her power like this before, and she started to feel drained. Within seconds, the wall snapped back into place, solid and unyielding. She sighed and stepped away. "I'm going to try something else."

She pulled her sword out of its scabbard, and directed her fey energy down through the dragonium blade, forged from some of the most powerful creatures to exist in her world—dragons. When the blade was humming with magic, she pushed it into a seam in the rock, satisfied when cracks started spreading across the surface. She focused even harder, aware of Gabe watching intently. "Nearly there," she said, now certain it was an illusion.

Within a few minutes, the wall vanished with a *crack*, revealing another passageway behind it.

"Yes!" she exclaimed.

Gabe grinned. "It's heading towards Belas Knap."

"Is it?"

"Yes. Can't you tell? Maybe his tomb is beneath the others. Come on."

This passage was bigger than the first. Again, the floor was of beaten earth, but the walls were made of layered stonework, and although some of the stones had dislodged, it was generally in a good state, allowing Gabe to set a quick pace. The path ran undisturbed in almost one straight line, deviating only slightly in a few places. Along the wall were recessed shelves where objects were placed: animal bones, bird skulls, unusually shaped crystals, and other decayed items. Finally, they paused on the threshold of the hidden tomb.

"As I thought," he said softly. "I think we're pretty much dead centre of Belas Knap. This place must have had great significance at one point."

The vault was circular in design, again made of layers of thick rock, rising to a shallow domed roof. In the middle of the space was a long, rectangular stone, like an altar, and on it was a human skeleton, grave goods arranged around it.

"Are you okay in there?" Harlan called, his voice faint.

"Yes, give us a few more moments," Shadow shouted back, and then said to Gabe, "Let's see what's so precious about this place first."

The roof was higher than that of the passage, allowing them to stand upright. Various objects were also on shelves in here, such as goblets, plates, dried things that may have been food, animal skins, and a carved walking stick that was almost as tall as Shadow. What looked like a leather bag lay upon the coffin itself.

"It all looks harmless enough, although this—" she said, pointing to the wooden staff, "has a hum of power about it." She examined it closely, seeing carvings along its length.

"A walking stick?" Gabe said, confused.

"It reminds me of staffs the shamans in our world carry."

"What about the jewellery? Any magic there?" He pointed to the rings and thick bracelets on another shelf.

"Faint only." She peered into the gloom. "I can't see anything suspicious, can you?"

Gabe shook his head. "No, nothing. I'll call Chadwick."

He headed to the end of the passage, leaving Shadow standing alone, and she flashed her torch around the tomb again. She noticed a small, polished flat stone sitting within the jawbone of the skull, and she picked it up, observing strange markings on it. Why was a stone placed in the jaw? But before she could consider it further, she saw a black shape manifest out of the bones, and she blinked, thinking her eyes were playing tricks.

Shadow backed away and kept her torch trained onto the area, holding the stone awkwardly. She held her sword in her other hand, ready to defend herself, although she wondered how a blade would help fight a ghost, or whatever that was. A wave of power rolled around her, and she stepped back again.

For endless seconds nothing seemed to happen, and she realised she was holding her breath. And then Gabe was next to her, Harlan and Chadwick behind him.

"What's up, Shadow?" Gabe asked, looking concerned at her raised sword. "Have you seen something?"

As soon as he spoke, the black shape manifested again and smacked Shadow in the chest, throwing her against the wall behind her. The torch and stone clattered to the floor. In seconds she was on her feet and she slashed forward, missing Gabe by inches as the mysterious entity retreated.

Harlan and Chadwick were still in the entrance, their torches flashing, and Harlan yelled, "What the hell is happening?"

Then it launched again at Shadow and Gabe, who was still standing next to her. This time, the two of them collided with each other against a far wall, and another wave of power rolled across the tomb.

"Is that a ghost?" Chadwick shouted, sounding both alarmed and excited. "It must be Kian! The Druid!"

"Why in Herne's balls is it attacking us?" Shadow said, outraged.

"I think it has a lot of pent-up energy," Gabe suggested, pacing the perimeter as he watched the black shape in the middle of the room.

"Yeah, well, so do I," Shadow replied. Determined not be defeated by a dead Druid, she pulled her fey magic towards her, and then sent it out like a punch, straight at the bulk of Kian's shade.

Within seconds the spirit disappeared, leaving all four of them looking around wildly. Harlan and Chadwick wouldn't have seen her magic, but they might have felt it. Hopefully, in the semidarkness they wouldn't notice.

"Where did it go?" Harlan asked, spinning around.

Chadwick trained his torch down the passage behind them. "Maybe it fled for the entrance?"

"In that case," Gabe said, "it's gone, and there's not much we can do about it."

"What about Niel?" Harlan asked. "For a ghost, it sure contained a lot of energy."

"Niel will be fine," Gabe reasoned, but even so, he looked worried. "Maybe you should do what you need to, Chadwick, so we can get out of here."

Harlan agreed. "Yeah. I'd rather be outside if he comes back."

Chadwick, however, didn't look so sure. In fact, he was grinning like a madman. "To have found his tomb is one thing, but his ghost! This is too good!" He looked at Shadow. "I'm impressed! You did it."

"That's what you pay me for."

Chadwick was already prowling around, flashing his torch everywhere and taking photos as he examined every inch of it.

Harlan frowned at her sword that she still held, just in case. "Where were you concealing that?"

"Nowhere special," she said, raising an eyebrow. "But it came in handy for breaking the illusion. It's not really that useful for ghosts."

"No, I guess not."

Harlan still looked uneasy, and he shone his torch around the stonework. "This is an impressive place. He must have been revered to have merited such a special burial."

"Yeah, but why hide the entrance?" Gabe asked uneasily.

"Because he was like royalty," Harlan suggested. "They didn't want anyone stealing his valuables and ruining his afterlife."

Chadwick was already gathering up all the grave goods and packing them in his bags. He grinned at them. "You did well. Harlan was right to choose you two."

"We'll finish the payment as soon as we leave the tomb, then," Harlan told him.

"Of course." Chadwick was barely listening, and when he came to the long wooden staff, he stroked it almost reverently.

Gabe pulled Shadow to the entrance and whispered, "Entities don't just disappear. I don't like this."

"We broke the seal. It has no need to stay here now."

Gabe looked doubtful. "Things that carry that much power don't disappear so easily."

"Maybe it's scared of my magic," she suggested, her voice low and her back to the others.

"Really? Or is he in one of those objects?" He nodded to where Chadwick was closing up his bags, laden with the stolen items.

"Then it will be his problem," Shadow told him. "Ready, Chadwick?"

He nodded, a satisfied smirk on his face, and Shadow led them out into the cool night air.

Niel sighed with relief when he saw them emerge. "I was just starting to get worried. Success?"

"Of course," Shadow said confidently. "You really shouldn't doubt me."

Niel gave her a withering look. "Silly me."

"I don't suppose an overly energetic ghost headed this way?" Gabe asked hopefully.

"Ghost? No." Niel looked confused. "What the hell did you do back there?"

"Kian didn't like his grave being disturbed," Harlan told him, still looking spooked.

Shadow started piling up the stone and debris against the hole in the bank again, and Niel helped her. "I think we should keep this sealed, but I have a feeling someone will spot it sooner rather than later."

Gabe turned to Chadwick, who was busy securing his bags. He'd given Harlan the staff to hold. "Chadwick, the Druid's ghost was in there, and it didn't seem to like being disturbed. You have his grave goods now, so be careful."

Chadwick straightened up. "I'm not scared of a restless spirit."

"Maybe you should be. It manifested enough energy to throw me into a wall." He rolled his shoulders. "That doesn't happen to me very often!"

Chadwick eyes travelled across Gabe muscular physique. "I guess not. But it didn't attack all of us!"

"True, but I'm just not convinced it's gone for good."

Chadwick was already turning away, dismissing his opinion. "Thank you, but I've been doing this for a while." He hoisted the bags on to his shoulders and set off through the trees, the staff once again in his hands.

Harlan watched his retreating back. "I'm sure he'll be fine. He really has been doing this for years. He's one of our oldest clients. I better go. We're in the same car. Thanks, guys! You'll get your payment later."

Harlan left, and Gabe helped Shadow and Niel close the tomb, muttering under his breath. "Well, don't say I didn't warn him."

Seven

When Harlan arrived in London the following day, he headed straight to the office, knowing that Mason would call him in at some point for an update.

He considered the previous night a resounding success. Chadwick was overjoyed at finally breaking into the tomb, and had babbled about it all the way back to the hotel. Harlan shuddered just at the thought of it, even as he looked around at his richly appointed office, which was soothing in its normality. He hadn't seen Chadwick at breakfast as he'd checked out early, returning to his Gothic pile in Highgate.

There were many things Harlan enjoyed about his job, and the money was especially good, but he hated ghosts. When he'd first entered this line of work, it was because he had a deep interest in mythology and mythical magic objects. Not only did he study them extensively, amassing his own impressive private library, but he'd also obtained a few of those objects for himself. Small goods much like they had found last night, but without the ghost that lurked in the tomb.

It was during the course of his grave investigations—he hated to use the term tomb raiding, he wasn't Lara Croft or Indiana Jones—that he'd come across the Orphic Guild. He'd never even thought this type of work existed until he'd been approached by a much younger Mason Jacobs, who had already given up fieldwork. He winced at how long ago that was. Olivia James, another collector, was his first contact, and they had met during the pursuit of a very interesting Incan statue with reputed strange powers. He had, by the skin of his teeth, beaten her to it. But she was the one with the better buyer and the higher profit margin. They had made a deal, and the rest was history.

Olivia was English, but based in San Francisco at the time, before she had been called back to the London branch. Within a few years, he had followed. The Orphic Guild was bigger than most people realised—by design. In addition to the London office, there was the U.S. branch in San Francisco, a branch in Rome, and one in Paris.

Harlan was still wearing his jeans, boots, and leather jacket, and he flung his backpack into the corner, threw his jacket over the closest chair, and then headed up to the Guild's library on the second floor. He wanted to research Kian, the Druid. He hated being a step behind, and last night he'd felt he was just that. Chadwick was infuriating, and he'd allowed his money and influence to stop him pressing for details long before he should have. He vowed he wouldn't allow that to happen again. That everything went well was more of a testament to Shadow and Gabe than his own efforts. The trouble was, he had to be careful with Chadwick, because he was a very old client and personal friend of Mason's. Damn politics.

He pushed through the double doors into the library, relieved to see that it was empty. The smell of old pages, musk, and vanilla filled his senses and he inhaled deeply, before heading directly to the section he thought would be of most use. With luck he'd get a few hours of peace before he needed to speak to Mason. He searched quickly, pulling book after book off the shelf, rummaging through them. He found half a dozen that should help, and then turned to some of the older texts and papers that he couldn't take home. Finding a comfortable chair, he settled down to read.

When his phone rang, shadows were stretching across the floor, and Harlan's shoulders ached. He answered quickly, the noise jolting him out of his studies. As predicted, it was Mason calling him to his office for an update. He confirmed he'd be with him in fifteen minutes, and then frowned at the papers in front of him. He had found virtually nothing on the Druid, other than passing references, and nothing that suggested his burial site. Maybe he should speak to Aidan Deveraux. He was another collector who specialised in that period. Not for the first time did he wish that Mason would employ a full-time librarian. It would make all their lives so much easier.

Aiden answered within seconds. "Harlan. It's been a while. How's London?"

"The usual. How's Scotland?"

"Freezing! The snow is virtually impassable in places, but I'm holed up at the castle, and fed and watered, so that's okay."

Harlan laughed. No one had wanted to be in the far north of Scotland at this time of year, but as Aiden was already there investigating the origins of the Crossroads Circus and trying to find the actual crossroads, it made sense he should stay and taken on the new case. "I trust there are roaring fires and whiskey?"

"Those are about the only plus points. The family is arguing non-stop. But that's tedious, and I doubt it's what you've phoned about."

Harlan told him about the tomb beneath Belas Knap, and how he wanted to find out more about the Druid, Kian.

"Belas Knap has a burial beneath it?" Aiden asked, shocked. "There have long been rumours of one! In fact, excavations years ago found the ruins of a small stone circle in the centre, but that was all."

"The entrance was well over a hundred metres away, and the tomb itself was very deep. Look, I know you're lacking in specific resources, but will you see what you can find out?"

"Sure. But why do you care? It's over now, isn't it? Chadwick has his treasures, and you've confirmed the usefulness of another hunter."

"You're probably right," Harlan admitted, "but I can't shake this feeling I have. Maybe I need a good night's sleep."

"All right, I'll see what I can find and I'll be in touch."

Mason had just ended his own call when Harlan walked into his office, and he was beaming. "Great job last night. Chadwick is very happy." He gestured for Harlan to sit. "Do you know how long he's been looking for that tomb?"

"No."

"Almost twenty years, but it's been his obsession for far longer, ever since he found some archaic old documents."

Harlan eased back in his chair, feeling the previous 24 hours catching up with him. "What's so special about Kian?"

"He's one of the great Druids of the dark ages. Rumoured to have been around slightly earlier than Merlin, although Merlin got all the fame."

"You believe Merlin existed?"

Mason laughed. "Of course, but probably not quite as the stories suggest."

"Why aren't there stories about Kian? I must admit, I've been trying to find some information myself."

"Chadwick hasn't told me much. It's part of his life's great work, but you know these alchemists...they have many, varied interests. He's planning to write about it, so he's understandably cagey. He doesn't want anyone stealing his thunder."

Harlan laughed. "Does anyone care, apart from him?"

"Maybe not," Mason said, shaking his head. "But, he thinks his own great obsessions are everyone's. Anyway, he wants to invite Shadow to dinner to thank her."

Harlan shifted uneasily in his chair. "Really? He doesn't normally do things like that!"

"Like I said, it's been a long time, and this is the end of his search. He knows it took a special kind of person to break the magic that sealed the tomb. He's planning to go back to the site at some point, to investigate it more fully—in private, you understand."

"Of course. But he should go soon. It's very obvious that the bank has been disturbed now, and quite frankly it's a death trap. The passageways are partially collapsed in some places."

Mason nodded. "I'll call Shadow and extend the invite, but I just wanted to say well done. I presume you have other jobs to keep you busy now?"

"Sure," Harlan said, rising to leave. "There are a few occult objects coming up for auction this week that I need to contact some clients about, and one of our long standing searches might have thrown up a few clues to an alchemical document."

"Excellent. I'll leave you to it."

As Harlan shut the door, he reflected on how little Mason seemed to know about Kian too, but he didn't seem to care. Maybe Harlan was reading too much into it. Their clients looked for all sorts of strange things; the Callanish Ring was only one of them. All had the power to wreak destruction, but they trusted their clients to do the right thing.

He headed to his office, shaking his head. He needed a hot meal, whiskey, and bed.

It was a slow drive back to White Haven for Gabe and the others, and Gabe fumed at the tail of traffic in front of him. He wanted to speak to Nahum, anxious to see if he'd found out anything interesting, but he knew ringing at lunch time was the best time to call.

When he pulled into the farmhouse courtyard, all of the cars and bikes were gone, except for Barak's, and Gabe realised he was probably sleeping after his night shift.

"What are you up to now, Shadow?" he asked, as all three headed to the kitchen.

"I need to ride Kailen. I hate being cooped up in that car. Then I'm meeting Dan."

"Dan from the bookshop?" Niel asked, opening the fridge and pulling out half a dozen eggs.

"Yes, we're going to Tintagel this afternoon."

Niel frowned. "I think I've heard of that. Has it got a castle?"

She nodded and leaned against the counter, watching him prepare a second breakfast. "Yes. It's very famous."

Gabe had settled at the table, and felt his stomach grumble. They'd all eaten earlier, but he was already hungry again. "Breakfast for me too, please, Niel. Is that the King Arthur castle?" he asked Shadow.

She nodded, starting to prepare cups for the coffee that was percolating on the bench. "And food for me!"

Niel groaned. "I'm not the bloody cook!"

"But your breakfasts are amazing, you know they are," she said cheekily, and dodged out of the way as he flicked a tea towel at her. "I'll make you dinner later. I'll bring back rabbits again, and start a stew before I go out with Dan," she added brightly. "And yes, it's the King Arthur castle, at least according to all those myths these people love so much."

By these people, Gabe knew she meant humans. Their layers of history were muddied and confused, a mixture of the real and imagined. It was a way of grounding themselves in the world, figuring out what was important, and a rare chance to keep some magic in their common lives. It was the same as when he was first alive, just the stories were different.

"Why are you going there?" he asked.

"Dan suggested it would be a good place to start with my investigation of places where boundaries could break. Although, he also said it was one of the most popular tourist attractions in Cornwall, and there were probably better spots to look for boundary magic." She slid a cup of coffee onto the bench next to Niel, and one in front of Gabe, and then sat opposite him, while Niel continued to cook. "But I thought I'd start there—even though it might not really be his castle."

The smell of bacon began filling the room as Niel started cracking eggs. "Who's this King Arthur dude?"

"He's a famous king who saved Britain from attack and united the people. He's in the Otherworld now, so I know that he's not made up. Which means," she said, her eyes wide, "if *he's* real, what else is?"

Niel looked at her, surprised. "He's in the Otherworld? How did that happen?"

She sipped her drink thoughtfully. "I'm not entirely sure. Something to do with a spell in exchange for his sword, Excalibur. It was created by the Forger of Light—he's very famous where I'm from. Or should I say infamous? Anyway, the Lady of the Lake wanted it to happen, so Merlin agreed, and they made a long-winded spell."

Gabe smiled. He doubted it was a long-winded spell at all, but Shadow loved to either play things down or exaggerate; there was no middle ground with her.

Niel nodded. "Interesting. So why do you think Tintagel Castle might not be his?"

Shadow snorted. "Because so many places here are associated with him! They can't all be true. But, Dan is happy to show me around, so why not?"

Niel finished plating up their bacon, eggs, and toast, placed a plate in front of them all, and joined them at the table. "Of course he is. He fancies you."

"Just a sign of his good taste, then," she said, as she tucked into her food.

Niel shot a look at Gabe and he laughed. It was a relief that they all got on so well. When he had asked Shadow to stay with them, he'd done so in a fit of guilt. He thought he had killed her, but instead she'd feigned death and escaped after the witches defeated the Wild Hunt, forcing it to return to the Otherworld. When he went back to move her body, and that of a male fey who had also been killed, she had vanished, and he had spent weeks tracking her down before finally capturing her in Old Haven Wood. A pure-blood fey was adept at hiding in woodlands.

He'd felt slightly guilty about keeping her in an iron cage in the basement for so long, but he'd had no idea what to do with her. It was Zee who finally made him free her, and much pressure from Alex and Avery, two of the witches. If he had just let her leave, where the hell else would she have gone? He'd rather she stayed here where he could keep an eye on her. And yes, she was nice to look at. But she also had a good sense of humour, was a great fighter, and wasn't intimidated by the overly-testosteroned Nephilim. She was a great fit.

"What are you doing today?" she asked Niel.

"Going back to bed before I head to the warehouse this evening. I need all my strength if I'm to put up with Estelle."

"That bitch," Shadow grumbled under her breath, but before Gabe could say anything to defend Estelle, his phone rang, and he left the other two sitting at the table in order to answer it. He leaned on the counter and looked over the fields outside, rubbing the stubble on his chin as he absently thought he must shave. "Morning, Nahum."

"Hey, Gabe."

"You sound tired."

"I had a late night watching Eaton Place. You don't sound so sharp yourself."

"I was tomb hunting, and we found a restless spirit."

"That's more interesting than my job." He sounded bored.

"No intriguing revelations about the Orphic Guild, then?"

"None. I watched it for almost 24 hours, just in case, and all I've seen are regular staff coming and going like clockwork. Mason Jacobs puts in the longest hours. He's there sometimes until nine at night."

Gabe was disappointed. "I guess I should be relieved that there's nothing out of the ordinary happening. Well, within reason."

Nahum laughed. "Yeah, running an organisation that hunts for the occult is anything but normal, but I know what you mean. I've noticed they have a rear entrance, accessed by another road, very discrete, but I guess that's only to be expected. I've only seen a couple of people go in that way, though."

"How did you manage that?"

"I flew up on the roof at night and found myself a nice spot to watch from all day."

"Very creative!"

"Do you want me to stay here?"

Gabe sighed as he thought about it. "Just for a few more days. I doubt you'll discover anything, but it will make me happy."

"Sure. I'll head there again shortly."

He rang off and Gabe turned around to see Niel and Shadow staring at him expectantly. "He's found nothing," he told them. "Which is a good thing, right?"

"Yes," Niel answered. "Your arrangement with them is already proving lucrative, so don't mess it up." He directed this at Shadow, and she rose to her feet disdainfully.

"How dare you. I'm going to shoot rabbits, so you better not get in my way, or you'll find an arrow in your back."

She turned and stalked out of the room and Niel grinned at Gabe. "I really enjoy winding her up. She bites so easily."

"You won't be saying that when she actually takes a chunk out of you."

Niel rose to his feet and dumped the dirty plates in the sink. "That's going to give me some very sweet dreams. Later, brother." And with that parting shot, he headed to bed.

Eight

Shadow stood on the cliff top overlooking the ruins of Tintagel Castle and gasped.

"That is quite impressive."

Dan grinned at her. "I knew you'd love it! Who doesn't, though? It's magnificent."

Shadow narrowed her eyes and tried to imagine how it would look completely intact. "It's in such a commanding place. No wonder history says King Arthur was born here."

It was a beautiful day on which to see Tintagel, too. It was early afternoon, and the spring sunshine was warm, the sky a pale blue, and clouds like feathers scudded across it. Shadow felt as if she were on top of the world. She turned to look along the cliffs that ran on either side, and then down to the waves crashing below.

"Come on," Dan said, eager to show her more. "Wait until you're inside it. We can go over the bridge. It's fairly new."

Shadow saw the steps below, winding up the face of the cliff. "But we have to walk the steps later."

"Of course. Merlin's cave is down there, too. The tide is out so we'll be able to get in."

She followed Dan, enjoying his infectious excitement. As he walked, he told her some of the tales, and she explored the ruined rooms, stroking the stonework. They eventually ended up on the beach, the cliffs towering over them, and she looked into the gloom of the cave, trying to find a quiet moment—which was difficult with half a dozen tourists around them.

"I don't think he really lived in this!" she said, turning her nose up.

Dan laughed. "Me neither. He'd surely drown at high tide. I doubt even his magic would keep him dry. But it's romantic, as so many of the King Arthur tales are."

He led the way inside, the damp sand squelching beneath their feet, and remembering their encounter in the tomb, she asked, "Have you ever heard of a Druid called Kian?"

"Kian? No, I don't think so. Should I have?"

"Not really, but I raided his tomb last night."

Dan spun around, his mouth falling open. "What on Earth were you doing that for?"

"Another assignment. We met his ghost, and he wasn't happy."

"I wouldn't be happy if you raided my tomb, either," Dan said. He looked at the other people close by, and pulled her out and up the stairs. "Let's find a nice patch of sun and an ice cream and you can tell me all about it."

By the time they were once again on the cliff top, Shadow was hot and breathless, and accepted an ice cream cone gratefully. The grass was warm beneath her and she gazed across the sea, feeling as if she could release her own wildness here, and blend in effortlessly.

"Go on," Dan prompted, sitting next to her, cross-legged.

In between bites, she told him what had happened the night before, and about Chadwick.

Dan frowned at her. "I can't say I approve of stealing from tombs. Those things are our cultural heritage! Everything we find tells us more about our past!"

She poked her tongue out at him. "Spoilsport!"

"Thief!" he shot back.

"If it wasn't for Chadwick's investigation, no one would have found it, anyway!"

Dan shrugged. "I suppose, but I still don't approve. But, if I'm honest, I had a feeling the Orphic Guild would do this sort of thing. Did you say Chadwick is an alchemist?"

"Among other things."

"Wow, Old School. I don't think there are many around anymore!"

Shadow felt she should confess her ignorance. "I must admit, I'm not really sure what one is."

"They were the forerunners of modern scientists, studying a strange mix of philosophy, magic, astrology and other esoteric things. They were chiefly known for searching for immortality and trying to turn lead into gold." He laughed at her puzzled face. "I have no idea if they still do that, or whether it's all just research-based now. If I remember correctly, they did have a resurgence in the early twentieth century, I think. That's about a hundred years ago for you!"

"We have fey who do such things, although it's less about the search for immortality. We already have long lives. It's more about the search for potent objects. Of course magic is normal in our world, although some of us possess more of it than others."

Dan looked surprised. "Don't you all have the same amount?"

"No. I can't do what the witches do here. My magic is attuned to the earth. I can't cast spells. But other fey who come from the powerful old families have special magic, enhanced by jewels or objects. But again, they don't really use spells. Of course we have a few witches and magicians too, and bards who weave magic with their words, and other types of fey who look quite different to me."

Dan's face took on a dreamy quality. "I wish I could go there. To think it even exists is amazing."

As he spoke, Shadow saw a pixie pop up in the distance, scowling at the humans, and she turned away, trying not to laugh. She wasn't sure whether to tell Dan or not, but decided against it. Maybe one day.

"There's still a lot of magic in this world, Dan. It's just hidden, smothered in technology. But you know that, you work with a witch! If you ever feel that it's missing in your life, just visit Ravens' Wood." She shivered, as a cool wind picked up and silvered the grass along the cliff top.

"True," Dan said, standing and pulling her to her feet. "Come on, let's go to the gift shop, and then I'll take you home. Over the next few days I'll read up on alchemists. You've piqued my curiosity now."

As they walked towards the shop, Shadow's phone rang, and she frowned at the unknown number. "Hello? Shadow speaking."

"Excellent, this is Mason Jacobs, my dear. Remember me?"

"Of course."

"I have spoken to Mr Chadwick today, who is so pleased with your help last night that he has invited you and Gabe to dinner, to show his thanks."

"Really? He's paying us!" Shadow said, not sure if she wanted to go to dinner with such an annoying man. "That's enough."

"No, no," Mason persisted. "He's really keen. This is something he's been looking for, for nearly half of his life. It could mean more lucrative work for you, too."

He left that comment hanging for a moment, and Shadow felt that to refuse would be rude, more than anything. They did not want to annoy Chadwick or Mason.

"Fine, that's very generous of him. I can speak to Gabe about it. When was he thinking?"

"Saturday night? He lives in London. You could book a hotel, make a weekend of it. There are many amazing sights to see around here."

She nodded, pausing outside the shop, and Dan waited with her, trying not to appear as if he was eavesdropping. "Okay. I'll call you to confirm."

She could practically hear Mason preening on the other end of the phone. "Excellent! I look forward to hearing from you."

She groaned as he hung up. Thank the Gods Harlan wasn't as formal.

"What's up?" Dan asked.

"I've been invited to dinner with the alchemist, Chadwick!"

"Great," Dan said, looking mischievous. "You can report back. Now come on in and I'll buy you a King Arthur key ring!"

𝕏 𝕏 𝕏

It was seven in the evening before Shadow saw Gabe again.

As soon as she arrived home, she started cooking her rabbit stew, and the rich smells drifted around the house. She knew it amused the Nephilim that she liked to cook, because she was anything but domestic; in fact, Eli had called her feral one night after she'd thrown her dagger at him and it had lodged in the wall mere inches from his head. But there was something soothing about the chopping, preparing, and balancing of flavours that quieted her overactive mind.

She could hear the shouts of Barak, Ash, and Eli from the living room where they were again fighting on the games console, the air ripe with insults that should have made her blush if she wasn't storing them for use later. Niel had already left for the warehouse, and Zee was at The Wayward Son, working the evening shift.

Gabe entered the kitchen, his hair still damp from the shower. He had jeans on and nothing else, and her eyes ran across his broad, sculpted chest before eventually resting on his amused face.

"Looked enough?" he asked.

"Well, if you insist on walking around displaying yourself like a prized cock, what do you expect?"

"I'm hoping you mean cockerel?" he asked, holding her gaze challengingly.

"What else would I mean?" She turned back to the pot and stirred it slowly, her tongue in her cheek as she tried to suppress a smirk.

"And for the record, I am not a cockerel, either. I'm looking for a clean t-shirt."

"I am not your laundry woman, so how would I know where it is?"

"If you remember anything at all, the laundry room is the other side of this one. I'm simply passing through."

He strode past her and she turned to watch his retreating back, admiring the sculpted muscles there too, and wondering where he put those huge wings. Herne's horns! These Nephilim stirred her blood like no other. Not that anything would ever happen between them, especially Gabe. They were housemates, with a business to run. But there was no harm in looking.

When he returned, he'd pulled on a clean white t-shirt, and if she was honest, that looked almost as good as his bare chest. She distracted herself from her thoughts by grabbing a loaf of crusty bread and started to slice it. "I heard from Mason today. We've been invited to dinner with Chadwick, on Saturday night."

Gabe groaned, as she knew he would. "You're kidding, I hope. That sounds like the most boring evening ever." He reached into the fridge and pulled out two bottles of beer, automatically popping them both and handing her one. "Why?"

"He's very grateful for our help."

"He paid us."

"I know, that's what I said. But Mason insisted, and it felt rude to say no. Especially if we want more business!"

Gabe grimaced. "Did you say this Saturday?"

"Yep."

"I can't go. I need to be at the docks, the one in Falmouth. There's another big shipment due, and Estelle wants me there."

"Does she, now?" she asked, wondering what else Estelle might want to do with Gabe. He frowned at her insinuation, and she moved on. "Great, I'll cancel."

"No. You should go. You're right. It's very important to keep our clients happy." He smiled smugly.

She threw her head back and groaned. "How very convenient! I don't want to go on my own! It could be awkward." She brightened then. "Nahum could come. He's already in London."

"No. I want to keep him an unknown entity. Perhaps Harlan could join?"

"That could work. I like Harlan."

Gabe clinked her beer with his own. "There you go, then. I'm sure Chadwick won't mind. Although, Harlan might."

"I'm so charming that I'm certain he'd love to accompany me."

Gabe's smile was tight. "You so are. Now, is that ready to eat, or am I going to die of starvation?"

Nine

S hadow negotiated the train and tube easily, checking into her hotel in London by mid-afternoon on Saturday.

She was staying at the same place as Nahum, and as agreed, at five on the dot, there was a knock at her door. She opened it to find him leaning against the opposite wall, and he gave her a lazy smile.

"You made it."

"Of course I made it, I'm not an idiot." She turned and headed inside as he followed.

"Always so touchy!"

"Only when people insinuate things."

He sighed. "I wasn't insinuating anything. It was just a greeting." He shook his head. "You are such hard work sometimes."

"Am not!" She headed to the mini bar and pulled out a beer. "May I offer you a drink in an effort to soothe your delicate sensibilities?"

"My delicate sensibilities! Yes, you can." He took the bottle from her, popped the cap, and sipped while he paced around the room. "Are you all set for tonight?"

She gestured to a black, slim-fitting dress hanging against the door, and strappy heels waiting on the floor. "Of course. I'm making an effort."

Nahum almost choked. "I never thought I'd see the day!" His eyes flitted from the dress to her and back again. "And heels? Can you even walk in them?"

Shadow glared at him over her bottle. "Of course I can." She winced. "Admittedly, I practised. El helped."

Nahum laughed. "Go El! Did she give you the outfit, too?"

"You don't think I'd buy one?" she asked, mildly affronted.

"No. You don't seem the shopping type."

"I am if it's for weapons! You should see the market in Dragon's Hollow. Weapons to die for!"

"Isn't that an oxymoron?" He smirked at her, and sat down in a chair next to a small table.

She grinned at him. "You know exactly what I mean." Nahum was very charming, just like the other Nephilim, despite the smirk on his face.

"So you're hoping to make an impression tonight?"

"I've already made an impression," she replied smugly. "But business is business. And besides, I could still kick your ass in a dress."

"Never suggested you couldn't. Although, I do wonder where you'll put your knife," he said, raising an eyebrow.

"Let me worry about that!"

"Is Harlan picking you up?"

She nodded, and sat on the bed. "At six-thirty. Apparently, Chadwick lives in a Victorian Gothic house on the edge of some park. I'm intrigued! I've never been invited to dinner before. Well, not here anyway. I just eat with you lot, or at the pub with the witches!" She reflected for a moment. "I think I'm quite excited. It will be interesting to see where he lives, what he cooks…"

Nahum smiled. "It's strange, isn't it, this new life?"

"Do you think so, too?"

"Of course! We all do. We're living outside of our time, and although I'm growing used to all of this," he gestured around expansively, "I still find myself needing to stop and orient myself sometimes."

Shadow regarded him silently for a moment, and then voiced something she had been thinking for some time. "I'm lucky to be living with all of you. You, more than anyone, understand how weird this life is."

"Well, at least we're in the world we were born in, unlike you," he said softly. "But it's virtually unrecognisable."

She frowned. "I actually don't know what I'd have done if Gabe hadn't asked me to stay! I thought I'd live in the wood, but that's ridiculous, really."

"You would have managed. You are fey, after all," he said, a hint of sarcasm to his tone.

Now she knew he was teasing her. "And you're cheeky."

He laughed and stood. "I better go. I just wanted to make sure you were okay. I'll be watching the Guild again later. Phone if you need me."

"Is it really worth watching it?" she asked, following him to the door.

"I don't think so, but it keeps Gabe happy. He's thorough, and he's always done the right thing, for as long as I've known him."

"He's a decent half-brother, then?"

"The best. But, we're all like brothers, regardless. We're unique. And we were all betrayed by those who supposedly loved us." His eyes darkened for a moment, and he opened the door before he could say anything else, as if he felt he'd shared too much. "Just be careful tonight. And yes—" he held a hand up, palm outwards. "I know you can look after yourself! More importantly, have fun!"

He winked and left the room, and Shadow watched him go, wondering exactly what he meant by *betrayed*.

Harlan pulled his car onto the gravelled drive in front of Chadwick's Gothic home, all turrets and arched windows and chimneys, and Shadow studied it for a moment.

"This is a cool place. It's a bit like a small castle!"

Harlan laughed. "It's not as old as it looks. In the nineteenth century, a lot of these were built by the Victorians after there was a resurgence of interest in all things Gothic."

"Have you been here before?"

"Once, years ago." He raised an eyebrow. "I feel very privileged to be asked again!"

"Thank the Gods I put a dress on then," Shadow said, amused. She pointed to the old Jaguar in the driveway. "Is that Chadwick's?"

"No, that's Mason's. It's his pride and joy."

They exited the car and headed to the front door that was positioned beneath a huge stone archway and rang the bell, hearing it tone deep within the house. In seconds, Chadwick was ushering them in. "Excellent, welcome!" His eyes swept across them both approvingly. "My dear, you look just fabulous in that dress!"

Shadow smiled, self-consciously smoothing it over her slender hips. "Thank you. I felt the occasion warranted it."

Harlan tried not to laugh. It might have fit like a glove but he could tell she was entirely uncomfortable wearing it. To be fair, he wasn't all that comfortable in his suit. Give him his jeans and bike leathers any day.

However, all thought of discomfort left him when he looked around. He'd forgotten how overpowering this place was. The house was decorated dramatically, with dark paper and gilt patterns. Side lights were dim, and the flooring was a mixture of tiles and thick rugs.

Shadow was equally impressed. "Wow. I even feel like I'm in a castle."

Chadwick looked smug. "I like to think I'm the King of the Castle when I'm home." He led them along the hallway and into a large drawing room, also dimly lit, and with a roaring fire in a stone fireplace that was easily half as tall as the room. Mason was standing in front of it, holding a glass of wine.

"Our guests of honour! Good drive over?"

"As good as can be expected on a Saturday night," Harlan said dryly. "At least it's not raining, but I don't think it will last. There are a lot of clouds out there."

"Forget the weather!" Chadwick said, pouring them white wine. "You're here now, and I have a selection of food you won't believe. Although," he looked sheepish, which was very unlike Chadwick, "I confess that I didn't cook. My chef came in earlier and prepared everything, assisted by my housekeeper!"

Shadow was pacing around the room, glass in hand, studying it with narrowed eyes. "You have a lot of things!" she observed.

The whole house was an exhibit, Harlan thought. Paintings and prints jostled for space upon the walls. Vases, figurines, and other objects, were crowded on occasional tables and shelves.

"I do love art and beautiful pieces," Chadwick admitted. "When I buy something, I have to display it to perfection!"

"There are so many different styles here," Harlan observed. "I had no idea you were such a magpie!"

"That's because he only uses us for certain items," Mason said. "Where do you keep your more unusual collections?"

"My arcane treasures? In other rooms, slightly less public than this one. I'll show you later." He looked at them knowingly, fellow conspirators in the occult business. "But first, *hors d'oeuvres!*"

For the next half an hour or so they all chatted politely, and Harlan had to admit Chadwick was the perfect host. He lead them to the dining room, also decorated dramatically, and they sat at a table covered with white linen and dressed with glassware and silver, while Chadwick carried in the dishes himself. That seemed odd, and gave Harlan the faintest prickling of unease.

He knew that Chadwick's housekeeper lived at the house and helped him with everything. He was a rich bachelor, and not used to looking after himself.

They had eaten the starters and the main course, when Harlan asked, "Where's your housekeeper, Chadwick?"

He answered quickly. "She has the night off! Heading to the cinema, I believe. I've had to manage."

"And doing so beautifully," Mason said smoothly, shooting Harlan a look of annoyance.

Chadwick pressed on. "Anyway, my dear, tell me a little about you." He fixed Shadow with an intent stare and she shuffled uncomfortably.

"There's nothing interesting about me. I was brought up a long way from here, but have recently settled in Cornwall. A place called White Haven."

"And what do you do, other than help find treasures?"

"Not a lot. I work with Gabe in his security business."

"The man you were with the other night."

"Yes, that's right, and Niel, who was also there." She was answering politely enough, but Harlan could tell she was wary about saying too much. He hoped Mason hadn't said anything about where she was really from, either.

"They are uncommonly large men," he said sharply.

"They are distantly related. Sort of cousins. They're all big."

"But you said Gabe couldn't be here tonight?"

"Unfortunately not. Gabe sends his apologies. He's tied up with his other business. Thanks for letting me come with Harlan instead."

"And how did you meet them?"

"We met on Halloween last year, at a party!" She shrugged, a hint of amusement in her eyes. "We hit it off! I live with them now."

"Just the two of them?"

"Yes." Shadow sipped her wine, and Harlan exchanged a nervous glance with Mason. "And what about you? Have you lived here long?"

He brushed it off. "It seems like forever." He pushed away from the table. "I'll bring dessert."

"Do you need help?" Harlan asked, moving his chair as if to rise. He felt guilty watching him trip back and forth to the adjoining kitchen on his own.

"No!" Chadwick smiled as if he realised he'd answered too abruptly. "I'm fine."

In the brief moments they had before he returned, Harlan said to Shadow, "Sorry. I wasn't expecting him to quiz you."

Shadow shrugged. "That's okay, it's just conversation. No harm done."

Mason spoke quietly. "I must admit, he doesn't seem quite right tonight. He normally loves to talk about himself."

Before anyone could answer, Chadwick returned with a tray of chocolate desserts in glass goblets. "I hope you all like chocolate. They're divine."

They all murmured their assent, and Harlan started to eat, the rich flavour filling his mouth. He barely noticed Shadow's frown as she looked across at Chadwick and placed her spoon down. And then he felt very dizzy, the room began to spin, and everything went black.

Ten

S hadow was on her feet in seconds, and she pulled her dagger out of the sheath strapped to her inner thigh.

Mason and Harlan were facedown on the table, unconscious, while Chadwick looked at her with cold, calculating eyes.

"You know, it's generally not polite to poison someone at dinner!" she said, half-inclined to slit his throat right now.

"I've never been one to follow convention. More importantly," Chadwick asked, "why aren't you affected?"

"I could taste the drug in my food." She could taste it still, a bitter residue disguised by the bitter chocolate. It had given her a faint buzz, but nothing more, and she shook her head, clearing the last of it away.

A slow, evil smile crept across Chadwick's face. "I knew it. You're fey."

"You're ridiculous. Have you gone insane?"

"Who else could have penetrated the magic that sealed my tomb?"

All evening she'd been looking at him, feeling something was amiss, and clearly so had Harlan and Mason. Suddenly, it hit her.

Chadwick wasn't Chadwick anymore.

"Kian, I presume?" She stood, frozen, her knife poised, deciding not to comment on his accusation.

He leaned back in his chair, watching her. "At your pleasure."

"I really don't think it is. What do you want?"

"My freedom!"

"You seem to have it. Why did you invite us here?"

"Because I wanted to speak to you!"

She shot a glance at Mason and Harlan, relieved to see they were still breathing. "You're not planning on killing them, then?"

"No. The poison was just to shut them up. You're the one I want."

"Why?"

He didn't answer. Instead, he studied her, and she wondered what he was waiting for. And then she wondered what *she* was waiting for. She should act now. Bury her knife in his chest and watch him die. That would be the end of it. Except that would also be the end of Chadwick, an innocent man, and potentially Kian's spirit would find another body to inhabit.

Shadow repeated her question, her irritation rising. "Why do you want me?"

"I needed to know what you are. And now I do. But your friends aren't fey."

"And neither am I."

"Liar." With a swift movement, he pulled an unusual-looking gun from under the table, took aim, and shot at her chest.

With lightning reflexes, she dived for cover behind a large stuffed sofa, and peeking around it, released the knife without hesitation. It flew at Chadwick, but he ducked and rolled out of the way surprisingly quickly, and her dagger missed him and landed in the wall.

Shadow could smell iron in the air. It must be the bullets. She didn't know much about guns, but she was pretty sure he didn't need an iron bullet to kill her. Any would do. He didn't seem to want to take a chance. Kian rose to his feet, raised the gun, and marched across the room, ready to fire again.

Shadow cursed the fact that she hadn't brought her sword, or another knife, and realised even with her speed she couldn't get to the one embedded in the wall that quickly. She picked up the nearest object to hand, which was a solid wooden-carved head on a small table, and threw it at Chadwick.

It hit his left arm, spinning him around, and he yelled in pain. The gun fired, shooting wildly up at the ceiling, and a shower of plaster rained down. He ran from the room and she raced after him, kicking her heels off, and retrieving her dagger as she went.

He dashed through the kitchen and out the other side, into a hallway. A couple of doors stood open, all with light coming from them, but Kian was nowhere in sight.

Shadow paused, catching her breath and listening for sounds of movement. A *thump* came from one of the rooms ahead, and she ran, only slowing as she reached the threshold. She edged forward until she could see the whole space.

It was full of Chadwick's collections. Plinths and tables had been placed with care, and objects were lit with soft spotlights. A collection of antique swords was on the wall, the familiar shape of the Empusa's blade in the centre. But there was no Kian.

Double doors leading to a connected room were on the left, and after satisfying herself that it was safe, she crossed to them, deciding to get another weapon on the way. She picked the Empusa's, wishing it was her own sword instead, but it would be better than nothing. She chided herself for not suspecting something sooner. Even Harlan had said that Chadwick was being surprisingly generous with his thanks. She remembered Gabe telling her he didn't think the spirit had gone, and she'd dismissed him, like an idiot.

The room beyond was in darkness, and she turned the lights off in the one she was in before she advanced, trusting that her eyesight was better than his. She dropped to the floor, waiting for her vision to adjust, and within seconds saw movement ahead.

She crept forward, wondering what to do with him. Her best options were to capture him or knock him unconscious, while they figured out a way to expel Kian from Chadwick. Alex, the witch, would know how.

She could see Kian clearly now, crouching as he tried to hide behind a piece of large, bulky furniture. She could just make out his leg, and crossing the threshold, she continued to ease towards him, only stopping when she heard a whirring noise and a clang overhead. She looked up in time to see a cage dropping on her.

Thank the Gods for high ceilings. She dived to the side and the cage crashed down, missing her by inches. Kian stood and shot at her, and she threw her knife at him simultaneously. It landed in the centre of his chest and he jerked back, hitting the wall before sliding to the floor, and she felt a searing pain as the bullet hit her left thigh. And then the most peculiar thing happened.

She watched Kian's shade leave Chadwick's inert form, its boundaries surprisingly clear. She could see his features, and a red gleam behind his eyes, before the spirit disappeared through the wall.

Damn it.

Despite the pain, she stood up, limped to the door, and entered the hall beyond. Kian was swifter than her now, already close to the kitchen.

Herne's hairy balls. He must be heading for Harlan and Mason.

Her wounded thigh burned, and blood dripped down her leg as she hobbled after him.

She'd just reached the dining room when she saw Kian's ghost grin at her from where he stood between Harlan and Mason. He was shockingly solid, and she briefly wondered why he needed to inhabit another body. He was of average height, with a dark shock of hair, thick eyebrows, and an intense stare. She could even make out his clothes—a loose shirt and trousers, covered by a long robe with a cowl hood. Mason was already rousing, his head lifting from the table, but Harlan was still inert. He was also closest to her, and she grabbed him, hauling him off the chair and onto the floor with her all strength. But she couldn't protect both of them. Not that she had any idea of how to protect a body from possession.

Kian sank into Mason, and with a jerky movement, he stood on shaking legs. He paused for moment, grinning maliciously at Shadow. "Until next time!"

He ran out the door, and within seconds she heard a car engine roar to life, the spatter of gravel, and then silence fell.

Bollocks!

She sat besides Harlan, feeling for his pulse. The beat was strong and regular, and with an inward sigh of relief, she called Nahum, relieved when he picked up quickly.

"Hey, Shadow. Isn't it a little rude to be ringing someone else at a dinner party?"

"Not when your host is dead."

His lazy, teasing tone disappeared immediately. "What? Are you okay?"

"I've been shot with an iron bullet and I'm bleeding all over the floor. Harlan's unconscious, and Mason has been possessed."

"Give me your address. I'm coming right now."

"No! I need you to wait and see if Mason turns up at the Guild. If he does, follow him. Besides, I have no idea where I am."

"You really don't do things by halves."

"No shit. I'll find the address and text it to you, but until then, watch for Mason."

She rang off, and slapped Harlan's face. "Harlan, wake up!"

He groaned and then went limp again.

Deciding to give him a few more moments of blissful unconsciousness, she examined her leg. The bullet had taken a chunk from her outer thigh, about two thirds of the way up, and it was still bleeding profusely. She grabbed a napkin from the table and pressed it to the wound, wincing from the pain, and then decided to call Gabe.

He answered quickly. "I've just heard from Nahum. You should have called me first."

Shadow's temper started to rise. "Well, excuse me! And yes, I'm all right, thanks, other than missing a large portion of my blood!"

He hesitated, and then said, "Sorry, worry makes me cross. Besides, you do sound fine!"

"Asking wouldn't go amiss, just so you know!"

There was a longer pause, and Shadow could almost see him trying to control his temper. "Nahum will bring you home."

"I think he should stay here, actually. To try to find Kian."

"Fill me in, on everything," he ordered.

Shadow took her time, describing the evening as best she could. "I'm going to wake Harlan now, I hope, and then... I don't know," she sighed, suddenly weary, "We need to decide what to do next."

"You shouldn't get involved with the police."

"I don't think I have much choice." Part of her wanted to run, but as the witches kept reminding her, that wasn't the way this world worked.

"No, probably not." His voice was serious, and Shadow knew he'd be weighing up the implications of this for all of them. "Ask Harlan for Mason's address, and tell Nahum. It might be worth him checking there, too."

"That's true. Harlan is still unconscious, but as soon as I have it, I'll send it. I'll call you later."

Shadow hung up and turned to Harlan again.

"Harlan! Wake up!"

She shook his shoulders, relieved to see his eyes finally flicker open. "Shadow? What's going on?" He lifted his head, confused. "Why am I on the floor?"

"You were drugged."

His eyes focussed and he sat up. "What? Ow! My head hurts, and I feel sick." He lifted his hand to his head. "I was eating. Did you say drugged?"

Shadow filled him in on what happened, and as she talked, Harlan started to look less pasty and more worried.

"Chadwick is dead?"

She nodded. "Sorry. It was him or me. As it was, he took a chunk out of me." She gestured to her leg.

Harlan leaned over. "Show me."

She lifted the napkin, showing him her wound, and fresh blood started to well again. "It stings, which I suppose is to be expected. I'm not sure if the iron bullet is making it worse."

He examined it and then said, "Did you say Mason is possessed?"

She nodded. "Again, it was either you or him, and I could protect you because you were closer." She paused, frowning. "Protect might not be the right word. How do you stop a ghost? Anyway, he was next to Mason, so... Not the most logical choice for him. You're younger, fitter—but there you go."

Harlan smiled briefly. "Thank you. I appreciate not being possessed, but," he glanced at her wound again, "we need to clean that."

Shadow pressed the napkin back into place. "Later. For now, can you find something to strap it up?"

Harlan nodded, and rising on still shaky feet, headed to the kitchen, returning with a fresh towel, which he proceeded to wrap tightly around the wound.

"That's the best I can do. We need to get you to a hospital."

"No way. I'd rather see Eli or Briar, the earth witch. She's the best healer I know. They'll ask uncomfortable questions in a hospital. What are we going to do about Chadwick?"

Harlan stood and extended a hand to her, pulling her to her feet. "Can you walk?"

"Just about."

"Lean on me." He proffered her his right arm, and they made their way slowly through the kitchen and down the rear corridor to the room where Chadwick's body lay. It was pretty obvious that he was dead, but leaving Shadow leaning on a chair, Harlan bent down and felt Chadwick's pulse. "He's definitely dead. Damn it."

A million things raced through Shadow's mind. "What now? Do we call the police?"

Harlan rubbed his face wearily. "There's a detective we use for cases like this. She's used to the paranormal."

"Someone like Newton, you mean?"

"Yeah." He turned to her, his eyes full of sadness. "I liked Chadwick, most of the time. He was annoying and impatient, but he didn't deserve this."

"I take it he doesn't live with anyone else?"

"No. He hadn't had time for relationships. He's a confirmed bachelor. His close friends were other eccentrics... And us." He looked around at the ornate furnishings and rich fabrics. "Ironic, isn't it? The very thing he's been looking for years to discover has killed him." He frowned as he focussed on a corner of the room. "Is that Kian's staff?" It was propped against shelving, as if it had been put there and then forgotten, and he collected it and handed it to Shadow. "I can still feel power in this, can you?"

She held it carefully, and nodded. "I can." She felt a faint hope stir. "You know, I think he forgot this in the rush to escape."

"Good. We can use it to bargain with." He pulled his phone out. "I'd better call Maggie."

"Is that the detective?"

He grinned for the first time since he'd regained consciousness. "Oh, yes. You're gonna love her!"

Eleven

G abe sat on the sofa in the living room of the farmhouse, and gazed vacantly at the TV. The sound was muted and he wasn't even focussing on the picture. He was deciding what do with the situation in London.

"Trouble?" Niel asked, handing him a beer and sitting in the chair opposite him. It was past midnight, but they all kept late hours, and he had just returned home from the warehouse.

"Yeah." He looked at Niel bleakly. "Shadow was attacked earlier this evening by the ghost of Kian—the spirit from the Druid tomb. Chadwick is dead."

Niel's jaw dropped. "How?"

Gabe ran through the details. "Nahum is trying to track Mason, aka Kian, without success, and I'm waiting to hear back from Shadow. She's being interviewed by the police. A woman called Maggie."

"This is really bad."

"I know. But Shadow says this detective knows the paranormal world, and hopefully she won't be arrested and thrown in jail."

Niel snorted. "Like that would hold her!"

"But it would make life tricky."

"What can we do?"

"Absolutely sod all for now. We need to figure out what Kian wants with Shadow. But she needs to heal first."

Niel frowned. "Isn't she like us? Can't she heal quicker than humans?"

"Not like we can. And she was shot with an iron bullet, which doesn't help."

His voice rose with surprise. "He knew what she was?"

"Apparently, yes."

"This keeps getting worse." Niel stood and paced to the fire.

Gabe thought through his conversation with Shadow again, feeling despondent. "She thinks Kian wants his own body, but we have no idea how he'll recover that. And in the meantime, we have to try to get him out of Mason's body without killing him."

"Why didn't he kill Harlan and Mason?"

"Good question. According to what he said to Shadow, he just wanted them out of the way so he could get her alone." He scratched his chin, perplexed. "He was either trying to kill her, or wound her badly enough to kidnap her."

Niel's back was to the fire, his voice grim. "We regained our bodies through blood. Is that what he'll do?"

Niel had voiced the very thing that Gabe was thinking. "We have to consider that it's a possibility. I'm pretty pissed that our first job has already caused bloodshed."

"You didn't do it on purpose."

"I promised Alex. I take my promises seriously."

"You couldn't have foreseen this," Niel said, trying to reassure him. "We'll honour our promises by stopping Kian. But, we need to know why he wants Shadow, and what he'll do next!"

Gabe nodded. "It must mean something that her magic opened his tomb."

"That's what worries me. He was sealed in for a reason. Why? What was so bad about Kian that his burial place was hidden with fey magic? Why would the fey even become involved in sealing a Druid's tomb?"

Silence fell as Gabe tried to make sense of Kian's actions. "Maybe fey blood is what he really needs, not human. That's why he made a cage for her. He must have acted quickly in the last few days since we released him. Make the cage, invite her to dinner, drug the others..."

"And now he's hiding, biding his time until he can trap her."

"We need to get her back here," Gabe said decisively. "She'll be better protected with all of us around."

Niel barked out a laugh. "Ha! I don't think she'll see it like that."

"She's not stupid. She'll know she's a target, and for all her skills, she'll still need help. I'll get Nahum to bring her home."

"Shadow might be right. He may be of more use staying in London, looking for Mason."

"No. Harlan can do that. He knows the city better, and has connections there. I'll call Nahum now."

$$ \text{大} \quad \text{大} \quad \text{大} $$

Harlan watched Maggie, officially known as Detective Inspector Milne, walk around the room where Chadwick's body lay.

She was what he called a 'ball buster,' in American slang. And he didn't mean that affectionately. She was of average height and size, with light brown hair and blue eyes, and at first glance, you'd almost dismiss her as insignificant. But those were the only average things about her. Once you got to know her, she was unforgettable. Maggie was intelligent, short-tempered, had a great sense of humour, and swore like a trooper. She was currently in full flow.

"Christ almighty, Harlan! You really are an A-1 shit! Look at this place!" She flung her arms wide. "It's the mother lode of all occult shit put together! And a cage? A fucking cage? Is this the fucking Wicker Man?"

Harlan had been trying to calm her down, unsuccessfully, for the last half an hour. "I know how it looks, but we'll find him. The whole thing has been unexpected!"

"Un-fucking expected? You really are taking the piss! And you!" She rounded on Shadow, who sat in a chair in the corner, looking far more amused that she should. "Your knife is in that man's chest!"

Shadow smiled smugly. "I know that. I put it there. It was an excellent shot, if I may say so. I was on the floor, bent and twisted, and had just escaped that landing on me." She pointed at the cage, which lay inside the entrance of the room, next to the connecting door. "I impressed myself."

Maggie stood in front of her, hands on her hips. "Well, lucky you! I now have all this shit to report on! And did you say a resurrected Druid?" She'd turned back to Harlan at this point, and glared at him.

Harlan, for all his bravado, wilted under her gaze. "Yes, we think so. The only person who knew much about him is dead."

"Fucking unbelievable!"

Harlan could feel his balls shrinking already. "I know, sorry." He sounded lame, even to his own ears. "But I have someone who's trying to track him down, and I can call Olivia to help. She's in town at the moment."

Maggie scowled. "That's all I need, more bloody Orphic meddling!"

"It's called help, Maggie. We like to clean up our own shit."

"No, no, no." She pointed at him. "You don't get away with this that easily. This will eat into my time. I'm already dealing with enough paranormal crap in this seething hotbed of weirdness that's called London, and you've just added to it!"

"What are you going to do about Shadow?" Harlan asked, trying to bring her back to his current concern.

Maggie addressed him with a narrowed eyed glare. "I'll need a statement, obviously. But because it's very clear that this was an attempted kidnapping and imprisonment," she swivelled to Shadow, "and that you were shot, I won't hold you or charge you. It's pretty obvious you were defending yourself."

Harlan sighed with relief. It was what he was hoping for, but he hadn't wanted to presume. "Thank you. We both appreciate that, don't we, Shadow?" He looked at her expectantly.

"Yes, thank you. I really had no choice." To her credit, she looked genuinely contrite. "I liked Chadwick, too."

"Can we give our statements here?" Harlan asked, eager to avoid going to the station.

Maggie nodded and yelled, "Walker! Get your arse in here and take their statements!"

A tall, skinny man with blond hair and a short beard appeared in the doorway, a look of weary resignation on his face. Detective Sergeant Ted Walker had worked with Maggie for a couple of years, and seemed to cope well with her regular verbal abuse. "I'm not deaf, Maggie." He looked at Harlan. "Who wants to go first?"

Harlan jumped in, "Do Shadow first, then she can get going and have her leg looked at. I'd like to stay and go through some of Chadwick's papers once my statement is done."

Walker glanced at Maggie, who nodded and said, "But keep out of the dining room for now, and this room, until we've gathered evidence." She pointed at the gun on the floor next to Chadwick's body. "Is that a Flintlock?"

Harlan nodded, thinking it was the perfect choice for using an old iron bullet—not that he'd tell Maggie that. She didn't need to know the significance of an iron bullet to Shadow. "Weapons were another of Chadwick's interests. Fortunately, their aim is usually off."

"Tell my leg that," Shadow said snarkily. She looked pale now, and tired, and Harlan guessed that even fey had their physical limits.

Walker must have thought so too, as he headed to her side, and sat in the next chair. "Let's get started. Name?"

"Shadow Walker of the Dark Ways, Star of the Evening, Hunter of Secrets. But you can shorten it to Shadow Walker, and then we'll have matching names." Shadow looked at him, amused.

Harlan saw Walker look at her with wide-eyed amazement, as if he was going to ask more, but then he just shrugged. "Yes ma'am."

Harlan suppressed a grin, and Maggie shot him a look. "Don't think I'm not going to investigate her."

He echoed Walker. "Yes ma'am." And then he sat down and waited his turn.

When Shadow emerged from Chadwick's home later that evening, she passed through the police cordon and official vehicles, limping on her now increasingly sore leg, and found Nahum a short distance down the road, as they'd arranged on the phone.

He exited the car and opened the passenger door. "I was getting worried." He frowned at the staff that she was using to lean on. "What's that?"

"It's from Kian's tomb. I thought I should bring it with me."

He jerked his head toward the house and the police cars. "Doesn't that count as evidence?"

She grinned. "Yes, but I disguised it with enough glamour to get it past them. It's too important to leave there." She eased into the car, and after Nahum put the staff on the back seat, he drove away before anyone could stop them.

The car was warm, and Shadow relaxed for the first time in hours. "That was an ordeal. Remind me never to be interviewed by the police again."

He shot her a swift look. "Try not to stab anyone again."

"It was kill or be killed! I'll miss that dagger..." Now that they were safely away from the house, she pulled the Empusa's sword from her jacket, where she'd hidden it with her magic. "I got this, too."

Nahum was concentrating on driving, but he looked at it with surprise. "You've stolen it?"

"Well, he doesn't need it anymore. And besides, I think it has more useful qualities than we initially realised." She leaned against the seat, the warmth of the heater making her sleepy. The evening seemed like a dream now, and she thought back to when she'd picked the sword up and saw Kian's shade fleeing

Chadwick's dead body. "I think it makes you see spirits more clearly. That's what it appeared like, anyway. The whole thing happened so quickly."

"Really? That's intriguing. Have you spoken to Gabe?"

"Only briefly, just after I phoned you. I haven't had time since."

"Okay. Tell me what happened, as much as you can remember, and then you can sleep on the drive home."

"Wait," she sat up, confused. "Aren't we going to the hotel? My bag's there."

"I've packed everything, and checked you out already. Is that okay?" He looked suspicious. "You haven't hidden anything in the hotel room, have you?"

"No." She leaned back again, relieved not to have to do anything else, and kicked her heels off. "Why do women wear these things?"

"Because you look hot as hell in them. Did you chase him in those?"

She laughed. "No! I took them off. Did you search for him? Mason, I mean?"

"Of course. I staked out the Guild for another hour or so, and then went to Mason's address. But he didn't show at either place, and there's nothing else I can do at the moment. Gabe wants us both home. Now stop getting distracted and tell me what happened, before you forget the details."

𝞜 𝞜 𝞜

They arrived home at four in the morning. A few lights were on in the farmhouse, the usual selection of cars and bikes on the driveway, and there was also a car Shadow didn't recognise.

As soon as Nahum pulled into the courtyard, Gabe opened the front door and ran over, closely followed by Niel. Gabe helped Shadow get out of the car, while Nahum headed to the boot for the bags.

"I'm fine, honestly," Shadow said, reassuring Gabe, but wincing. She felt horribly stiff and slow.

He ignored her. "Liar. Briar's already here." He glanced at Nahum. "Any updates?"

"No, nothing new. The drive was uneventful." He turned to Niel. "The staff and the Empusa's sword are on the back seat. Can you get them?"

"Sure," Niel said, already opening the rear doors. "That's all we need, Kian's magic stick."

"It's important!" Shadow said, frowning.

"Yeah, yeah," he muttered.

"Send Briar and Eli over," Gabe said to him, and then led Shadow to her own room in the outbuilding she had made her home. It was warm and the lighting was low, and he escorted her to her bed.

"Wait," she said. "I can't sleep in this dress. I'll ruin it. It's probably already ruined, actually—there's blood all over it. Can you grab me a t-shirt? Top drawer."

She struggled with the zip, and when Gabe returned, he placed her clothing on the bed and turned her around. "Allow me."

Shadow was suddenly self-conscious—which was ridiculous. She felt a tingle run through her as air rushed across her skin when Gabe unzipped her dress down to the small of her back.

"Can you manage?" he asked, a rough edge to his voice.

She looked over her shoulder to find his dark eyes fixed firmly on her face. "Yes, thanks." She wriggled out of it and it fell to the floor, and Gabe quickly turned his back. She smiled to herself at his unexpected gentlemanly behaviour, and then chided herself. Why was she surprised? Gabe was always a gentleman. She swiftly pulled the t-shirt over her head and slid into bed, stacking pillows behind her. "All done."

Gabe picked the dress up off the floor, and placed it on the back of a chair. "Do you need anything? A drink, some food?"

She smiled at him gratefully as she considered her options. Whiskey was tempting, but instead she said, "Hot chocolate, really hot and sweet please."

"Sure thing." He paused for a moment, his gaze serious. "I was very worried. I'm glad you're okay."

"Thanks. I'm sorry to be a pain. I've caused us all a lot of trouble, haven't I?"

"No. You were defending yourself."

"But the police—"

He cut her off. "Stop. We'll talk about it tomorrow."

Nahum interrupted them as he brought in her bag and dumped it on the floor. "You'd be better off staying in the house, where we're closer."

"I'm going to sleep in here, too," Gabe told him.

Shadow protested. "Why? I'll be fine!"

"If by some weird chance Kian's found where you live, I don't want you to be attacked in the middle of the night."

"But—"

"No! I've made my mind up. Nahum, get the guys together. I'll be over in a moment."

Nahum nodded and left them to it, and Shadow noticed a pile of blankets and pillows stacked on the sofa next to wood burner on the far side of her cabin. A few weeks before, Gabe had insisted she have the wood burner installed, rather than deplete her magic to keep the smokeless fire going in the middle of the room.

She looked at Gabe. "Seriously, you do not need to do this."

"You're weak. You couldn't possibly defend yourself if something attacked. I've got this."

Shadow's natural instinct to argue reasserted itself. "I don't need protecting! I could still fight!"

"We don't even know what we're fighting. I don't know if I could fight it. It's some weird ghost with a powerful energy." He ran his hands through his hair, frustrated, and turned as there was a soft knock at the door.

Briar peered inside. "It's only me and Eli." She entered, Eli on her heels, and headed to Shadow's side.

Eli had been an apothecary, amongst other things in the past, and that's why he liked to work with Briar. He was one of the calmest Nephilim, quiet and considered, and an undeniable ladies man. His soft brown eyes were made for seduction. He wore his hair tousled, but was clean-shaven usually. Not tonight, however. Stubble grazed his cheeks.

"Hey, you two," Shadow said, trying to sound brighter than she was feeling. "You could have seen me in the morning, you know."

"No, we couldn't," Briar replied, as she pulled a table close to the bed, set her bag on it, and opened it up. "We need to act now. You look a peculiar colour."

"I do?" Shadow's hands flew to her face.

Eli laughed. "You're very pale, and I think there's a tinge of green there, too."

Gabe was already heading to the door. "I'll leave you to it." He looked at Shadow. "I'll be back with your drink."

Before he'd even left, Briar was easing the blankets back, revealing her injured leg, and she started to unwrap the towel. Eli, in the meantime, was filling a bowl with hot water from the sink in the corner, and he brought it to the table. He threw a handful of herbs in, and added some clean cloths. A rich smell filled the air, something honeyed and sweet.

Briar frowned. "You bled a lot. This towel is stiff with it."

Shadow winced as Briar pulled it off her wound, taking scabs and clots with it. "I didn't think it was that deep."

Blood immediately started to well again, and Briar tutted. "Liar. It's going to leave a nice scar."

"That's okay. I have a few. Sword fights will do that to you."

Briar looked up at Eli. "Can you prepare the poultice? I'll clean the wound."

He nodded. "Sure."

Eli worked silently, but Briar whispered under her breath as she cleaned the dried blood away. Shadow felt Briar's magic swell, and a lightness came over her as the throbbing in her leg began to ease. "That's better already."

Briar smiled. "Good."

Gabe returned before they'd finished, and handed Shadow her drink. He looked at the wound and frowned, shaking his head as he left again. Sleep started to steal over Shadow, and she sipped, savouring the rich hot chocolate. It was delicious. Gabe didn't mess about. It was actual melted chocolate and cream, with a dash of cinnamon, exactly as she liked it.

She watched Briar put the poultice on her leg, and felt warmth spread up and across her body, meeting the hot balm of the chocolate in her stomach. By the time she'd drained the cup, she couldn't keep her eyes open, and easily fell into a dreamless sleep.

Twelve

Maggie glared at Harlan as he signed his official statement. "We've checked the rest of the premises, and there are no more bodies anywhere, thank Christ, or the lurking shades of the fucking undead. Just watch what you're doing!"

"Scout's honour," he said, saluting.

She shot him a filthy look and marched back to the kitchen, and after a quick search on the ground floor, trying to find Chadwick's study, Harlan headed upstairs.

Other than the living room, drawing room, dining room, and the two rooms with the connecting door, there was only the kitchen and utility room downstairs. By the time he'd finished his statement, the coroner had arrived with SOCO, and Harlan was keen to keep out of the way.

The stairs were in the middle of the unusual house, and they swept up into darkness. Harlan paused as he reached the landing, listening carefully, but other than the muffled voices coming from below, he could hear nothing. From first impressions, the overpowering decorating didn't stop on the ground floor. Richly patterned wallpaper, ornate woodwork, and oriental furniture was clearly going to be a feature everywhere.

Harlan moved methodically, opening one door after another, finding Chadwick's bedroom at the rear of the house overlooking the garden. He also found a spare bedroom, followed by another room that housed more of Chadwick's collected artefacts. Finally, he found the study, lined with books and prints.

Harlan sighed with relief, slipped inside, and shut the door firmly behind him. Chadwick had obviously been in there earlier that day. A fire was smouldering in the fireplace, and lamps were lit. And, it was a mess. Books and papers were strewn everywhere, and Harlan wasn't sure if this was Chadwick's normal way of working, or if Kian, in Chadwick's body, had been looking for something specific. Harlan hoped for the former.

Logic dictated that as Chadwick's latest discovery, the details of Kian's burial must be accessible on his desk somewhere, although as he started searching, Harlan became more and more convinced there was little order applied to the mess. Chadwick was a magpie.

There were old books, new books, first editions, illustrated manuals, and arcane papers that should really have been in a museum. The source for the burial and any information about Kian must be old, surely. Harlan abandoned the desk after a fruitless search, and headed instead to a large table in the centre of the room. Under the chaotic paperwork, he saw what looked like the edge of a map, spread across the surface. What he had assumed to be objects on display were actually holding down the corners, to stop it rolling up again. He quickly pushed the papers aside and frowned. It was a map of Belas Knap and the surrounding area, and there were marks all over it.

It looked as if Chadwick had narrowed his search down to the Neolithic burial site a while ago, and had been testing theories ever since. Harlan rummaged around some more, finding book after book on Neolithic burials, and then books on Druid religions. He was getting closer. And then a thought struck him. Where were the other grave objects? Shadow had taken the staff, but what about the old leather bag, the pottery and the jewellery?

Harlan sighed. He could be here for hours.

A headache was beginning its slow, insidious advance when Maggie found him in Chadwick's bedroom. He'd figured that this was the next best place to look when the study refused to reveal any secrets.

"I wondered where you'd snuck off to." She looked around. "Christ. How did he sleep in here? It's as creepy as hell."

Harlan straightened from his examination of the chest of drawers, amused. "I don't know... It has a certain charm, if you like Hammer House of Horror films."

"I don't. I have enough of this crap in my day-to-day life. I feel like Peter bloody Cushing is about to leap out on me."

"I wish he would. I could use some help right now."

Maggie walked around the room, her sharp eyes everywhere. "What are you looking for?"

"Grave goods, taken from the tomb of our ghost. They could be important."

"You're sure he didn't take them?"

"No, he ran out of here too quickly, in Mason's body. They have to be here somewhere. And so does information on who Kian was and why he was sealed in his tomb, despite the fact that he was dead."

Maggie shook her head. "You probably should have asked that before you opened it!"

"You know how it works, Maggie! We're hired to help find these objects, and we trust our clients have done their homework."

"And you don't double check?" She snorted. "That's a big fat fucking recipe for disaster, isn't it?"

Harlan took a deep breath, and repeated what he'd said to others before. "We check up on as much as we can. But we've worked with some of our clients for years! Chadwick is not a demon-raiser! He loves the occult, the old, and the arcane, like we all do. He wants to—" Harlan corrected himself, "He wanted to unlock life's secrets. It's what many of them want. All of the members of the Order of the Midnight Sun are the same, too."

"That bunch of new age alchemists. Of course they are." She was dismissive of the group.

"They are actually intelligent people, who follow the old teachings, and their predecessors were the forerunners of scientists!"

"Yeah, yeah. Well, now Chadwick's dead, and we have a rogue ghost on the loose." She frowned. "Where did you find Shadow?"

"Ah!" He'd been expecting this question, and had decided to keep it simple. "In White Haven. She helped me on another job. She's very resourceful."

Maggie crossed her arms in front of her and tapped her foot. "That Cornish village?"

"It's a town."

"I've been hearing things about that place. They had a vampire issue just before Christmas."

"Really? I had no idea. I was there because of the Crossroads Circus."

She raised her eyebrows as understanding dawned. "Oh! You dealt with whoever had caused the deaths that had been trailing after that show?"

He winced. "Not exactly, but I helped, in my small way. That's how I met Shadow."

"She doesn't live in London?"

"No. White Haven."

"Good. She's trouble, I can tell." She changed the subject abruptly. "Have you looked under the bed?"

"Isn't that a bit obvious?"

"I suggested it for a reason!"

Harlan frowned at her, and feeling foolish, dropped to the floor, lifted the valance, and squinted into the darkness. He groaned. The bed was old-fashioned with a high base, and underneath it were shabby boxes. He pulled them out and laid them on the richly coloured eiderdown.

Maggie grinned. "Told you."

"They could be old clothes!" Harlan protested, but he opened one that was the least covered in dust. A worn leather bag and the other grave goods were inside. "Bingo! But this doesn't make sense. Why would he hide them in his own house? Chadwick would be examining these like a kid at Christmas!"

"Perhaps Kian hid them?" Maggie shrugged. "Whatever—you owe me." She leaned closer. "I'm amazed they aren't more decayed!"

"Me too," Harlan murmured, lifting them gently. "They're dirty, and although the leather bag is rotting, it's in far better shape than I'd have thought. Maybe it was the magic protecting the tomb?"

Maggie pointed at the rings, torques, and a large, ornate cloak clasp. The metal was dull, but their engravings were intriguing. "He had influence, and money. What's in the pouch?"

Harlan opened it gently, dislodging a flurry of dust. Inside were old bones—a bird skull, a skull of some type of small mammal, claws, feathers, and beads.

"Looks more like a shaman's bag to me," Maggie suggested, "but what do I know?" She walked towards the door. "You've got fifteen more minutes, and then we lock up and you have to go. I've put an alert out for Mason's car, but haven't heard anything yet. I'll tell you if I do."

"Sure." Harlan nodded. "I'll hurry. And thanks, Maggie. I appreciate this."

"Just try not to leave a trail of death in your wake!"

Gabe and the other Nephilim were beyond tired, and their tempers were short.

They were in the living room, and music played softly in the background while they argued about the meaning of the symbols drawn on the staff and the translations of the words they had deciphered. Being a Nephilim meant they understood all languages, modern and ancient, and that applied to written languages, too.

Nahum frowned. "'Those who choose the dark path will reap its rewards.' Well, that's suitably cryptic and ominous. Sounds like mumbo jumbo to me."

"But do you feel its power?" Gabe asked.

"Sure. But I don't know where its power is coming from." Nahum held the staff under the light. It was the height of an average man, and made of what looked to be oak. The symbols were carved down the entire length. Some were delicate, others made with thicker stokes.

Ash took it from him. "None of these symbols look particularly magical to me. Some are just images—these are of the moon," he pointed to them. "And these are rudimentary animals —this one's a deer, and these are the carvings of stag horns."

Zee was sprawled on the sofa. "Was it used in rituals? I mean, I presume it's more than a walking stick with some dire warning on it!"

"Possibly," Ash said, nodding. He placed it against the wall, next to the fire, where they all could see it, and sat down again.

"Perhaps we're focusing on the wrong thing," Niel suggested. "It may have power, and we know what's written on it, but there might be other important things we're missing."

"Yeah, like why he wanted to get Shadow," Ash pointed out. "And why didn't he kill Harlan and Mason while he had the chance."

"Let's not forget that he shot her," Gabe said.

Nahum shrugged. "Sounds like he was only intending to wound her—it would have been easier to catch her if she was injured. The gun was insurance, and sensible self-defence."

"He knew she was fey, though! How?" Zee asked.

"Because she broke the seal on his tomb," Niel reminded them. "There were other objects, too. We should find them. It would help to know more about who he was."

"Let's hope Harlan is on to that. In the meantime, what else can we do?" Nahum asked.

Gabe stood and stretched, touching the ceiling with his outstretched fingers. "I think we need to go back to the tomb. See if there's something we've missed. We can go tonight." He checked his watch. "Briar and Eli should be finishing up soon. I'll sleep over there, and see you all in a few hours. Who's up for later?"

There was a show of hands, and Gabe grinned. "Road trip, then!"

ᚠ ᚠ ᚠ

Gabe had only been asleep for a short while when he heard movement in the room and he sat up quickly, blinking in the gloom.

But it was only Shadow, stirring from her bed. She sat on the edge of it, reaching for water, and nodded at Gabe. "Morning. I can't believe you slept on that sofa—it's barely big enough! So we weren't attacked, then?"

He groaned as he stretched. "I'm not sure I'd call it sleep. And no, we weren't. How's your leg?"

She stood, testing her weight. "It feels so much better. The pain is dull rather than sharp. That has to be good, right?"

"I'd say so." Gabe tried not to stare. Her t-shirt was long, but he could still see a lot of thigh. A bandage was wrapped around the wound. "Briar will be back to check that later today. I don't think she completely trusted Eli."

Shadow laughed. "Poor Eli. Although to be fair, he doesn't have Briar's magic."

Gabe checked his watch and found it was almost ten in the morning. Five hours of sleep would have to do; he managed on far less in the old days, when they waged war. He was growing soft with age, he reflected, as he stood up and gathered his blankets, rolling them neatly and putting them in the corner. He hesitated to tell Shadow the plans the group had discussed, but he couldn't really keep them a secret. "We're going back to the tomb tonight. I'd like to suggest you stay here—"

She didn't let him finish his sentence. "No way! I'm coming, too."

"You're injured!"

"Don't nanny me!"

"Shadow, will you please see sense? First, there's that hike up the hill from the car park. Your wound could start bleeding again!"

She grinned at him. "Or, you could fly me up there! If you're strong enough."

She was baiting him, and he knew it. "Of course I'm strong enough."

"It will be night, and no one will see us. That place is deserted! And surely you want to stretch your wings?"

Damn it. He hated it when she was right, but he wasn't about to concede that now. "I'll think about it."

"Sure you will. Are you going to cook me breakfast, too?"

"Don't push your luck. I'll meet you in the kitchen. Do you need help getting dressed?"

She just stared at him. "No."

"Fine!" He didn't know whether he was relieved or disappointed. He chided himself on the way out of the door. You're relieved, you idiot!

Niel was already cooking, and the smell of bacon filled the room. He looked up when Gabe entered. "She okay?"

"Fine. As annoying as usual. She wants to come tonight."

Niel laughed, his white teeth flashing. "Did you really expect anything else?"

"No." Gabe headed to the coffee machine and made a drink, strong enough to stand the spoon in it. He inhaled deeply, and took a sip; it was so hot it almost scalded his tongue. "Are you making some for us?" He nodded to the breakfast supplies.

"Of course. The others are getting up, too. Only Barak is out."

Gabe was about to say more when his phone rang. He glanced at the screen. "It's Beckett." He answered quickly. "Morning, any news?"

"Only bad, I'm afraid. The police haven't found Mason's car yet, so we have no idea where he is."

"Shit." Gabe moved to the window and looked out across the fields. It was raining, and the moors disappeared into a hazy mist. "He could be heading to us, but we have no way of knowing."

"Presume the worst, but hope for the best." Beckett sighed, and Gabe could hear the worry in his voice. "Mason knows where you live. I have no idea how this possession business works, but he must have access to whatever is in Mason's head—if his possession of Chadwick's body is any indication. How's Shadow?"

"She's fine." Gabe paused. "Thanks for getting her out of there with no charges."

"We have Maggie to thank for that. Listen, I managed to find those grave goods last night, but I still haven't found anything that could tell us who Kian is. I'm going to keep looking. They've sealed the house, but I'll try and sneak back in anyway."

Gabe was unsure of how much to share with Beckett, but he seemed to be fairly upfront with him. "We're going back to the tomb tonight. I want to give it a thorough check."

"Is that wise?" Beckett asked.

"Maybe not, but like you, I want to cover all of our bases."

"All right. I'll let you know if I find anything else. I may even drive to White Haven."

"Fair enough. You be careful, too, Beckett. He might come looking for those grave goods."

Gabe rang off, and turned to find Shadow already sitting at the table. She was fully dressed, and the Empusa's sword was next to her. She was sipping her coffee and watching him with a speculative look on her face, while Niel continued to cook. Gabe heard movement on the floor above, and the sound of feet on the stairs.

"What's happened? Is Harlan okay?" she asked.

"He's fine. Let's hang on for the others, and I'll update you all at once."

"I have news for you, too," she said enigmatically.

"Great," Niel groaned. "Sounds like life is about to get more complicated."

Thirteen

Shadow finished listening to Gabe's updates, and studied the other Nephilim.

They had all just eaten, and their plates were pushed into the middle of the table. Their appetites were huge. Shadow couldn't fathom why they weren't obese. Must be their sylph ancestry. It was rare to see a fat fey. Their genetic makeup didn't work that way. And yes, she was still sure their fathers were sylphs. She sensed a kind of magic in them, and was convinced it was fey blood. But the language thing was weird. As far as she knew, speaking multiple languages was not something sylphs could do—unless they were some sort of super-sylph.

Gabe interrupted her thoughts. "What's your news, then?"

Shadow lifted the Empusa's sword from where it rested next to her chair, and placed it on the table. "I had a strange experience with this last night, when I was chasing Kian's ghost. I pulled it off the wall, because I only had my dagger and wanted to have another weapon." She paused, remembering the moment when Kian's spirit left Chadwick's dead body. "It was really odd. I killed Chadwick, and Kian's ghost left it, but the weird thing was that it wasn't a shadowy shape like it had been before. It was almost solid—like an actual body. I could see that he had dark hair, a thin face, and a wiry build. By the time I'd scrambled to the door, he was at the far end of the corridor, but I could still see him clearly." She looked at the Empusa's sword. "I think it's because of that."

Nahum was sitting next to her, and he picked it up. "I thought you and El had examined it and decided there was nothing special about it?"

"We did! I even went to her friend Dante's forge the other day to double check. He agreed that it wasn't unusual in any way. Dante said it was virtually impossible to say where it had been forged or how, though."

"But I guess there wasn't a ghost in the room, was there?" Nahum asked.

Zee leaned on the table, his chin on his hands. "You're saying that sword allows you to see the dead?"

"It seems to." She shrugged. "Well, that's my impression. I obviously haven't had a chance to test that theory again. But once I got to the kitchen, I saw him, just as clearly as I do you, before he sank into Mason's body."

"I think it's great news," Gabe said. "I wonder if it would injure a spirit, too."

"A sword that fights ghosts!" Eli laughed. "Wow! *That* would increase its value."

"I'm not selling it again!" Shadow exclaimed. "That's mine now. It's not like Chadwick will miss it. I'll see if I can borrow El's too, just for the next few days."

Nahum passed the sword around the table for the rest of the Nephilim to examine it. As Niel held it, he said, "You know, that does make a lot of sense. The Empusa was Hecate's servant, is that right?"

"Yes, straight from the Underworld," Shadow told him.

Niel nodded. "It makes sense she would carry weapons that would allow her to see the dead and fight them."

"But she was from there," Eli said. "Surely she wouldn't need that kind of help?"

Gabe shrugged. "Maybe she was like some kind of Underworld enforcer."

"Whatever the reason," Zee said, "it puts us at a distinct advantage to have them." He turned to Shadow. "Did Kian know you could see him properly?"

"Hard to say. I don't think so. I didn't do anything that gave it away...well, other than talking to him. But," she said, taking a deep breath, "that brings me to the next thing I noticed. Kian was fey."

"What?" they exclaimed, pretty much as one.

Shadow continued. "I could tell from his ears, and the way his face was shaped. He had a long, narrow chin like some fey do."

"Well shit, that puts a new perspective on things," Gabe said. "Are you sure?"

"Very sure. I've been thinking on it all night. Well, before I fell asleep," she conceded. "I've been trying to decide if I was imagining it. But it also makes sense for other reasons. Did you know that Avery's ancestor, Helena's ghost, is in her flat?"

Eli nodded. "I did. Briar has mentioned it. Sounds freaky to me." He shuddered, as most people did at the mention of ghosts.

"I asked why she allowed her to stay, because you know—creepy, and apparently Helena possessed her once. I wondered why Avery wasn't worried that she'd try to possess her again, but Briar told me that you have to invite a ghost in. That they just can't slide in whenever they want. Alex prepared a potion for Avery, and then she said an invocation that allowed it to happen." The Nephilim were silently watching her, a couple starting to nod with understanding. "It's been playing on my mind. I couldn't work out how Chadwick had been possessed. He wouldn't have invited Kian in—I doubt it, anyway. He was a collector!"

"Of course," Zee said thoughtfully. "But a fey spirit might not need to be invited in."

"Exactly!"

"That's just brilliant," Ash said, not sounding like it was at all. "Does that mean it could possess any of us?"

Shadow winced. "In theory. But who knows how weird you are? You might be immune to possession. Or it could be he triples his powers if he possesses one of you!"

"Please stop talking," Zee said, rising to his feet and gathering the plates up. "This keeps getting worse."

"Better we know what we're up against!" she shot back.

Eli stood, too. "I'm heading to the barn to work out. Anyone want to join me?"

Shadow knew what that meant. It was sparring time.

"Sure," Niel said, "give me five."

Zee shook his head. "Not me, I need to go to the pub. I'm covering the lunch shift. I don't think there's anything else I can do here—Gabe?"

Gabe nodded. "No, go ahead. I'll have to decide what we do next. I'll ring Barak and update him, too."

Shadow stood as well, trying to hide the grimace when she felt the injury to her leg tighten. "Can you take me to White Haven with you? It will save Briar coming here to check my wound. And then I can see El."

Zee nodded. "Sure. Ten minutes?"

"Great."

She headed to the door, but Gabe called her back. "Are you going to get the second sword?"

"Yes. Why?"

"Be careful. Kian could be here, and he could be anyone!"

Harlan looked at Olivia's worried face, and wondered what, if anything, he could say to reassure her.

"He needs him. He won't kill him."

"But Mason might be killed accidentally, just like Chadwick! Poor Mason!" Olivia rose from the leather chair where she'd been sitting, and started to walk around his office, picking things up and putting them down randomly. "We have to tell the staff."

"Do we?" Harlan asked, watching her. "Or will we scare them unnecessarily? Most people who work here just have admin duties, filing, bills, or look for acquisitions. Most of them have no idea of some of the things we really deal with! Half the staff would probably resign! And," he raised his hand as Olivia rounded on him, "I know that's their prerogative to leave, but they won't be at risk. They know nothing, and can't achieve anything for Kian."

Olivia paused, her face pinched, and her lips pressed together tightly. "No, you're right. Although, I wish you'd told me sooner."

"Yes, sorry. That was an oversight. I should have spoken to you before I called Maggie." As he said it, Harlan half-wondered if Olivia could be Kian right now. And then he shook his head. No. Chadwick was different last night. There were subtle clues that he wasn't behaving normally, but he would never have presumed possession. Now, of course, it all made sense. But Olivia was her usual self. "We need to work out how to save Mason and catch Kian without further bloodshed."

Olivia nodded. "Where are the grave goods?"

"In my safe." He headed across the room and pulled aside some books from the shelves, exposing the safe behind. He punched in his code and drew out the box he'd put everything in, and then placed it on the round table he used for meetings.

Olivia started rifling through the objects. "Just the usual grave goods, really. Nothing that rings any alarm bells."

"There was also a staff that was marked with strange symbols, but Shadow has that. She claimed it had power."

Olivia looked startled. "That sounds more interesting!"

"Bollocks!" Harlan said, exasperated. "Why the hell didn't I ask Chadwick more about this tomb?"

"Because you trusted him. I take it you aren't any wiser as to who Kian is?"

"Other than some Druid who clearly pissed a lot of people off? No. I need to get back into Chadwick's house."

"Breaking a police cordon?" Olivia raised an eyebrow, a smirk on her face. "What would Maggie say to that?"

"What Maggie doesn't know won't hurt her." Even as he said it, Harlan wondered how he was going to manage it. In theory, by tonight, no police would be there, but Chadwick had an alarm system…

"I know his security code."

"You read my mind! For the alarm? How?"

"He's good friends with Mason. Best buds. He sent me round there once to get something when Chadwick was away on one of his trips."

Harlan looked at her sceptically. "And you remember it?"

She rolled her eyes. "I wrote it down! I'm not stupid. These things come in handy—like for now!"

Harlan winked at her. "Oh, Olivia. How are you still single?"

She grinned. "Like you, I take my job far too seriously, and get my pleasure along the way." She ran her finger across his chin. "Would you like some company tonight?"

He blinked and stuttered as several images flooded his mind from one night years ago in a hotel room, during a snow storm. His one and only night spent with Olivia, and it had been memorable for so many reasons. She'd worn her very sexy Louboutin shoes, and not much else.

"Naughty." She wagged a finger. "Breaking into Chadwick's house, I mean."

"Oh, that. I suppose so. I preferred the other option."

"It was not an option. That was your mind teasing you." She stepped away, amused. "Give me all the details. I can tell I need to get your thoughts out of the gutter."

Briar looked at Shadow's wound. "Excellent. This looks so much better. Far more so than I expected, actually."

"I'm fey," Shadow said nonchalantly, already feeling stronger. "I've always healed quickly, and beside, you are a very good healer."

Briar's eyes were wide, and she looked as if she were trying to suppress a smile. "Thank you. I wish I could say you were a better patient. You shouldn't be walking on it so often."

"There's too much to do!"

They were in the sunroom at the back of Briar's house, and Shadow was lying on the low couch pushed into the corner. While Briar worked Shadow looked around at the herbs growing on the sills, and the eclectic mix of decor. It was very Briar. Outside the window, in her tiny courtyard, a tangle of vines and climbing plants were already sending up bright green growth.

Briar said, "I'm going to put another poultice on it and strap it up, and then I want to see you tomorrow." Her small hands were deft and sure, and as she dressed the wound, she uttered a spell. Once again, Shadow felt warmth creeping up her leg and across her body.

"Your magic is strong. I feel the Green Man's spirit in you."

Briar looked up. "He's never far away anymore."

There was a ring of bright green around Briar's dark eyes that Shadow didn't remember seeing before. "Your eyes have changed."

"I know." She dropped her gaze, concentrating on finishing the dressing. "He's getting stronger with the arrival of spring."

"Not like possession?" Shadow asked, suddenly anxious.

Briar laughed. "No, not at all. He's just—around. It's like his sap runs through my blood."

Shadow smiled. "That's an interesting way of putting it."

"It's the only way I can describe it. I've always felt an affinity for spring—most gardeners and earth witches do. It's just enhanced now." She finished the dressing and straightened up. "I have to remember to rein him in. Anyway, you're done," she said, changing the subject.

Shadow stood, pulling her combats trousers on. It was difficult to wear her tight jeans at the moment because of the bandage. "Which one of you witches is the best at dealing with spirits? Is it Alex?"

Briar nodded. "You thinking about your wayward spirit?"

"Yes."

"Definitely Alex." Briar checked her watch. "He'll be in the pub now. You could get lunch in there. And any of us will help if you need it."

"Thanks, but we're trying to clean up our own mess."

"Sometimes things just happen, despite our best intentions. It has to us. I mean it. We're happy to help." She paused, frowning. "How are you getting to the pub if Zee dropped you here?"

"I was going to walk."

Briar tutted. "No! It's too far."

"It takes ten minutes!"

Briar lived on one of the charming, winding lanes around White Haven, and it was a short stroll to the town centre.

"You'll aggravate your wound. I tell you what—I'll take you. Any excuse for a lunchtime tipple!"

Shadow smiled. "I could meet El there, too! I love pubs! We have them in the Otherworld too, you know."

Briar laughed. "Well, you're hanging out with the right people, then! I'll grab my keys."

Fourteen

Shadow sat at the bar on their usual stools at The Wayward Son, and scanned the room.

It was Sunday lunchtime, and very busy. The smell of roast meat scented the air, and the pub was loud with chatter. The English loved their Sunday lunches. It was something she'd learnt very early on, and she had to admit it was a tradition she liked. Not right now, though. Niel's breakfast had filled her up.

Zee headed over to take their order. "I should have known you'd come here. Pint of Skullduggery Ale, I presume." He smiled at Briar. "And white wine?"

Briar laughed. "You know me so well."

"How's your patient?" he asked, filling her glass.

Briar wrinkled her nose. "Not being nearly as compliant as she should be."

"Nothing new there, then."

Shadow shot him a filthy look. "I'm right here!"

"I know. And here I was hoping for some peace and quiet." He placed her pint in front of her. "Did you get in touch with El?"

Shadow bit back a rude response. She was trying to be less argumentative, and it didn't sit easily with her. "She's on her way. Is Alex here?"

"In the kitchen." He leaned forward. "If you're going to talk business, head to the rear lounge. There's a table free. I'll send El and Alex through."

"Good suggestion," Briar said, and grabbing her drink she led the way to the room Alex had spelled to keep quiet for the locals.

Within minutes El arrived, looking very glam for a Sunday, and Alex was right behind her. He slid into his seat staring at all three of them, intrigued. "You all look like you're up to something!"

"Me?" Shadow said, wide-eyed. "I'm never up to anything!"

"Oh, please. Pull the other one!" Alex had shoulder-length dark hair and stubble always grazed his chin. He favoured old jeans and older t-shirts, and despite the wet, miserable day, he wasn't wearing long sleeves, revealing his tattoos, although he had nowhere near as many as some of the Nephilim. "Zee has told me about your wayward ghost."

"Ghost?" El said, suddenly paying attention.

"Should I wait for Avery or Reuben?" Shadow asked. Alex lived with Avery now, and El and Reuben were a couple. Together with Briar, they made up the White Haven Coven.

"No, Avery is seeing her grandmother, and Reuben is surfing," Alex said, sipping his pint. "I'll tell Avery later."

El nodded. "I can fill Reuben in. Now, tell all! What's happened?"

Shadow relayed how they'd found the tomb and released the spell on it, and then the attack by Kian's ghost the night before. "Now we have to find Kian, and get him out of Mason's body without hurting him. If he's even still possessing him. We have no idea where he may be, but suspect he'll probably come here, after me."

"Wow." El leaned back in her chair. "And you think this ghost is fey?"

"Yes. I can tell—just like you can tell that I'm not human without my glamour. There are subtle differences."

"Not so subtle if you ask me," Alex said. "It's a bit worrying to know a fey spirit can invade your body without your permission."

"Are there any circumstances where that could be true for any ghost?" Briar asked.

Alex looked out of the window, deep in thought. "I couldn't say categorically no, but it would be unusual. Possession is usually demonic. I have spells that can help with exorcism, but I'm not sure how effective they'd be in this circumstance. I'm sure I could adapt one. Of course," he said, brightening, "there is another, simpler option."

"Yes?" Shadow watched him, hoping it was something they could do without needing the witches.

"You could drug Mason, then Kian couldn't use his body."

Briar frowned. "I thought you said that he possessed Mason when he was drugged, and he woke up when Kian was inside him?"

"He was already rousing," Shadow reminded her. "They only had a light sedative. He wanted to get me on my own. Maybe a stronger one would work. But it would have to be safe, too. I have no problem killing anyone, but Mason is an innocent man. I could do without a second death on my hands. The whole police thing really complicates matters, too." She said police distastefully, as if the word was bitter on her tongue.

"I could make a potion that would work," Briar said. "You could slip it in a drink, or food. But, it would be hard to get close enough to do that without him knowing."

"I could poison an arrow tip!" Shadow suggested, becoming excited. "I could craft a fine one, like a dart. That would be easier. Could you make something powerful enough to work in a tiny quantity? Or even something that could go on the end of my knife? One small cut would be sufficient to administer the drug."

"Wow. You do like your hands-on weaponry, don't you," Alex said, amused.

"It's what I do best. I've always been told to work with my strengths!"

"Sage advice," El agreed.

"Yes, I could do that," Briar said, thoughtfully. "I could reduce it to absolute potency and put it in a cream or gel. When do you need it?"

"As soon as possible. Kian seems to want me, and we think that's to resurrect his own body using some unknown ritual."

"But what happens when he's in spirit form?" Alex asked, dropping his voice.

"How do you stop him then? I could at that point banish it, probably. I've done it before with human spirits."

Shadow grinned. "Oh, that's where the Empusa's sword comes in. I've found out what it does!"

El looked at her, shocked. "It does something? But we tested it!"

"There's no way we could have known this until we tested it with a ghost. When I held it last night, I saw him clearly. I think I could injure the spirit, too. Or else, what's the point of it?"

"Chadwick, the man you killed, he was your buyer?"

"Yes. I've stolen it back. And I'm wondering if I could borrow yours? It may be that its effects are enhanced when used together."

"Consider it done!" El said, suitably intrigued. "But you should set some kind of trap. You want to fight him on your terms, not his."

"That's a great idea," Briar agreed. "Either by the farm, or Ravens' Wood. You draw strength from there."

Shadow nodded, as she thought it through. If she could lure him to her preferred place that would be better. "I like the idea of using the wood. But he's fey, too. It could work to his advantage."

Alex looked confused. "How the hell did a fey end up beneath Belas Knap? And did you say it was fey magic that had sealed the tomb?"

"Yes, part of it. It is odd. We have no idea who he is, or why he's there. Harlan has found the grave goods, but he's still trying to find Chadwick's research. That should tell us something about him."

"Do you like Harlan?" El asked.

Shadow nodded. "Yes, he's seems honest enough. He helped me out last night. Gabe likes him too, and that doesn't happen often. He's usually very suspicious!" She checked her watch. "I'd better not be too late. We're travelling to Belas Knap again tonight."

"All right," El said. "Let's drink up, and we'll go get the sword."

Harlan pulled up halfway down the street from Chadwick's house, deciding to advance on foot. It was just past ten at night, and very dark. It had been raining for most of the day, and thick clouds still covered the sky.

He glanced at Olivia. "Are you ready?"

"I was born ready," she said, already exiting the car. "It's a good thing this place is so green. At least we'll have some cover."

Harlan locked up and nodded, falling into step next to her as they strolled down the road. The houses all had drives, and plenty of shrubs to offer privacy.

Olivia tucked her arm into Harlan's, in an effort to look like they were a couple out for an evening walk, and when they reached Chadwick's drive, they ducked under the police tape, and kept to the shadows along the edge. The drive ended in a small turning circle, and a side gate led to the rear of the house. As soon as they got closer, a sensor triggered the security light, and they hurried to the front door.

"Bloody hell!" Olivia said, annoyed. "This place is lit up like a sodding Christmas tree!"

"Very sensible, really," Harlan said. "He has a lot to steal!"

Harlan had managed to swipe the spare keys before he'd left the previous night. He'd spotted them on a hook in the kitchen, and he used them now. The alarm started to beep, and Olivia quickly entered the code, both sighing with relief when it worked.

"Thank God he hadn't changed it," Olivia said. She paused in the darkness, and Harlan could barely see her.

The house felt eerie, its silence thick and heavy around them, the smell of the food they'd eaten the night before still lingering. "Shit. I feel terrible doing this."

"It's the right thing to do. We're avenging Chadwick's death, and let's face it, only he knows anything about Kian."

"We think," Harlan reminded her.

"Oh, come on," Olivia said in hushed tones. "We know these guys. They don't share anything if they think they're on to something big, and this was his life's passion. Where to?"

"The study again. There were papers everywhere. I didn't have long enough to get a proper look."

"Okay," she said, pulling a torch out of her bag. "Why don't you head up, I'll check the rooms down here, and then join you."

Harlan nodded, and taking out his own flashlight out, headed up the stairs and down the hall. When he reached the study door, he pushed it open, keeping his light pointed down. The windows were screened with heavy velvet curtains, and when he'd made sure they were drawn tightly, he flicked the lamps on.

The table was still covered with papers and books, slightly obscuring the map. He was relieved to see the police hadn't taken everything. But why would they? It was well away from the crime scene and probably seemed unconnected. He looked at the documents despondently. He must have missed something last night; he just needed to be more organised. He quickly started making orderly piles of related work, but most of the books were obscure texts on the end of the Roman Empire in Britain. That was interesting. Chadwick had suggested that Kian was from a similar time to that of Merlin, and of all the research that had been done, the most likely time frame for that was around 500 AD—if you believed King Arthur was a real figure. The myths were boundless.

Harlan looked at the map again. Kian was buried long after the original building of Belas Knap, but research of the site suggested that it had been used for centuries afterwards. *Why was Kian buried beneath it? Was he greatly respected, or more likely, feared?*

Harlan stepped back from the table, frustrated. Chadwick must have had handwritten notes somewhere. He slowly turned, scanning the room. There must be a safe, or a secure hiding place. He was halfway through pulling out books and lifting pictures off the wall when he heard a shout from downstairs. Olivia.

He raced on to the landing and peered over the bannister, down into the darkened hall. There was another shout and loud thumps. Someone was attacking Olivia, and with luck they may not know he was here, too. *One good thing*, he assured himself as he sprinted down the stairs, *was that Olivia was very capable of looking after herself.*

He headed in the general direction of the noise and Olivia yelled out, "I know it's you, Kian! Don't think I'm fooled by your new skin suit!"

There was another *thump*, and Harlan ran, finally pausing outside an open doorway. A fallen torch illuminated two figures wrestling on the ground. He raced in, threw his arm around the neck of the man straddling Olivia, and hauled him off her.

They stumbled and fell, and the man rolled onto Harlan, trapping him. He repeatedly jabbed his elbow into Harlan's gut, forcing him to let go, before jumping to his feet to grab a bag that was lying to the side. But Olivia was now standing and she tackled him unexpectedly, and they crashed into a bookcase. The man threw Olivia off, pushing her with such force that she fell onto a table and landed on the floor, winded. Before Harlan could get close, the man rushed out and down the passageway.

"Grab him!" Olivia yelled.

But Harlan was already in pursuit, and in the seconds it took him to reach the kitchen, their attacker had escaped through the back door and was sprinting across the garden.

Harlan watched him go. It was pointless to follow him. He risked being possessed himself, or injuring the man who was now possessed. And besides, he knew his identity. It was Kent Marlowe, a member of the Order of the Midnight Sun.

Olivia joined him, wincing as she put a hand to her lower back. "Bollocks! That hurt. Why aren't you chasing him?"

"Because that's Kent Marlowe. Don't you recognise him?"

Olivia groaned. "Shit. I do now. I haven't seen him for ages. What the hell is Kian doing in Kent's body?"

Harlan locked the door. "And importantly, where is Mason?"

"Oh crap! He better not have hurt him!" She fumbled in her pocket. "Bollocks. I've lost my phone." She headed down the hall to the room where they'd been fighting, and Harlan followed, thinking furiously.

"Why Kent Marlowe? He's a research guy, not an action hero."

"Oh, really," Olivia grumbled. "He seemed pretty action-heroey to me. I think I've broke a rib." She retrieved her torch and flashed it around the room, eventually getting onto her hands and knees to look under tables. "Got it!" she said triumphantly as she picked it up.

But Harlan was distracted by the upended bag that Kian had abandoned, and a sprawl of papers on the floor. He shone his own torch down, feeling a flutter of excitement as he knelt and searched through them. "Hey, Livy. I think we've found Chadwick's research. He must have come back for it."

Before she could reply, her phone rang, and he paid scant attention while she answered, until he heard her exclaim, "Mason! Are you okay?" Harlan looked up at her anxious face, relieved when she said, "Thank God. Where are you?" There was a pause before she nodded. "Yes, of course. We'll call Maggie and we'll be there soon!"

She ended the call, and Harlan asked, "Is he really all right?"

"I think so. He sounded shocked and confused. He's just woken up in a dark house, and he had to go the street to work out where he was."

"Which is, of course, Kent Marlowe's house?"

"Bingo." Olivia was already heading to the door. "Come on, we have to go. Bring the notes."

"Give me a minute," he told her. "Help me search. We don't want to miss anything, and I am not coming back here again!"

Olivia shot him a long look. "One minute, and then we leave. And you need to call Maggie to get her to meet us there."

Fifteen

Gabe exited his SUV at the base of the Cotswold Way, the path leading to Belas Knap, and stretched as Shadow, Niel, Ash, and Barak exited, too. It was close to midnight, and after their almost four-hour drive, he felt cramped.

There was a light breeze, and clouds were heavy overhead, the air carrying the promise of rain; he inhaled deeply, savouring the night scents.

"I'm looking forward to seeing this place," Barak said. "It sounds suitably ghostly."

Gabe grunted. "And small! I had to crouch to get in."

Shadow nodded in agreement. "But only the Gods know why someone would make the tomb so inaccessible."

"So it's hard to raid and steal grave goods, obviously," Ash told them. "Although, it clearly didn't work."

"It did for a long time!" Niel argued, walking to the path.

Gabe was about to follow, but then noticed Shadow's hand touch her leg wound, and he remembered her earlier suggestion. "Why don't we fly, boys?"

"Is that wise?" Barak asked. He turned, scanning the car park and the sky above them.

"There are no other cars here," he pointed out.

"But there's a path from the other direction," Niel reminded him.

Gabe grinned, sick of following rules and playing human all the time. "I don't care. Let's live a little." He pulled his jacket and t-shirt off, throwing them in the SUV. "I'll take Shadow for a ride." He looked at her, eyebrow cocked. "Ready?"

Her gaze drifted down his chest and back to his eyes, amused. With one quick flex of his shoulders he unfurled his enormous wings, and enjoyed seeing Shadow gasp as they spread out, twice his height on either side of him, and thick with tawny feathers that swept to his feet.

Gabe groaned with pleasure as he lifted them up and down, feeling the wind already ruffling them. "That feels good!"

Barak whooped, and throwing his t-shirt off, did the same, unfurling wings that were as black as the night sky. "Brother, that's the best suggestion you've made all day!"

Without waiting, Barak lifted into the air with ease, manoeuvring himself with dexterity and grace. Ash and Niel quickly followed suit, until Gabe was the only one still standing. He held his hand out to Shadow. "Want a lift?"

"I think I should walk." Her eyes did not echo her words. She watched the others circling the car park, envy in her gaze, and glanced back at Gabe. "You make it look so easy."

"It is, to us. It's like walking is for you. Or sword fighting. It's instinctive." They flew often at the farmhouse. It was secure there, private and protected from prying eyes. It was one of the reasons he'd chosen it. But although they lived with Shadow, they didn't usually fly in front of her. It wasn't for any other reason than the freedom of being with his brothers.

She studied his wings, taking in their span, and then circled behind him. He smiled, enjoying her admiration. "How do you hide them?" she asked. "They're huge!"

"Magic," he said, winking. When she stood before him again, he held his arms out. "Come on. I promise I won't drop you."

She gave him a long look, her violet eyes almost hooded, and then stepped close, her back to his chest. Gripping her tightly, he rose into the air, laughing at her sharp intake of breath.

"Herne's horns!" she exclaimed. He felt her stiffen and tense, her arms wrapped around his strong ones that were circling her waist. Her fingers dug into his skin and liked it more than he should. She was breathless when she whispered, "This is so freaky."

"Relax," he murmured in her ear. "I've got you."

"Easier said than done!"

He smiled. She was light and easy to carry, and he lifted them higher. In seconds they were above the tree line, and the road, car park, and fields were laid out around them. The rise of Belas Knap was ahead, black against the night sky.

"Looks good to me," Niel said, flying closer. His wings were a pale grey on top and darker underneath, which made it harder to detect him from below. "Let's go."

Gabe followed the others, but rather than land straight away, Gabe circled above, his keen eyes taking in the landscape and design of the burial site. "I can see why humans think it looks like a kneeling woman."

Shadow huffed. "People love to see the female form in everything! I find it demeaning."

"You should find it flattering. And besides, she's called Mother Earth for a reason. She was even called that, or a version of it, when I was first alive. She gives life to all. Perhaps the shape of Belas Knap is about returning the dead to the womb of the Earth."

Shadow didn't answer, and he flew over the fields and then the woods that lay alongside them, which were larger than he first realised. The roads beyond were quiet, and he saw only occasional headlights winking through the lanes as they dipped behind hedges. Niel had already landed and was checking the small tombs, but Ash and Barak were still circling over the area. The night air caressed his skin, and the feel of it through his feathers was almost as pleasurable as a woman's touch. *God knows it had been a long time since he'd experienced that.*

He'd been like a monk since they'd arrived back from the spirit lands. Most of them had, except for Eli.

Pushing those thoughts behind him, he asked Shadow, "What do you think of flying?"

"I like it, although I'd much rather be doing it myself. It's scary putting my life in someone else's hands." She shivered slightly, and he gripped her tighter.

"Just like it?" He sounded annoyed, but he wasn't really. He was teasing her. He had decided long ago that teasing Shadow was one of his life's greatest pleasures. "I am flying, woman!"

"All right. It's amazing! I love it. I'm jealous." She twisted her head to look at him. "Bastard."

He laughed, pleased to have provoked her, and then a piercing whistle from Niel gave them the all-clear. They swooped down to join him, landing on top of Belas Knap, and Gabe released Shadow, a beat slower than he should have.

"No one's here," Niel told them. "I've read that sometimes people spend the night in one of the tombs, but not tonight. The wood should be deserted, too."

"Let's go, then," Gabe said, reluctantly hiding his wings. He led them down the bank and onto the narrow path through the trees, but Shadow slipped ahead of him, and once again, she disappeared, despite his good eyesight. Her capacity to just vanish was unnerving. She might have been jealous of his ability to fly, but he was jealous of her vanishing tricks.

He continued regardless, remembering the way easily, and within ten minutes they were back at the blocked entrance to the tomb. They quickly dismantled the stones, revealing the passage beyond.

"You weren't kidding about the size," Barak said. His hand was on the bank as he bent down to peer inside.

"Just be careful with those ridiculously oversized shoulders of yours," Shadow said. "You might get stuck! I'll go first."

As she entered, Gabe said, "One of us should wait here, anyway. I don't want to be sealed in there, and it *is* a tight space."

"I'm happy to wait," Barak said, already pacing around.

"And me," Niel agreed.

"Good, I need to see this," Ash said, and he followed Shadow, leaving Gabe to enter last.

Once inside, Gabe was quickly reminded of how dirty and ruined the initial passage was. As they crouched, walking awkwardly, trickles of earth slid down, and Ash broke away roots that had breached the walls, something they hadn't bothered doing before, trying to make their progress easier. They reached the false tomb with relief.

"What exactly are we searching for?" Ash asked, looking around.

"Anything!" Gabe said. "Marks on the stonework or floor, or something unusual about the objects, although I don't think there'll be much of significance here. These items were designed to fool anyone who found it into thinking this was the tomb proper."

Ash nodded. "While we're here, though, we may as well check."

They spent a short while examining the small alcoves, finding cups, bowls, and small animal bones, before Shadow sighed, frustrated. "There's nothing useful here. Let's carry on." She hadn't bothered using her torch up to this point, but now she pulled it out, and flashed it down the passageway, explaining, "I don't want to miss anything."

Every now and again they stopped, noting symbols etched onto the stones, swirls and shapes that made no sense. Gabe rested his hands on them. "These feel like they were carved only recently. They're pristine."

"That's because no one's ever seen them before," Ash pointed out. "We had many such tombs where I came from, but they were ornate, and lots were lined with gold. That's Kings for you. " He pulled his phone from his pocket. "I'm going to take some photos. I'd like to see if we can find anything out later."

Gabe nodded. "I'll follow Shadow, she's disappeared. Again. "

"It can't be easy knowing that a fey ghost wants to capture you. I'd be pretty pissed if a ghost Nephilim was trying to catch me for some dodgy reason." He gave Gabe a knowing grin. "She certainly makes life interesting."

He grunted. "That's one way of putting it." He left Ash laughing and headed to the main tomb, where he could see torchlight flashing around. When he reached Shadow's side, her expression was bleak. "Are you okay?"

"Not really. I still feel his energy in here. It's dark, twisted. I should have paid more attention to it before." She looked at him, meeting his eyes. "You were right, and I should have listened. Restless ghosts don't just disappear."

He placed a hand on her shoulder and squeezed. "But what would that have changed? Nothing. Chadwick would still have taken the grave goods, and we can't perform exorcisms. If that would even work." He recalled what Shadow had told him about her chat with the witches.

She nodded, turning her attention back to the room, and sweeping the torch up to the roof. "Did you notice the flat stone in the dome centre? It's different to the rest."

Gabe squinted upwards. The roof was high at the point, well beyond even his reach, and it was impossible to fly to. His wings were too big for the tight space. "It has spirals marked on it, too. Get on my shoulder—see if you can touch it."

He crouched down and once she was in place, he gripped her legs and lifted her slowly. "You okay?"

"Fine, I can reach it."

Ash joined them again. "What are you doing?"

"Checking the roof, dummy, what does it look like?" she called down.

"I can see that!" he said, impatiently. "Why?"

"That is not what you asked first," she retorted. "It has marks on it. Do you think it opens?"

Gabe couldn't look up, it was too hard with Shadow on his shoulders, but he frowned at Ash. "Isn't that likely to bring the roof down on our heads?"

"Yes! Hey Shadow, don't do anything rash!"

"But it's in a sort of frame. I can see it. I'm going to try." She thrust the torch at Ash and he took it, aiming the beam of light where she worked.

Before they could object, Shadow was already pushing at the central stone, and Gabe could feel her wriggling above him. "Seriously? Shadow, what the hell are you doing?" Gabe yelled, debating whether to lower her to the floor, although part of him was intrigued. Was there something above them? A trickle of earth and tiny stones showered down. "Shadow!"

Ash's eyes narrowed with worry. "She's going to kill us all!"

"Will you please trust me?" she said, annoyed, and then grunted. "Damn it. Nothing's happening!"

"Good," Gabe said, and squatted before she could cause any damage.

Shadow huffed as she slid from his shoulders. "There must be something else here, apart from his bones!"

"It's a bloody tomb. What else do you expect?" Ash asked.

Her eyes widened. "Oh, no! I just remembered what happened right before Kian's spirit rose out of those bones." She started to examine the floor methodically, sifting through the debris of earth and small stones.

Gabe willed himself to be patient, trying to ignore Ash's obvious amusement. "Shadow, can you explain what you're looking for?"

"In all the excitement of being attacked by a murderous spirit, I'd forgotten that I found a stone in Kian's jaw. It was polished and flat, with strange symbols on it."

Gabe groaned. "You took it out, didn't you?"

"Of course! I wanted to see it. But then the spirit rose up and assaulted me, and I dropped it."

"For fuck's sake! That's what probably triggered its escape, you bloody Muppet! Why didn't you say so before?"

She stood up and poked him in the chest. "I am not a Muppet! I just forgot! I was attacked, remember." And then she scowled. "What is a Muppet, anyway? It sounds derogatory."

"It's meant to be. They're stupid, brainless puppets."

"Calm down children," Ash said, stepping between them, his lips twitching. "Why don't we all look for it now, and we can debate Muppets and their merits later." He turned to Shadow. "Where were you?"

She pointed to the wall on their right. "Over there, but it could have gone anywhere."

"Let's take a section each then, and get this done," Ash said, immediately heading to the far corner.

Shadow gave Gabe one final scowl before turning her back on him, and he took a deep breath and counted to ten, before starting his own search.

It wasn't long before he heard a shout from Ash. "Is this it?" He pointed his torch at the stone in his hand.

Shadow sighed with relief. "Yes. Can you interpret those symbols?"

Ash nodded, looking grim. "It's a rune sigil for silence—a sort of binding of the tongue and body."

"And you took it out of his mouth!" Gabe said, shaking his head.

"Well, I didn't know that at the time, did I?" Shadow said, annoyed.

Ash pocketed the stone. "At least we know what triggered Kian's escape, but it won't help us find him." He examined the doorway. "The swirling signs that are all along the passageway are inscribed here, too. I think this is purely decoration to honour the dead, before they sealed him in, but there's nothing here to indicate why he needed to be locked away for eternity."

"I think we should take his bones," Shadow said, dusting her trousers off.

"Why?" Gabe asked.

"I just think we should. His spirit is separate from his body now, but maybe we can use his bones to control him or banish him. And if I'm honest, I don't really want to come here again, so we should take everything."

Gabe felt increasingly uncomfortable about the tomb. Kian's dark energy still seeped from the stones. Tombs often were elaborate and detailed, celebrating the dead within them, but this was different. "Maybe Kian had some power over death. Maybe that's why they had to treat his body so carefully. Maybe death wasn't merely death for him? We've already messed so much up, is taking the bones really a good idea? And just to remind you, he's hunting you for some reason. This could make him even more annoyed."

"It's the only thing left to take. The significant grave goods have gone, including the staff." Shadow paused thoughtfully. "I just think we should."

Ash shrugged. "I'm not convinced. I'm with Gabe—this feels wrong!"

Shadow ignored their protestations and started to collect the bones anyway, placing them in the bag she had brought with her, before flashing them her most dangerous smile. "Trust me! I'm fey!"

"Yeah, and look what happened..." Gabe muttered to her retreating back. He stared at Ash. "The next time I suggest going into business with a fey, remind me of this moment."

Sixteen

Mason looked grey, and far older than his years.

He was slumped in a chair in Kent's living room, staring vacantly at the wall. Olivia sat next to him, holding his hand. "Can you remember anything?"

Mason shook his head. "Not really. I felt as if I was buried alive. I had flashes of awareness. Of being in my car, and then I was gone again. Until about an hour ago, when I woke up on the floor." He swallowed and took a few deep breaths. "I feel sick."

They had arrived ten minutes ago, to find Kent's door wide open and Mason sitting in the hall, shivering. As yet, Maggie hadn't turned up, and while Olivia had settled Mason in the lounge, Harlan prowled around the house, looking for anything that might help them. However, he'd found nothing of note, except for a half-consumed meal that must have been interrupted.

Kent Marlowe was well respected in the Order of the Midnight Sun. He was a similar age to Harlan, he would guess, and was known for his love of the occult, particularly magical rituals. All of the Order had eclectic interests, some more than others. Kent was an academic though, not a practising magician, and his home reflected that. It was far more ordinary than Chadwick's house.

Mason started to shiver, and Olivia looked at Harlan anxiously. "He's in shock. We need to get him seen by a doctor." She picked up a woollen blanket that was placed across the back of the sofa, threw it around Mason's shoulders, and then stood decisively. "I'll make some tea."

Harlan rolled his eyes. "Sure. Tea solves everything!"

"He needs something hot and sweet! It always works."

"Maybe throw a shot of brandy in it," Harlan called after her.

While Olivia headed to the kitchen, Harlan paced off his nervous energy, trying to work out where Kian would go next, but it was impossible to know at this stage. "Mason, can you remember what Kian was thinking, or doing?"

Mason blinked once and shook his head. "I don't think so. I felt he was sifting through my brain for things."

"That's because he was. He was looking for someone to help him, and Kent Marlowe is it." He rubbed his face wearily. "He headed back to Chadwick's, too. Fortunately, we interrupted him."

The screeching of brakes called him to the window, and he saw Maggie's car in the drive. Harlan took a deep breath, steeling himself for what was to come. "She's here," he shouted to the kitchen, not needing to explain what he meant to Olivia.

He headed to the door to let Maggie in, but she was already hammering on it when he got there. "All right, all right. I'm here."

Maggie barrelled into the hall, shaking the water off her jacket as she went. It had started raining since they'd arrived. "Bloody hell," she said, not wasting time. "Another kidnapping! For fuck's sake. You and your sodding Orphic Guild!"

"Can I remind you that I am not responsible for this? This was Chadwick's doing. I did what I always do, enable an acquisition!"

"Without any thought of the consequences!"

"And I help, too!" he yelled back, now very grumpy. "We keep objects of power away from the general population. Objects that could do immense harm in the wrong hands. You're happy for us to do our job then, aren't you?"

Maggie paused and took a deep breath. "Sorry. I'm tired. I had just got into bed when you called."

Harlan calmed down, slightly mollified. "I'm tired, too. And I'm worried. I have no idea where Kent Marlow has gone, but he will be in his own car. That's something."

"Okay. At this stage if we find him, I don't think we'll stop him, just monitor him," she said thoughtfully. She glanced down the hall. "What state is Mason in?"

"Not a good one. We might have to take him to the hospital." He led the way to the elegant sitting room and found Olivia pressing a cup of tea into Mason's hands.

Olivia nodded. "Hey, Maggie. Life is getting weird."

"Not for me, it's not. It's always this bloody weird. Christ!" She looked at Mason, focussing on him fully as she took in his appearance. "He looks like shit."

Mason stared into the mug, mute.

"Maybe you should get him checked out," Maggie said. "Although, he might be better after getting a good night's sleep in a warm bed. And food. Has he eaten in the last twenty-four hours?"

"Hard to know," Harlan told her. He leaned against the wall, his arms folded across his chest, exhausted. If he sat down now, he might never get up again. "He can't remember anything."

Maggie sighed. "Okay, let me get my head around this. You manage to wake a spirit from his tomb, who has become actively aggressive. He inhabits Chadwick, who tries to catch Shadow. She kills him and he hops into Mason, and now body-hops again, into Kent. What is he trying to achieve? And why does he want Shadow?"

Harlan exchanged a worried glance with Olivia. "I don't know why he wants Kent, but I presume it's because he studies ritual magic. He's an expert on it. Maybe his knowledge compliments Kian's. We believe Kian was a Druid who would have protected his tribe and his King." He'd already decided he wouldn't tell Maggie about their encounter with him at Chadwick's house. Not yet, anyway.

"So he would have practiced magic, of a sort," Maggie said thoughtfully. She narrowed her eyes at Harlan. "What aren't you telling me about Shadow?"

"Nothing. She's new to the Guild, but she has useful skills and will, hopefully, continue to help us in the future."

Maggie tapped her toe. "You're a shit liar. I checked her out. There's nothing about her anywhere until a few months ago. And nothing much about this Gabreel, who she lives with, either. He didn't exist on paper until September of last year! The same story for the other six guys registered at that address."

That gave Harlan a momentary shock, and his eyes must have betrayed it. He hadn't checked on Gabe, particularly. It didn't seem necessary. The Guild wasn't the police. They didn't run background checks on their contractors. They couldn't.

Maggie laughed. "So, you didn't know! You're slipping, Harlan. You get your contractors to do all sorts of things. Surely you should investigate them!"

"I had first-hand experience of working with Shadow. I trust her, and I trust Gabe."

"But you know nothing about him, or the other six men. That's eight of them living in a farmhouse, with no background at all! But they all have IDs and they all pay taxes!"

"Well, there you go then," Harlan said, relieved ever so slightly.

"Just because they pay their taxes doesn't make them good guys! It makes them smart! Do you even know who they work for?"

"Gabe? No idea." He shot a look at discomfort at Olivia, but she was mute, listening with interest.

"Kernow Industries. He and his crew do surveillance for them at their main warehouse in Harecombe."

"Great! I'm sure they must have done security checks on them. They have to be legit."

She was silent for a moment, considering him. "I have a contact down in White Haven. DI Newton. I haven't met him personally, but I hear good things about him. He's heading up their recently formed paranormal division. I bet he knows something."

"I met him after the Crossroads Circus problem ended. He seems decent." Harlan cast his mind back to the night of the fight with the Empusa, when Ravens' Wood had sprung up in a matter of hours. "He's good friends with the witches down there."

"Well, in that case, I must ring him." She gave Mason another long, speculative look. "We have to presume that having failed to catch Shadow once, he'll try again. That's good. She's bait."

"Maggie!" Harlan protested. "That's not cool."

"It is if it means catching some bastard rogue ghost. We need to exorcise it!"

"We are working on it. Trust me. Shadow will have a plan! She has no wish to get captured."

"I guess not," she agreed, begrudgingly. "Well, it's clear I'm getting nothing out of him now. Where's he going tonight?"

"He can come to my place," Olivia said. "I have a spare bed, and I'm happy to look after him."

Harlan nodded gratefully. "Thanks. I'll help you get him settled in."

Maggie headed for the door. "I'll have a quick look around and then lock up. I'll call you in the morning, Livy. Now, you three get out of here, and if I hear anything about Kent's car, I'll let you know."

𝝠 𝝠 𝝠

Shadow finished her conversation with Harlan, put her phone in her pocket, and stared at Kian's bones, which she had laid out in a corner of their barn.

She hadn't bothered to place them in order, but had instead piled them on each other, his skull on the top. The sockets looked back at her balefully, and she glared at them. "What are you up to, you devious old fey?"

"I don't think he's going to tell you," Gabe said from behind her, and she spun around.

"How did you sneak up on me so quietly?"

He smirked as he stood next to her, his arms folded across his chest. "I'm Nephilim, remember?"

"And huge! You're rarely quiet."

"Just goes to prove I can be when I want to be! Why are you talking to the bones?"

"Obviously I'm not expecting them to answer me. I'm musing out aloud."

"Good. Just checking that the iron in your blood hadn't addled your brain."

She decided to ignore his sarcasm. "I'm trying to recall what I know about certain rites that allow the spirit to transcend death in fey. It would involve dark magic, but I guess it could be done." She studied the hard planes of Gabe's face, and the stubble that grazed it. He looked tired, but she guessed she did, too. It was lunchtime on Monday, and those who had gone to Belas Knap had grabbed a few hours' sleep like her, and woke late. "You transcended death. How?"

Gabe met her eyes briefly and then looked at Kian's skeleton. "We didn't really. We died in the Great Flood that swept the Earth. It was sent as a punishment by God to kill us and the rest of the population who were deemed unworthy." Gabe had a good sense of humour, but it was often buried beneath what seemed an unequal burden of grief, and it showed now. His eyes were haunted.

"And what did you do that deserved that?"

"Rebel against our destiny."

"Wow." For a second, words failed Shadow, but if she didn't ask now, she may never get another opportunity. It was rare for Gabe to open up. "And what was your destiny?"

"We are half-angels, a bridge between the divine and the human. We could walk the Earth, unlike our angel fathers. We were bred for fighting, and to do our fathers' bidding."

He fell silent, and Shadow had to prompt him again. "Which was?"

"Controlling people, making war, herding the innocent to follow God's will. Our size and skills gave us a superior advantage. For a while, it made me arrogant. All of us, in fact." He was still staring at the bones, but it was clear he was seeing something entirely different. "I didn't like it, in the end. It felt wrong. I don't like to use my strength against others who are weaker and don't deserve it. We stopped following our fathers' orders and were punished for it, and those we then tried to protect were punished for our rebellion."

"I've read about the flood in history books. How big was it?"

"It pretty much killed everyone in the Mediterranean and the Middle East, except a chosen few. I don't believe that it really was worldwide—I think that's myth. But, what do I know? What I do know is that our fathers let us drown." Shadow felt the enormity of the event roll through her, and she was speechless. He finally turned to look at her. "Harsh, wasn't it?"

"That's one word for it."

"I drowned, as did all of my brothers, and our spirits ended up in the spirit world. An eternity of nothingness, in a dark place. And then we saw our chance, a glimpse of life and light again."

Shadow nodded, recalling a conversation she'd had with the witches. Curiously, they had been cagey about it, too. "Alex's spell that opened a portal."

"Yes. But only seven of us escaped."

"There were more of you?"

"My brothers were many. They are there still."

Shadow leaned against the barn wall, thinking that Gabe's history was far more complex than she could have imagined. She would probably only ever know a fraction of it; the histories she had read revealed only fragments. "I'm sorry they were left behind. But how did you regain your bodies? I don't understand how that's even possible."

"I had to kill someone and take his blood. It gave me enough strength to finally transform my spirit form into my physical body. We killed cattle, when we could."

"Oh. So that's why Newton doesn't like you. How many people did you kill?"

"Enough. We broke our centuries-old pact when we took innocent mortal lives to regain our bodies."

"Is your father alive?"

"He was immortal, so he should be. But I have not heard from him, and I'm glad of it. And neither have the others."

"I still think they are some kind of fey, a sylph."

"I no longer care what you think. I know what I know."

Shadow felt guilty. "I don't mean to demean your parentage. You may be right. Maybe this God of yours did have winged servants who bred with humans, but I really do sense some kind of fey blood. Fey bred with them, all the time at one point, when the veil between worlds was thin." She nodded at Kian's bones. "Look at them. Look at me. Look at you! We are like humans in many ways."

"We used human blood to regain our bodies. I fear he will do the same. With yours. Fey blood for a fey body."

"I have no intention of letting him do that. Briar is making me something to drug him. I aim to kill his spirit when he emerges from whoever he's possessing."

"Sounds easier said than done."

"I know." It was a half-formed plan, at best. "Harlan has phoned me. Kian moved bodies again, into a man called Kent Marlow who is an expert on ritual magic. He must need to use his knowledge. The good news is that Harlan has found Chadwick's notes—or some of them, at least. He hasn't read them yet, not properly anyway."

"Good, that's something. Kian has stayed in London then?"

"I suspect he will be here soon enough."

Gabe nodded. "Let's hope that he won't try to jump into our bodies."

"But what does he want?"

"Ultimately? To live like anyone else, surely? We'll keep a watch now and every night until this is over."

Shadow looked at Kian's remains. *Did he need these? Should she destroy them?* Gabe was spirit-only and he had regained his fully physical form without them, but he was Nephilim. *What was a Druid capable of? Whatever it was, she would stop him.*

"I need to get out," she said. "I'm going for a ride. I'll be safe enough on horseback."

He considered her for a moment. "I suppose you will. But don't stay out long, and take your bronze swords."

She nodded, heading to the stables. However, before she saddled Kailen, she spent some time with the horse of the fallen fey warrior. Shadow didn't know either of their names, but she had decided to call the beast Stormfall, after the night of their arrival. She stroked his soft nose and looked into his eyes. "I'm sorry your master is dead," she whispered. He was a fine animal, as tall as her own and as swift, like all horses from the Otherworld. Fortunately, the Nephilim were good riders, and many of them took him out for exercise, particularly Ash.

She didn't know his rider, so it would be wrong to say she'd grieved for his death, but she had grieved for the loss of one of her kind. Like her, he had been recruited for the Hunt at Herne's request. He'd been tall, fair-skinned, with fire in his eyes. He'd been the one to break the circle, and she followed, foolishly, as had one other. But he had died, killed by the Nephilim. She suspected it was Niel, but they hadn't said, and she didn't ask. The other fey had managed to get back to Herne and to the Otherworld when the witches forced them out through the doorway between worlds.

What if Kian did regain his body? What then? Would she forever fear him, or would he become an ally? She sighed, resting her head against Stormfall's neck. Just because he was fey didn't make him trustworthy, or a friend. He had been enough of a threat to others for him to be sealed in with fey magic. Perhaps he had crossed to this world because other fey had been hunting him. *Had he died naturally, or had someone killed him?*

Shadow thought again of Kian's remains. She had given them a cursory examination, but there were no obvious signs of trauma. No smashed bones or tell-tale cracks across the skull. He could still have died a violent death, though. A knife between the ribs, along the throat, or into the stomach would leave no marks on bone.

She took a deep breath and turned away. She didn't need to know who he was or what he'd done to kill him. She saddled up Kailen and headed out into the fresh air, leaving her speculation for another time.

Seventeen

When Harlan arrived in White Haven, the shops were just closing. He headed for the one place he knew he'd find a familiar face and some food before he visited Shadow—The Wayward Son, Alex's pub.

Harlan hadn't left London until the early afternoon, having been late to bed after helping Olivia with Mason the previous night. Olivia had already phoned to say that Mason was much better today, but he hadn't heard from Maggie yet. He'd decided to travel to White Haven anyway, and rather than examine Chadwick's notes at home, planned to do it once he arrived. They were in the trunk, with his overnight bag. Tucked inside the latter were his shotgun and a pack of salt-filled shells. It was the best protection he had against a rogue ghost.

He managed to find a park along the quayside, and when he stepped outside, he inhaled the fresh sea air. This place was a balm for the senses after London. He wasn't sure if it was his imagination, but he thought he could feel magic. When he'd come here a few weeks ago chasing the Crossroads Circus, he'd been suspicious of the town after everything he'd heard, but not anymore. Even the presence of powerful witches didn't put him off. Was that a mark of how he lived far more in the magical world than he did the normal? Maybe. White Haven felt remarkably safe, despite the magic, and that was a credit to the witches.

He pushed through the door of Alex's pub, relieved to see that it wasn't too busy. There was a table by the fire that would do nicely for his purposes. He headed to the bar to place his order, immediately seeing Alex serving another customer, and he waited patiently for his turn, scanning the menu to pass the time. But it wasn't Alex who served him; it was a tall man with broad shoulders, a scar down his cheek, and brooding eyes.

He nodded at Harlan in greeting. "What would you like?"

"The steak, medium rare, and a pint of Skullduggery Ale, please." The beer seemed fitting, considering his situation.

"Sure," he said, starting to ring up his order. "You're American."

"I am."

"You wouldn't happen to be Harlan Beckett, would you?"

Harlan looked at him, shocked. "What if I am?"

The man laughed and he instantly looked far less formidable. "Don't worry, you're not in trouble. I live with Shadow—as a housemate only, you understand!" He looked as if the alternative was horrific.

"I get it." Harlan laughed as he relaxed. "How do you know who I am?"

"We don't get many Americans this time of year. And Gabe said you'd be coming." He placed his pint in front of him. "I'm Zee."

Harlan shook his hand, remembering his conversation with Maggie. This man was as tall and broad-chested as Gabe and Niel, which was unusual. He couldn't help wondering about the rest of them. "I understand there are a few of you in that farmhouse."

Zee nodded and cocked an eyebrow. "Yeah, eight of us. Fun times."

"Never a dull moment, eh?"

"That's one way of putting it. Where are you staying?"

"I haven't decided. There are a couple of hotels I thought I'd try, but I needed food first."

Zee leaned on the bar and lowered his voice. "Have you come to help us find our rogue ghost?"

"Sort of. I've found Chadwick's papers, but I haven't had a chance to read them properly yet. I'm hoping they will tell us something useful." He broke off as Alex approached, a wary look in his eye. Harlan reached over and shook his hand, keen to establish good relations. "Hey, Alex. Great to meet you again."

"You too, I think. You're not chasing anything else, are you?"

Harlan laughed. "Just the ghost. I was telling Zee that I found Chadwick's papers. I need to study them, but I'd like to see Gabe and Shadow later."

"We keep late nights," Zee told him. "Give him a call after you've eaten. He won't mind."

"You still driving that Mercedes?" Alex asked.

Harlan had a jolt of surprise as he wondered how Alex knew what car he drove, and then realised they'd probably researched him, too. "It's outside now."

"Well, if you value your suspension, I suggest you take it slow. Did I hear you say you need a place to stay?"

"Yeah. I'd hoped I'd get a room easily at this time of year."

Alex looked uncertain. "You might, but my flat, upstairs, is empty at the moment. It's furnished, and it will take only a few minutes to make up the bed if you want to stay there. No charge, either. As long as you don't raid the alcohol stores tonight."

That sounded perfect. "You don't mind? It's not like you know me that well."

"I know you well enough. And besides, I think you know better than to cross a witch." He said the word witch quietly, an amused look on his face.

"I sure do. Thanks, Alex. And you can trust me with your whiskey."

When Harlan pulled into the farmhouse's courtyard a few hours later, he found a large man blocking his way and he halted, uncertain, as the man strode around to his window.

He was well built and again very tall, and very similar in appearance to Gabe—olive-skinned and dark-haired. Were all these men related?

Harlan introduced himself. "I'm expected, I hope."

"You sure are," he answered. "Park over here and head to the front door."

Harlan felt like saluting, but he resisted the urge, and instead did as he was told. He hoped he was guarding the gate just because of their unusual situation; otherwise, things were really odd here. When he exited the car, the man had already disappeared, and he crossed the yard feeling invisible eyes on his back.

Shadow answered his knock within seconds and led him inside. "Hey, Harlan. You want a drink?"

He looked around with curiosity as she brought him down the hall, which was bare, except for a couple of prints on the wall. "You got any beer?"

She laughed. "Of course we have. I'll grab a few before I introduce you to everyone." He followed her into the kitchen, which was far cleaner than he expected for a house full of men. He must have looked surprised, because she said, "Gabe keeps these guys on their toes. Although, to be honest, they're all house-trained. More than I am, anyway."

She flashed him a cheeky grin, her beauty catching him off guard. She had relaxed her glamour, or whatever it was she used to mask her Otherness, and he felt lost suddenly in her violet eyes. Her Otherness was uncanny, though he knew it was stupid to say that. Of course she was uncanny, she was fey, but her glamour was so effective it was easy to forget who she really was. He took a deep breath to ground himself, and when she passed him his beer, he clutched it like a man clinging to a life raft, and swiftly took a gulp.

"You look like you've seen a ghost." She grinned again. "Sorry. Poor choice of words."

Harlan decided honesty was the best policy. "It's easy to forget you're fey when you cover it up, and tonight you haven't. It's unnerving. Sorry if that's uncool to say."

"It's fine. I'm home now, so I don't need to bother."

"And the guard in the courtyard. Is that normal?"

"No. That's Nahum, and it's just what we're doing while Kian is on the loose. No one wants any nasty surprises at night."

He leaned against the counter, glad to have the chance to speak to her on her own. "Gabe and the others know you're fey, then."

Shadow watched him steadily, gauging his reaction. "Of course. They're fine with it."

"And you're okay with them knowing?"

"I had no choice when we first met," she said enigmatically, "but yes, I am. I'm okay with you knowing too, and the witches, but it was Avery and Alex who told me to use glamour. Of course they're right. I'd never fit in, otherwise. Gabe agrees. He says I'm too rash. So, from now on, I'm very choosy as to who knows about me!" She shrugged. "This place is not like home. I'd be a freak if everyone knew."

"Well, I feel very privileged, then," he said, raising his bottle in salute. "But there are a few of us who straddle two worlds, you know, and you happen to have stumbled upon some of them—me and the Orphic Guild, included."

"So I gather. I'm lucky to be in White Haven, and have Ravens' Wood to visit." She frowned. "I'm surprised more people here don't see the magic that still exists, despite mankind's attempt to bury it."

"People like to rationalise everything away. If science can't explain it, then it must be your imagination."

"How very sad and dreary they are."

He laughed. "They are indeed. Tell me, these men you live with. Are they paranormal in any way? The ones I've met so far are big guys."

"They're all big. Come and meet the rest," she said, and she led the way back down the hall, ignoring his question, Harlan noticed.

He heard them before he saw them. Loud shouts and swearing filtered down the hall, and when Shadow opened the door to a large living room on the side of the house, he paused for a moment, taking stock of the space.

There were four men sitting either on the sofa or floor cushions, cursing each other as they played a game screened on the TV dominating the wall. The lighting was low, a fire burned in the fireplace, and he noted the room had an oriental feel to it. There were two huge maps of the world on the rear wall, one modern, and the other old. A few pins were on it and he wondered what they were for. Gabe was on the sofa next to Niel, and two men he hadn't met before were on the floor. Both looked to be from the Mediterranean from what he could discern, Greek maybe. One had long hair, and the other's was shorter. And yes, they were also big, broad-shouldered, and clearly very competitive.

"Oi!" Shadow shouted to be heard over the noise, and she headed to the sofa and gestured Harlan toward the armchair. "Harlan has arrived."

Gabe barely glanced at him. "Hey Beckett, be with you in a minute!" The others grunted their greetings as a volley of gunfire filled the room.

They were all playing together, some combat game he didn't recognise.

Shadow rolled her eyes. "They're obsessed. Don't worry, they're generally civil when they're not trying to kill everything in sight. Do you play?"

"Not for years. Do you?"

"Yeah, I like to remind them who's the better fighter every so often."

The man on the floor in front of her laughed dryly. "Sure you do. I am fey!" he mimicked.

Shadow smacked a cushion off his head. "Sod off, Eli," she said. "Why aren't you out seducing unsuspecting women tonight?"

"So I can annoy you, Shadow, why else?" he retorted, without taking his eyes off the screen.

Harlan stared at him for a few moments. "I know you. You work with Briar!"

"Sure do," he said, shooting him a grin.

Shadow pointed to the other man on the floor. "That's Ash. He works with Reuben, and sometimes at Caspian's. And you saw Nahum outside. There are only another two who you haven't met. Barak is at the warehouse right now, and Zee's at the pub."

"I met Zee, actually. I'm staying at Alex's old flat tonight."

Shadow gave him a wry smile. "So you've seen most of our happy household, then."

Harlan tried to relax, but it wasn't easy with so much testosterone in the room. "It's an interesting setup you have here."

There was a final flurry of gunfire and a lot of cheering as they completed the end of the scene, and then the screen suddenly froze as someone paused the game. There was a general shuffling as they all grabbed beers and swivelled to look at him, and Harlan tried not to show his discomfort at the intensity of their stares. There was something about these men, something strange he couldn't place.

"Sorry," Gabe said again. "That level's been killing us. We had to get through it."

"I know the feeling, although I haven't played for a while," he answered. "Sorry to have disturbed your evening."

"It's fine," Niel answered, looking at him curiously. "Have you found our missing ghost?"

"I'm afraid not, but he's in another body now. A man named Kent Marlowe."

Gabe nodded. "Shadow told us, thanks for phoning. Who is he?"

Harlan paused, wondering how accepting of unusual news these men were. They lived with a fey and knew about an escaped ghost, so they must be broad-minded. "Kent is a ritual magician, although less of a practicing one than someone who researches the knowledge. He's a member of the Order of the Midnight Sun. It's an organisation that devotes its time to esoteric learning."

Gabe glanced at the others. "What kind of esoteric learning?"

"Alchemy, astronomy, divination, communing with angels and demons, unlocking the secrets of eternal life, ritual magic...and more, no doubt."

Eli raised an eyebrow. "That's quite a list."

"They're an interesting bunch," Harlan acknowledged. "But generally harmless. Well, they have been so far."

"You think Kian has stolen Kent's body because of his knowledge?" Gabe asked.

"It's the only reason I can think of. Kian is a Druid, and I imagine would be an expert in magical rites, but what the hell do I know? Maybe he needs a refresher? Maybe he just needs someone to understand what he wants to do? I mean, what can a ghost see or do in someone's body?"

Ash spoke for the first time, a trace of an accent in his voice. "He's got a plan though, that's for sure. He's setting things up carefully."

Harlan nodded reluctantly. "Yes, you're right. He was very determined last night, too. We ran into him when me and Olivia went back to Chadwick's house to find his notes. He attacked us both."

"Who's Olivia?" Niel asked.

"My colleague. She's a collector, like me. She's good, and can take care of herself—which is lucky, because he assaulted her while she was on her own. Fortunately, we got what he found, and he escaped empty-handed." He pointed to the bag at his feet. "Chadwick's notes on Kian."

"Why would he have wanted those?" Eli asked, puzzled.

"I can only assume to stop us from seeing them—to keep us in the dark."

"Have you read them yet?" Gabe asked.

"Just started, but if I'm honest, I can't find anything that will benefit us. They're just notes about his life, the approximate time of his existence, the king he was linked to—a local king you understand, the head of a tribe in the dark ages. It looks like they're assembled from hundreds of different sources, some the barest of references. It will be my bedtime reading later." He shrugged. "I know I'm staying in a spell-protected pub, but I didn't want to leave them there."

"Sensible," Niel acknowledged. "With luck, if Kian is being methodical about his plans, he won't attack tonight."

"Unless he prepares very quickly," Shadow said. She'd curled up in the corner of the sofa, listening to the exchange. "I'll be carrying the Empusa's swords everywhere with me now."

"Maybe you should leave one in here, for us," Eli suggested. "Just in case."

"Nahum's got one at the moment, and the other one is there." She pointed to where it sat on the side table, its curved blade wickedly sharp.

Harlan held his hand up, confused. "What's the relevance of the Empusa's swords?"

Shadow looked at him, wide-eyed. "Shit! Haven't I told you? I found out what they can do. The bearer can see spirits —and hopefully, banish them. When I accidentally killed Chadwick, I saw Kian's ghost! So clearly that I could tell that he's fey."

Harlan thought he was imagining things. "Fey?"

"Sorry. I'd forgotten I hadn't told you."

"That's pretty important, Shadow!" he said, annoyed.

At least she had the grace to look embarrassed, and she repeated, "Really sorry! That's why we think he wants me, in particular."

"But what if we're wrong?" Ash said to Shadow. "He might not be coming for your blood. He might want something else. Or someone else."

Harlan tried to bury his annoyance, feeling like he was playing catch-up with this evolving situation. "I've brought the grave goods with me, if anyone wants to see them. I'm not sure how they'll help."

"No harm in looking," Ash said, and pointed to the long, low coffee table in front of the fire. "Put them here." He started to clear cups, bowls of crisps, and empty beer bottles from the surface, and Eli quickly helped him as Harlan unpacked.

He placed the old leather bag out first. "It's rotted quite a lot, but not as much as I expected."

The others crowded around, picking up the items as Harlan unloaded them.

"Rings and torcs," Niel noted. "The torcs look like silver. He was wealthy."

"Or had a wealthy benefactor," Ash said. He had spread out the contents of the bag. "These look like herbs, and these are runes." The *click-clack* of wood on the table drew Harlan's attention. "For divination."

"If he was considered dangerous, and his tomb sealed, why bury his personal items with him?" Gabe asked. "Wouldn't you destroy them?"

Shadow stood to get the staff, which was still propped in the corner of the room, and she laid it next to the other objects. "Why insult the dead more than you need to?"

"Exactly," Ash said. "You still honour the dead, for fear of retribution. We did."

Harlan looked at him, wondering what the hell he meant, then decided now was not the time to press for information. "Did you decipher anything on the staff?"

"We did," Gabe nodded. "'Those who choose the dark path will reap its rewards.'"

"Great. Suitably ominous, then," he said, feeling more unsettled.

"I see nothing in here of particular concern," Eli said, still sifting through the items. "It just confirms he's a Druid, or a shaman."

"A fey shaman," Shadow reminded them. "I'm more interested in knowing why he was here." She turned to Harlan. "We found something else in the tomb—something I'd forgotten about when we were attacked." She fished in her pocket and then handed him a small, flat stone. "I took this out of Kian's jawbone. A few seconds after that, his ghost attacked us." She leaned back, frowning. "I should have known better."

Harlan looked with curiosity at the seemingly innocuous object, examining the marks etched into its surface. "What do the symbols mean?"

Ash answered. "It's a sigil that binds the tongue and the body. We think removing it broke a spell on Kian's spirit."

"Wow. They really didn't like him, did they?"

"Apparently not," Gabe said, shooting an impatient look at Shadow. "And now he's out, thanks to us!"

"To be honest," Harlan said, "there was nothing in the fake tomb to suggest of what was beyond it. Nothing. How were we supposed to know what the magic was hiding? It could have just been a very wealthy burial! And who would think a stone would have bound him after death? It's very easy in hindsight to criticise our behaviour. I've been annoyed with myself ever since, but the reality is, we couldn't have known unless they had slapped a big warning on it."

"Which would have told everyone that something was there, anyway," Niel said, nodding.

"And," Harlan continued, "if you hadn't been here, Shadow, we couldn't have gotten through the fey magic."

"It's fate," Shadow said, her eyes widening.

"More like an unfortunate confluence of actions," Eli said.

Harlan addressed Ash, confused. "How do you know what the marks on the stone mean?"

Ash shot an amused glance at Gabe before answering. "It's a skill."

"To read old markings that haven't been read for hundreds of years?"

Ash shrugged. "Yes."

Harlan studied them all again, one by one; their height, build, and the intensity that lurked behind their eyes. Now that he was with a few of them, he sensed a latent power. Something different. He couldn't help himself. "Who are you?"

"We're nothing and no one," Gabe answered flatly.

"We're working together. Honesty would be nice," Harlan pointed out.

"Honesty has a time and a place," Gabe said. "We're cautious, that's all." He moved on swiftly, instead asking his own questions. "How is Mason now? Does he remember anything of what Kian wanted?"

Harlan paused, unwilling to change the subject, but faced with their blank but pleasant expressions, he realised he didn't have a choice. "I wish," he said, regretfully. "He feels like he's been hit with a sledge hammer. He doesn't remember much at all, unfortunately."

"Damn it," Gabe said, sighing. "Tell us more about the Midnight Sun."

"They've been around for a very long time, hundreds of years. The Order was formed in the sixteenth century, and then became very popular in the 1800s. They were all alchemists originally, searching for the meaning of life, but they also studied metaphysics, astrology, divination, and astral travel." Harlan shrugged. "I think that's still the focus for quite a few of them, but other members are interested in other occult things."

Gabe sipped his beer. "How many are in the Order?"

Harlan laughed. "That's difficult to say for sure. They're very secretive. I know a few of them, but most I have no idea about. And I believe there are various initiation levels, too."

"There have always been such organisations," Eli said, "for as long as man has existed. They may call themselves different things, but their intent is the same."

Ash agreed. "To unlock the secrets of the world. And some secrets are dangerous."

There was something about the way they looked at each other that unsettled Harlan, as if they knew facts he didn't. "I think the danger is part of the appeal. They may look like regular men and women, but those appearances are deceptive. However," he shrugged again, "that's what the Orphic Guild does, too. We search for the lost items of the world, to buy them for others."

"The secrets just below the surface of everyday life," Niel said, wryly. "Be careful what you wish for, isn't that the saying?"

Harlan tried to shrug off his unease. "It's certainly led me to a few interesting experiences, and the situation with Kian is one of them. And of course I'm sitting here with a fey," he said, looking at Shadow. "I wasn't expecting that."

"An unexpected pleasure, though," she said, a challenge in her voice. "You're very privileged."

Eli groaned. "Will you shut up? Privileged? You're a pain in the ass. We have a watch on the house because a fey ghost wants your blood. If you ask me, he's welcome to it."

In seconds, Shadow's dagger appeared in her hands as if from nowhere, and she whipped it to Eli's neck, but equally quickly, in a blur of movement Harlan barely saw, he grabbed her wrist in his hand, staring her down.

"You do that again, and I'll break your arm, Shadow."

"Trust me, if I wanted you dead, you would be. That's a warning."

"You could try," he said softly.

At this moment, Harlan wasn't sure who he would put his money on to come out on top; he was just glad they hadn't turned on him.

"Shadow, put your damn blade away," Gabe said, glaring at her. "You really need to learn to take a joke."

"He wasn't joking," Shadow retorted.

Eli looked amused. "No, I wasn't."

"Shadow is one of us now," Gabe said staring at Eli, and then at the other two. "You know that, and if you've forgotten, get used to it."

Shadow smirked at Eli, and her dagger disappeared again. "We're in business together, remember?"

"How could I forget?"

Gabe ignored both of them and addressed Harlan. "Have you any idea what to do with Kian? Our plan is vague, at best. Stop him from kidnapping Shadow whilst trying to kill his ghost without harming the host."

"I haven't got much else to offer, unfortunately, other than to try to find out more about him."

"Briar's making me a potion to drug him," Shadow said. "Well, a paste I hope, something to put on my knife, or a dart. I'm picking it up tomorrow. If I can drug the host, Kian will have to leave the body, and I can slay him using the Empusa's sword."

"You trust the fact that he'll arrive here at some point, then?"

"If he wants me, he'll have to."

Harlan nodded, thinking of what Maggie had said. "So you're the bait."

"I guess I am."

"You look way more comfortable with that idea than I would be."

"Without wishing to annoy my colleagues," she shot a vitriolic look at Eli, "I have faith in my abilities."

"Even with your injured leg?"

"I've had worse, and it's healing well. Thanks to Briar."

"And me!" Eli said, refusing to let her get away with anything.

Harlan tried not to laugh. "Maggie is keeping an eye out for Kent's stolen car, so if she finds it, I can warn you. But her resources are small when it comes to surveillance cameras and such. I should caution you about her, though."

"Why?" Shadow asked warily.

Harlan paused, debating just how much to say, but had to admit he wondered how they'd react, especially considering their response to his earlier question. "She's very interested in all of you, particularly because she believes that none of you existed six months ago."

"She can be as interested as she wants," Gabe said evenly. "We work, pay our taxes, and don't cause trouble."

"Who's Maggie?" Ash asked.

"The detective who leads the paranormal team in London," Harlan told him. "She's well versed in the occult world, and likes to know everything. She's going to speak to Newton about you."

"So be it," Gabe said, looking more at ease with the news than Harlan expected. "Our arrival caused some initial concerns, but since then we have only helped the witches here."

Harlan noted that he didn't say where he'd arrived from or why they'd raised concerns, but he wasn't going to ask anymore. *Not yet.* He finished his beer, and placed the empty bottle on the table, along with the stone. "Well, it's good to have met you all. I wanted to let you know that I'm here, and happy to help. I'm as responsible for this mess as anyone, and I'm not going until it's over. Shall I leave the grave goods with you?"

Ash answered, "Yes, please." He was still examining the items.

"You have his bones too, is that right?" Harlan asked.

Shadow nodded. "I decided that we needed them, I'm not sure why."

"Maybe you should try putting the stone back in the jaw," he suggested.

"Maybe we should," she said thoughtfully.

Harlan stood to leave, and realised he was exhausted. He wanted nothing more than bed, but that would still be a few hours away. He had more reading to do first. "I'll keep you updated with what I find out."

The other men stood as well, all reaching to shake his hand, and Gabe said, "Thanks, Harlan, we appreciate it. If we ever form a more concrete plan, we'll tell you."

Shadow escorted him to the door, and after he'd said goodbye, he headed swiftly to the car, aware that Nahum was out there, somewhere, still watching. If anything, the meeting with Gabe and the others had raised more questions than provided answers, but he was glad for one thing. At least they were on his side, because he definitely didn't want to be their enemy.

Eighteen

Gabe joined Nahum outside once Harlan had left. He was sitting on the roof of one of the outbuildings, leaning against the chimney, his wings wrapped around him for warmth.

"Anything out there?"

Nahum shook his head. "Nothing but the wind and a few cars heading into White Haven."

"Good." Gabe shuffled himself into a more comfortable position. "I wonder if Kian knows where we live? It's hard to know how much he extracted from Mason."

"Unless Mason has a phenomenal memory, it's unlikely. But maybe he went by the office in the middle of the night. It's possible, I guess. He could have looked at the files."

"If he doesn't know, he'll have to ask around. That will slow him down."

"What did Harlan have to say?"

"He's found Chadwick's papers, and will tell us if he discovers anything useful. He also told us the detective, Maggie, is interested in who we are."

Nahum gave him a crooked smile. "We knew it would happen eventually. She'll talk to Newton, I suppose."

"Yes. That's okay. She knows more about the paranormal world than he does, by the sound of it. She's worked in it longer. We'll just be one more non-human group to know about."

"But Nephilim? Do you really think she's come across us before?"

"It would be something if she had, brother," Gabe said softly. "But I doubt it. No one had escaped before us."

"You've read our vague history. It sounds like some of us didn't die in the flood."

Gabe looked to the horizon, a distant black line barely discernible from the dark, cloudy sky. He could see the sea from here, but not White Haven; it was tucked in the folds of the valley. The farmhouse was high on the hill, and it caught the wind, but it afforded them views across the moors, as well as the sea. It was open, and Gabe liked that. You couldn't be trapped up here. It was the perfect spot.

He thought on what Nahum had said. "It's speculation, nothing more. The flood took everything."

"But there are written records, and we're in the Bible!"

"Stories to promote a God, that's all. The tales about us are wrong and vague at best," Gabe insisted.

"But there were hundreds of us, spread across the east, Canaan, and the Mediterranean. We didn't know all the Nephilim. Some might have survived if they reached the mountains in time. Or our fathers could have found more willing females and created more of us."

Gabe looked at Nahum, his expression barely discernible in the dark. "Say some of them did. They would be long dead by now. Our lifespans are great, but we are not immortal. You are talking about thousands of years. The land doesn't even look the same. It's impossible to know where we were with any accuracy." He was frustrated, and he knew he sounded it. For months they had been trying to work out where their old home was in the modern world, but everything had changed. "I don't even see any place names that are familiar."

"We'll find out one day," Nahum said, reassuringly. "We're collecting books and old maps that will help. But if I'm honest, I don't know why it worries you so much. We're here now, and in a good situation. That's all that matters."

Gabe nodded, knowing Nahum was right, but he couldn't help it. He had a need to establish himself in the modern world. "I think it's because we were ripped from our existence so quickly. I feel I have unfinished business."

"With what? Who? We were fighting battles that didn't mean anything to us, other than the money. Except for Eli, who was smart enough to stay out of it. At least we're not doing that anymore."

"You know who I have unfinished business with."

"With our father? Forget him. He's not worth our time. We were tools for him, nothing else. And he was fallen, damned."

"He let us die."

"He let lots of people die. They all did." He snorted. "They were never Angels of Mercy. The flood was probably sent to kill them, as well as us. They had angered their God and created us out of spite. A merciful God, my ass. You've heard the witches talk, and Shadow. Gods have their own agendas, and ours was no different. Let it go, Gabe."

"I can't. Since we've been here, our time before the flood seems like a dream. I can't help but think that we must have been created for more than to be our fathers' weapons on Earth."

"You're looking for meaning where there is none. Our destiny was to bring death and destruction, and at one point we did it well—too well. And then we sought independence." Nahum smiled. "We were kings and princes, once."

"We'll never be that again."

"And I wouldn't want to be." Nahum's eyes gleamed. "We have more freedom now than we ever had. No responsibilities, no one to dictate what we do. Our plan with Shadow is a good one."

"It is. I've been thinking about this Guild. It has resources, arcane knowledge."

"You want to use it for your own research."

"Our research, our history."

"We know it, we were there!"

Gabe fell silent. He wasn't the only one to think this way. The more he thought back on their old life, the more he realised there were secrets they weren't privy to. Some of the others thought so, too. If they had resources, they should use them. But he would let it drop, for now.

He surveyed the hushed landscape, and knew he wouldn't sleep for hours. "I don't think Kian will come tonight, but I'll take your place. Head inside and rest."

"Thanks," Nahum said, and passed him the curved bronze sword. "You'll need this, just in case. But Gabe, don't get caught up in our past. It's behind us now."

Gabe watched him jump from the roof and land as lightly as a cat, and wished he could feel the same way.

Shadow looked at the thick paste in the pot. "How much do I need?"

"A smear, only. It's concentrated, but even if you use more than you need to, it won't kill anyone. It's a heavy sedative, but it shouldn't interfere with breathing," Briar told her. "And of course, there's magic in there, too. It's very effective."

"Thanks," she answered, slipping it into her pocket. "With the sword and the paste, I feel like we have a chance of success."

Shadow and Briar were talking in Briar's herb room in her shop. It was early and Shadow had arrived with Eli, riding on the back of his bike. Despite yesterday's argument, she liked Eli. They may spat occasionally, but he was generally even-tempered and a good healer, just not quite as good as Briar. She knew he wasn't particularly excited by their deal with Harlan, but he went along with it anyway, and she sensed he blamed her for the arrangement. He was right about that. She was responsible, but Gabe had agreed quickly enough. Eli was in the shop now, opening up.

"Just be careful with it," Briar warned her. "If you get some in a scratch, you'll end up putting yourself to sleep. Right, let me see your leg."

Shadow slipped her trousers off and sat on the small sofa in the corner of the room, watching Briar deftly pull the bandage off. "It feels much better already," she told her.

Briar looked pleased as she examined the wound. "It looks good. I'll put the salve on it and another light dressing. You should be able to do it yourself from now on. Or ask Eli." She grinned. "Just don't mix the pots up."

Shadow laughed. "I won't."

"What are you doing now?"

"Heading to Avery's shop to see Dan. I want to ask him about tombs and bones."

"I hear he took you to Tintagel the other day."

"It's a beautiful spot," Shadow admitted. "I can see why people love it. But no portals to the Otherworld there."

Briar tightened the dressing and stood up, giving her space to dress. "Did you think there would be?"

"No, not really. I guess I'm getting used to this place, anyway." Shadow headed to the door. "I'd better let you get to work, and I need to go, too. Gabe is picking me up soon, and we're going to the warehouse."

"I hear Caspian is back. Say hi to him for me, and tell Avery I'll see her later."

When they re-entered the main shop, a couple of people were already browsing the shelves despite the early hour, and one young woman was leaning on the counter, looking doe-eyed at Eli. He chatted to her easily, and Shadow could tell he had another admirer.

"Does this happen often?" she asked Briar, nodding at them talking.

She rolled her eyes. "All the time, but it's good for business, and he treats them well. I guess it's a win for everyone."

Shadow laughed, waved goodbye, and stepped outside. It was another brisk spring morning, and she strolled up the winding lanes to Happenstance Books. But she hadn't gone far when she saw Harlan sheltering in the doorway to a gift shop, staring down the street, and she hurried to his side. "Can you see Kian?"

He barely glanced at her. "I thought I had, but now I'm not so sure." He rubbed his face with his hand. "I think I'm overtired."

His chin was covered in day-old stubble, and there were dark rings beneath his eyes. "Did you sleep at all?" she asked.

"For a few hours. I was reading until late. I want to see Dan, and Avery too, I guess, so I'm heading there now. I'm starving as well, which doesn't help matters. I should have eaten first."

"I'll treat you. I'm going your way, and I'm buying cakes for bribery purposes."

Harlan walked up the street with her. "You want to see Dan, too?"

"He said he'd do some research for me, so I just want to learn what he's found." She spotted the shop she wanted, and stopped. "Wait here, I won't be a minute."

She ducked inside and chose half a dozen pastries, feeling her stomach rumbling already, and then bought a coffee for her and Harlan. By the time she got outside again, he was sheltering within the deep porch, and gestured to her to get behind him.

"He's here."

She tried to peer over his shoulder. "Where?"

"Walking up the street, just dawdling, really."

"He hasn't seen you, then?"

"Not yet, and I'd like to keep it that way."

Shadow chaffed at not being able to see. "Should we try and follow him?"

"It's tempting, but the street's not busy enough. If we step out now, he's likely to spot us. At least we know he's here, in White Haven."

"I feel we should do something!"

"Like what? We can't challenge him. Oh, hold on."

"What?"

"He's going into a shop, now's our chance." In a split-second, Harlan grabbed her arm and pulled her up the road at a fast trot. "At least Avery's shop is along the next street."

"Shouldn't we be going the other way?" she protested. "We can spy on him!"

"No. We're not ready."

"I'm not saying we engage in battle right now!"

"If he spots us and feels cornered, who knows what might happen? We must wait."

Harlan's hand was under her elbow, almost propelling her around the next corner, and then he pushed her behind him in a way that Shadow had to admit made her feel both resentful and protected. He looked back down the street, ignoring the strange glances they were getting.

After a few moments he was satisfied, and he sighed. "Good. We dodged him for now."

He tried to walk on, but Shadow stopped him, feeling increasingly annoyed. "Harlan, I need to see him. I have no idea what he looks like, and meeting him in the open is actually the safest thing to do! He's not stupid. I'm going to find him."

She turned and marched back down the road, Harlan hot on her heels.

"Shadow, this is dumb!"

"No, it's not! Which shop was he in?"

"I'm not telling you," he said petulantly.

She stopped in the middle of the pavement, glaring at him. "Don't be ridiculous!"

"You're the one being ridiculous. How can you protect yourself carrying pastries and coffee?"

Shadow itched to drop the goods, grab him, and throw him against the wall, but decided to soften her approach. "If I don't know what he looks like, how will I defend myself?"

Harlan sighed heavily. "Damn it. He was in the little occult shop that sells crystals, incense, and things."

"There are a million of those in White Haven!" She thrust his coffee at him, freeing up one hand. "Take that and show me!"

He walked around her, leading the way. "He went into Spells and Shells."

The shops were in old buildings with doors set back from the road, and they were close to Spells and Shells when Harlan paused, hand on her arm. "That's him!"

A man with fine, sandy blond hair emerged from the entrance, a package in his hands. He looked up, saw them, and froze, and then glancing around at the other shoppers, stood his ground, a grim smile on his face.

Shadow didn't hesitate, and trying to ignore the twinge in her leg, marched to his side. "Kian, how nice to see you again."

"And you Shadow, Harlan."

"Whatever you're planning, I'll stop you," she told him coolly.

"But that's the problem, isn't it?" he said softly. "You have no idea what I'm planning."

Shadow glanced at the package, wondering what was in it. "I presume it involves me."

"Maybe, maybe not. I may not need you."

"Then why are you here?"

"That's my business. But I will thank you for my freedom. I wasn't sure I would ever get it again."

"My mistake," Shadow admitted. "Which is why I'll make sure I put you back where you belong."

Kian looked infuriatingly smug. "You'll try, of course. I'm going to walk away now. Please don't follow me, if you value Kent's life."

Harlan leaned into him. "You'd better not hurt him, Kian."

"Or what?" he sneered, oblivious to the curious onlookers. "You have no way to stop me, and the more you annoy me, the more likely Kent will get hurt, understood? Although, I'm not the one who killed Chadwick." He shot

Shadow a vicious smile, which sent her hand reaching for her knife, and then walked away, leaving Shadow and Harlan staring after him.

"Bollocks," Shadow said, using her favourite English curse. "I really wanted to sink my knife into his gut."

"I'm very grateful you didn't," Harlan said with a tight smile. "And at least you know what he looks like now. Let me see if I can find out what he bought."

He left Shadow watching Kian until he was out of sight, and when he returned, he said, "He bought some herbs—wormwood and valerian."

"What will they do?"

Harlan directed her back up the hill. "We'd better ask a witch!"

By the time they got to Happenstance Books, they were both stewing on their encounter, and they pushed through the door with relief.

Avery, the redheaded witch who owned the shop, was already heading towards them, a worried look on her face. "What's happened?"

"Kian is in town," Harlan told her. "We've just had an unpleasant chat outside of Spells and Shells. I assume Alex has told you what's going on?"

Avery ushered them into the recesses of the shop. "He did. Anything I can do?"

"Not at the moment, other than offering some shelter in case he decides to follow us. He suggested he didn't need Shadow, but I'm not convinced." He looked at the section of books surrounding them. "The Gothic and Horror section. How apt!"

Avery laughed, but Shadow protested loudly. "I don't need sheltering, thanks! I'm not a child. And besides, you're squashing the cakes."

As if he had supersonic hearing, Dan appeared from behind the stacks. "Did I hear the word cakes?"

"You have a one track mind," Shadow told him, and then squinted at his t-shirt, reading the words out loud. "When I think about books, I touch my shelf." She groaned. "Seriously?"

He grinned. "Always."

Harlan looked perplexed and annoyed. "You should be taking this more seriously, Shadow. The man who wants your blood is out there now, planning his next move!"

"And so are we!" She passed the cakes to Dan. "We were coming to see you two anyway, especially you, Dan."

He nodded. "I've found out some stuff, but I'm not sure how helpful it will be." He peered into the paperback bag. "I spot a custard tart. You've done very well."

"Thank you. Now can we move away from The Mysteries of Udolfo so I can drink my coffee in peace?"

Nineteen

While Harlan stopped to speak to Avery, Shadow headed to the kitchen with Dan. As soon as the door was shut, she sat at the table and took a long sip of coffee. "I needed that. It's a bit annoying that Kian is here already and we didn't know."

Dan was getting plates out of the cupboard, and he put them on the table, and then set out the cakes on an oval platter. "You know now! And you're in White Haven. I think that gives you the advantage."

"Only just," Shadow moaned, reaching for a sticky chocolate brownie. "I'd like nothing more than to just fight it out, rather than deal with all of this subterfuge and threats."

Dan sat down opposite her. "But you'll endanger the man who Kian is hiding in. Who is it?"

"Kent Marlowe, a member of the Order of the Midnight Sun." She raised an eyebrow. "Alchemist, magician, astronomer, and other things."

"Really? Since I saw you last, I did as promised and read up on alchemists, and I've heard of the Order. They've been going for years. Very shadowy!"

"Dodgy shadowy?"

"More like secret handshakes, special rites, initiations, and all of that baloney."

"Baloney?"

"Rubbish," Dan explained. "It's an organisation that has levels of secrecy built into it, and you have to achieve certain things to move up the levels."

Shadow chewed her cake, considering his words. "You sound like you don't like them. Do you know them?"

"No, of course not. But it smacks of the Masons. It's like an old boys club, where you get perks for being a part of it. Like avoiding arrest, and getting promotions you don't deserve."

"I think women are in the Order, too."

"Doesn't matter, it's the same principles."

Intriguing. "Do you know what rites they do?"

He swallowed his mouthful of cake. "No idea, I'm afraid—and that's the point. No one does, except for the initiates, and they don't tell anyone. It perpetuates the secrecy and intrigue, and makes everyone feel very important."

"How do you know it's true, then?"

"You can Google it. There are all sorts of articles about them on the net. To be honest, they all share the same basic information, and focus more on the history and old members than current concerns, but they definitely talk about initiation and levels of knowledge. I think their headquarters are in Marylebone, in London."

"Well, I look forward to meeting Kent Marlowe then, when he's no longer possessed. Let's hope he survives."

"I don't want him to die!" Dan looked horrified. "Who knows, I may even like him."

"The witches here have a coven, isn't that the same thing?"

"Not at all. I would imagine Avery has more magic in her little finger than all of those members put together. They don't need initiation rites to make them feel special. They are special."

Shadow hadn't seen this side of Dan before. He was normally so accepting, and yet today he was sceptical. She trusted his judgment, so maybe it was something to consider. Before she could say anything else, Harlan joined them, looking reassured.

"Hey, guys." He slid into a seat and reached for a pastry. "Avery and Sally are keeping watch, which gives us a chance to talk about Kian."

"Did you read Chadwick's research last night?" Shadow asked.

"I did. It seems that there are a few obscure tales attached to him."

"Like what?" Shadow and Dan asked together.

"Like he can summon the dead, and use them for his own bidding."

Dan's eyes widened. "Like a zombie army?"

"Something of the sort."

"Necromancy, then," Shadow said. "We had such sorcerers in our world. They would use the dead to find secrets, hidden treasure, for divination purposes, and other such things."

Dan dipped his pastry in his coffee, looking thoughtful. "There are many instances here, too. Necromancy goes back thousands of years. I must admit, though, I couldn't find out anything about Kian, not even a morsel."

Harlan shrugged. "I'm not surprised. Chadwick's documents are old and obscure, and would have taken him years to find. The references are oblique, and tangled within other tales." He rubbed his stubble. "I have to confess, I'm a bit annoyed with myself, actually. I should have suspected something like this sooner, because Death Magic was one of Chadwick's special interests."

"I bet Gabe would know something about that, too. Necromancy was mentioned in the Old Testament, and Canaan was discussed in my research," Dan suggested, but before he could say anything else, Shadow shot him a look of warning and catching her eye, he clammed up.

Harlan looked between them uneasily. "Is Gabe some kind of Bible aficionado?"

Shadow tried to brush it off. "Sort of. He has many varied interests, all of them sort of Biblical in nature."

Harlan stared at her. "Gabe has Biblical interests?"

She inwardly squirmed. "He's not particularly religious, however. It's just a hobby!" She flashed him her most beaming smile. "Useful for treasure hunting, don't you think?"

"Very," he replied, unconvinced.

Dan leapt in to relieve her. "Back to Kian. He's a fey necromancer, highly regarded, and greatly feared. No wonder they sealed his tomb. They must have been afraid he could come back from the dead."

"No shit," Harlan said dryly. "He has!"

"Because you broke the seal!" Dan pointed out. "You shouldn't mess with tombs!"

"I've been messing with them for a long time, and this has never happened before!" Harlan reached across for another cake. "I need food. I'm getting a headache."

"Can you have a look at these, Dan?" Shadow searched for the photos she'd taken on her phone, and quickly found the images of spirals. "These were everywhere. Are they significant?"

Dan squinted at the screen. "I've seen lots of these shapes—you see them in many megalithic sites. There are some great examples in New Grange. People have been wondering about their significance for years. They may be decorative, or something else."

"What's New Grange?" she asked.

"Another tomb in Ireland. It aligns with the winter solstice, and it's very famous," Dan told her. "The spirals there are very ornate, and it's quite old."

"I agree with you there," Harlan said. "Whatever they meant, it was a great honour to have such a burial."

Shadow looked between them both. "It changes nothing, though. The most important information is that he's a necromancer, which explains the power he has over his own spirit. It won't stop me killing him. Again."

"Are you sure the Empusa's sword will work?" Dan asked.

"I can see him as easily as I can you."

Harlan looked worried. A deep crease divided his forehead, and the cake didn't seem to help. "It doesn't mean you can harm him with it, though. You're assuming a lot."

Shadow's phone buzzed with a text message, and she gratefully picked it up. She hated being questioned. "My lift's here. Must go, boys. Thanks for the update—I'll pass it on to the others. Now that we know he's here, it's time to trap him."

As Gabe pulled into the car park at the Kernow Industries warehouse, he saw Caspian's Audi, and he pointed it out to Shadow. "Caspian's here. We'd better update him on the latest."

"Will he care?" she asked. "He's been away for weeks. I'm sure he'll have plenty of his own business to catch up on."

"You'd be surprised what Caspian cares about," he said, exiting the car and locking it.

"You mean Avery?"

"I mean lots of things," he replied enigmatically and then winked, knowing it would infuriate her. She hated not to know everything.

He grinned as she fell into step beside him. He'd learned early on that Shadow was a force of nature who would bulldoze everything in her path if given half a chance, acting first and thinking later. He'd decided to limit those chances, for her and everyone else's safety.

She prodded him for details. "I suppose you mean business concerns?"

"Business, witch stuff, family stuff...you know," he said vaguely.

They passed through the security checkpoint at the entrance to the building, nodding at the guard on duty. Caspian still employed a few guards who'd been with the company for years, and they mostly worked during regular hours, operating the main gate and the second checkpoint into the main building.

The other security work, such as monitoring the perimeter and patrolling the grounds, was left to the Nephilim.

Although Gabe was teasing Shadow, during the past few months of working with Caspian, he had come to know him better, and he liked him. Like the Nephilim, he had a strong work ethic and a complicated family. And also like them, he'd had a very difficult relationship with this father, Sebastian. Since Helena, Avery's ghostly ancestor, killed him, it had freed Caspian to become the man he wanted to be, rather than the man his father had tried to shape.

The warehouse was full of crates and boxes of all sizes, and although it looked haphazard, there was a system in place. A few employees were moving crates using a forklift, and making sure to keep out of the way, they headed up the stairs to the mezzanine floor and the two offices that overlooked the whole operation. Barak, Niel, and Nahum were already seated in the security office, monitoring half a dozen screens on the wall, and Gabe raised his hand in greeting, but first he needed to speak to Caspian, so he headed for the bigger office. He could see him through the large window, seated at the computer; he knocked and entered.

"Hey Caspian, welcome back."

Caspian was dressed in his characteristic dark suit with a white shirt, and was perfectly groomed, his dark hair swept back and face clean-shaven—unlike Gabe, whose stubble was now thick. He looked up and smiled. "Gabe, Shadow. It looks like there have been no major issues while I've been away."

"None," Gabe reassured him. "Estelle runs a tight ship."

Caspian's lips set in a thin line. "She certainly does. I hope she hasn't given you any problems?"

Estelle was well known to be prickly and abrupt, and there was no love lost between the siblings. If anything, they seemed to rub each other up even more lately.

"No, I've got used to her, and I think Barak quite likes her prickliness."

Shadow grunted. "I think she's a pain in the ass."

Gabe glared at her, but Caspian looked amused. "I think the feeling's mutual."

Shadow's mouth fell open. "She thinks *I'm* a pain? I don't know why," she said, leaning against the doorframe. "I'm always polite."

Gabe nearly choked. "Liar. You antagonise her deliberately."

A small smile crept across Shadow's face. "Only occasionally."

"You questioned her about an address the other day. It's none of our business!"

"It was just a question!" Shadow went still for a moment. "That reminds me of something..."

She fell silent then, and Gabe looked at her, puzzled, before turning to Caspian. "You should know there are other things going on with us at the moment, in White Haven. It won't affect this business, though."

"What things?" Caspian asked, worried. "Is Avery okay?"

"Avery's fine."

Caspian instantly relaxed, and Gabe realised that whatever feelings Caspian had for Avery were still there. He knew that look, and he'd experienced those feelings, and they would pass, eventually. But Caspian wouldn't thank him for that advice. Instead, Gabe explained about Kian, and he listened closely, nodding and asking questions.

"My family has dabbled in necromancy in the past," Caspian told him, "but nothing recently. A fey necromancer is different though, and potentially more dangerous."

Shadow abruptly interrupted them. "Marylebone! You ship to an address there sometimes. I saw it the other day, and when I asked Estelle about it, she snapped at me."

Caspian looked confused. "We deal with lots of addresses. Why do you care about Marylebone?"

"Dan said the Order of the Midnight Sun is based there, and I remember the name on the package. Do you work with them?"

Caspian shrugged. "I've heard of them, so maybe. But we ship lots of things, some of which come through other companies. Why are you asking about them?"

"Because Kent Marlowe is a member."

"You aren't suggesting that I've got anything to do with this current situation are you?" Caspian asked, a dangerous edge to his voice.

Shadow looked impatient. "No, of course not. But they intrigue me. Do you know any details about them?"

Caspian leaned back in his chair. "Nothing. I'm a witch, not a new-age alchemist. And I'm a business man. I'm not responsible for peoples' orders. We just receive shipments and distribute them."

Gabe shot her a warning look. "Shadow, they have nothing to do with Kian's reappearance—we're responsible for that. What does it matter?"

"It doesn't, I guess. I just like to connect the dots and know how things work."

"Most of our business dealings are with legitimate companies who have nothing to do with the paranormal world. But yes, we do have *other* connections. And shipping is just one of our business arms. There are others," Caspian explained. "We're called 'Kernow Industries' for a reason."

Shadow nodded, "Of course, I'm just curious."

While Gabe talked to Caspian about a few other things, he kept an eye on Shadow. She looked restless, and Gabe knew what that meant. She would be pacing around and getting under his feet for hours, and they had work to do. As much as he didn't want to leave her on her own, he had to admit that she knew how to look after herself.

They left Caspian's office to return to the security office, and he stopped her. "You've got that look in your eye."

"What look?"

"You know what look. You're not paying the slightest bit of attention."

She had the grace to appear marginally guilty. "I'm sorry, Gabe. I can't concentrate right now. I know it's important, but it's driving me mad."

He thrust the keys to the car at her. "Take them and go home. I can go back with the guys. As long as you promise to be careful. No hunting Kian alone!"

She grinned at him as she grabbed them. "As if I would!"

Shadow virtually skipped down the steps, and as Gabe watched her go, he hoped he hadn't just done something really stupid.

Ҡ Ҡ Ҡ

The farmhouse was quiet by the time Shadow arrived back there. All of the Nephilim were out. Eli, Ash, and Zee were working for the witches, and the other four were at the warehouse.

There were just a couple of bikes in the courtyard and no signs of intrusion, so it seemed like the perfect afternoon for a ride. She felt restless with excess energy. All of this waiting was frustrating. They knew Kian was a necromancer and potentially dangerous, but despite that, he was a ghost, and she was going to get rid of him. All they needed was his address. If necessary, they could break in and drug Kent, and they could all finish this tonight.

She saddled Kailen up quickly, feeling his impatience, too. He was skittish and needed exercise, and within minutes she was on the moors with the wind in her hair, urging Kailen to ride faster. The fields flew by, and she knew exactly where she was headed. Ravens' Wood. She needed old magic, fey magic, around her.

When she entered the wood, she expected Kailen to settle down. He'd been hard to control on the ride, but if anything that made it more exhilarating. Now, however, it was annoying. "Kailen, calm down," she chided, trying to slow him down.

But he was wilful, pushing beneath the trees as he headed to the middle of the wood. He was following a track she hadn't seen before, which she liked. Ravens' Wood was constantly changing—to her, at least. Paths would appear and then disappear, and just when she expected to come out in one place, she found herself in another. It was a reminder of the Green Man's magic, and the fact that the wood was based on crossroads magic—boundary magic. Did humans find it as bewildering sometimes as she did? Or was it just the fact that she was fey that it misbehaved for her?

Kailen picked up his speed, and she had to duck to miss a branch. She pulled tight on his bridle, trying to slow him, but if anything he sped up, and Shadow had a horrible feeling that something was wrong.

Was Kian in the wood, spooking her horse?

They entered a small clearing and Kailen bucked wildly, throwing her to the ground.

She landed awkwardly in a heap, winded, but dragged herself to her feet. With a hand on the hilt of her dagger she ran to Kailen, concerned that he was injured. But before she could reach him, he collapsed to the ground, unresponsive.

Shadow fell to her knees, stroking his neck. Kailen could not die. He was the one thing she had that she truly cared about. Had he been poisoned? And then she heard a laugh from behind her, just before everything went black.

Twenty

W hen Gabe arrived at the farmhouse with Nahum and Niel, the place felt empty. There were no lights on in the main building or Shadow's quarters, and Shadow was nowhere in sight.

"This is odd," Gabe said, as he looked through the window of her building. "She should have arrived back hours ago."

It was close to seven o'clock now, the light was fading, and the temperature was falling.

"The car's here. She's probably out riding," Nahum said. "You know how obsessed she is about that. And she was restless earlier—you said so yourself. I'll check the stable."

"Or," Niel pointed out, "she might be asleep on the sofa, in the dark."

Nahum crossed the courtyard to the stable while Niel headed into the farmhouse, Gabe right behind him.

Gabe shook his head. "You know that's unlikely. I'm worried something has happened."

There was no sign of Shadow in the living room, and Niel ran to check the rest of the house. Gabe had a horrible feeling that something wasn't right, but there was no sign of a fight. He stood in the kitchen, looking over the fields beyond. She was out there, somewhere, in trouble. He pulled his phone from his pocket and called her number. It rang and rang before finally going to her voicemail. Damn it.

Nahum joined him in the kitchen. "Kailen is gone," Nahum told him. "She must be in Ravens' Wood, that's her favourite place. But," he hesitated, his face creased with worry, "there's something else."

"What?"

"Kian's bones are gone, too."

"Shit! He's found us!" Gabe was furious with himself. "We underestimated him! I said we shouldn't bring those damn bones here."

"Too late now," Nahum said. "It's done. He must need them to resurrect his body. Anything else missing?"

Before Gabe could answer, the kitchen door flung open and Niel said, "The window in the back door is broken. He must have smashed his way in. I rechecked the living room, and the staff is missing."

"Fuck it!" Gabe said angrily, marching to the living room, the others right behind him. He headed to the table where the grave goods had been spread out and sighed with relief. "At least nothing seems to have been taken from here. What the hell does that staff do?"

"He's a necromancer," Nahum reminded him. "Maybe it helps him summon the dead."

"Great, just great! We've made everything so much easier for him by bringing it all here! He must have thought it was his lucky day!"

Nahum and Niel looked completely unconcerned at Gabe's outburst. They'd both seen it happen too many times before.

"On a positive note," Nahum said, pointing at the side table, "the Empusa's sword is where we left it. Shadow must be carrying the other one."

Niel gave a wry smile. "He must have no idea what that can do."

"Unless he has no fear of it," Nahum suggested.

"Hopefully that's one thing on our side," Gabe said, quickly deciding on a plan of action. He strode across the room and picked up the sword. "Shadow isn't answering her phone, so I'm going to Ravens' Wood, and I'll take this with me, just in case."

"You can't go alone," Nahum said, watching as he strapped the sword in its scabbard around his hips. "I'll come with you. For all we know, Kian is in the wood with her right now."

"What do you want me to do?" Niel asked. "I could speak to Harlan, see if he's heard from her."

"Good idea," Gabe said. "He'll know what car Kian now has. If they're not in the wood, with luck we can try and track it down."

Niel looked doubtful. "You really think he has Shadow?"

"I hope I'm wrong, but I don't think I am. If, however, she's still riding around and not answering her phone, I'll kill her." All three headed out of the house, and while Gabe and Nahum went to the car, Niel sat astride one of the bikes.

Gabe yelled, "Be careful! Don't do anything without backup."

Niel just nodded as he pulled the helmet over his head, fired up the engine, and exited the courtyard in a squeal of rubber.

"Are you sure we shouldn't take Stormfall? It might be quicker," Nahum asked, referring to the other horse as he slid into the passenger seat.

"Not once we're under the trees. Besides, I don't want to have to worry about bringing the horse back here if we have to start driving around." Gabe drove quickly, familiar now with the twisting, turning lanes around the house.

"I'll call the guys," Nahum said, pulling his phone out. "Just in case they've heard from Shadow."

But no one had heard from her. It took about ten minutes to reach the edge of the wood, and they parked on the grass verge by one of the pathways that wound beneath the trees, quickly exiting the car and jogging down the track. This area was closest to where Shadow would have entered the wood from the fields on the opposite side of the lane.

"It's not dark enough to fly," Nahum said regretfully.

"I doubt we'd see under the branches anyway," Gabe said. "They're too thick."

In the twilight, flies buzzed, and the birds were noisy as they settled for the evening. Bats were already swooping through the air. They passed a few people walking their dogs, and Gabe smiled and nodded. It wouldn't do to look too alarming at this time of night. He knew their size was scary enough for most people.

Nahum grumbled next to him. "Any idea which direction she may have gone in?"

"Into the middle. She always says that's where it's quieter, and she feels fey magic more."

They came to a junction in the path, and Gabe followed the direction that led further into the wood; it became darker with every footstep.

"I'll phone her," Nahum suggested. "We may hear it." He punched the number in and yelled out, "Shadow! Where are you?"

He waited a beat before calling again, but there was no response, and no sound of a phone either. They carried on, shouting intermittently, and Gabe became increasingly frustrated. *There was no way she'd still be here. There was nothing fun about riding a horse through a wood at night, even for a headstrong fey.*

Then they heard the crack of a branch, and the high-pitched whinnying of a horse, and Gabe headed into the undergrowth as he followed the noises, slapping away branches aggressively before finally coming into a clearing.

Kailen was tied to a tree and he was pulling and sweating, his eyes wild with panic. Gabe ran over, laying his hand on his neck and rubbing gently. "Calm down, it's okay, boy." He turned to Nahum. "Where the hell is Shadow?"

"She'd never leave Kailen willingly," Nahum said, already looking for her. He crouched to poke around in the undergrowth, and then searched in an ever-expanding circle.

"And this isn't our rope, either," Gabe said. He'd already untied Kailen, and he examined the blue nylon cord. "Someone came prepared."

"Kian must have her," Nahum announced, his voice grim. "He must have surprised her. There's no evidence of a fight, and we know she'd have fought if given a chance."

Kailen had calmed down now that Gabe was soothing him, and Gabe examined the ground. "I can't see any blood, either."

Nahum finished investigating the immediate area and joined him. "He either followed her from the house, or followed her once she arrived at the woods."

Gabe shook his head. "There's no way he could have followed her over the fields, not in Kent's body, anyway. She would have seen him."

"Let's face it—it doesn't matter how he got her. Now we just need to find her."

Gabe rubbed his hair, frustrated. "She could still be here, in another clearing."

"Unlikely. It's obvious we would have come looking for her. There's no way he'd stay here. If he's going to start a ritual to get his body back, he needs space and time."

"You're right." Gabe pulled Kailen onto the path. "You ride Kailen home, and I'll drive into town."

"And do what?"

"Hunt for Kian, what else?"

"He could be in *any* house, probably on the outskirts. There are lots of holiday cottages that would fit that bill. We need to narrow it down, Gabe. Once I've secured Kailen, I can take a bike and look, too."

"No, wait at the farmhouse. I'll call you if I need you. You never know, she could arrive at home needing help."

Nahum mounted Kailen, swinging easily up onto his back. He was natural horseman, but Kailen still fretted beneath him. "Something has certainly spooked him. He's normally much calmer than this. I'll call when I get back. Good luck, brother."

Within seconds he'd disappeared into the darkness, and Gabe ran back to the car.

𐐇 𐐇 𐐇

Harlan was in The Wayward Son, sitting at the table closest to the fire. He had Chadwick's notes spread in front of him, hoping to find out any nugget of information that could help, but he was failing miserably.

Now that he knew Kian was a necromancer, many more things made sense. For instance, Chadwick's fascination with him was evident, as he'd said to Shadow and Dan earlier—Death Magic was one of Chadwick's favoured subjects. That's why he had a wall of gruesome masks in his home, and endless books on the subject in his study.

He'd driven around White Haven that morning, hoping to see Kent's car, but he'd found nothing. And knowing what Kian had bought from the shop didn't help, either. Avery told him that the herb ingredients could be used for a number of spells.

A shadow fell across his table as a plated burger and chips was slid in front of him. He looked up at Zee and smiled. "Just in time. I'm starving."

"You're going to need it," Zee said, sitting opposite him. "I've just heard from Niel. He'll be here soon. Shadow's gone missing."

Harlan was already lifting the burger to his mouth, but he stopped, shocked. "Missing? Since when?"

He shrugged. "We're not sure. Lunch, maybe?"

Harlan went to put his burger down, as if he was going to rush out the door right then, but he realised he had no idea where to go. "Shit. Do we think it was Kian?"

"It has to be, but Niel will talk to you. I'd better get back to the bar." He nodded at the plate. "Eat up. There's nowhere to go yet."

Harlan watched him go and took a mouthful of food. The burger was delicious, and just what he needed, but he couldn't enjoy it now. He refused to believe that Shadow was dead. She must be locked away somewhere, injured maybe, but she had to be alive.

He was halfway through his meal when Niel came in. If the situation weren't so dire, Harlan would have laughed, because the room fell silent for the briefest moment as every head swivelled to look at him. He was wearing heavy work jeans and big, black boots with a worn leather jacket, and tucked under his arm was a helmet. His blond hair was shaved at the sides, and he had a decent beard and sideburns. You could just about see the tattoos edging up his neck, and more than one or two women were open-mouthed.

Niel ignored them all, looking for Zee at the bar, who pointed to Harlan. He marched across the room to him and sat, helping himself to a chip. "Harlan, we have a problem."

"So I heard."

"Gabe and Nahum are in the wood right now. Her horse is missing. Have you heard anything?"

"Nothing at all. I didn't even know until Zee told me. But, you know I'll help in any way I can."

"We need an address."

Harlan nodded as he swallowed a mouthful of burger. "I searched most of central White Haven this afternoon, but I think we both know he won't be in the centre of town."

Niel sighed, narrowing his eyes. "Give me a moment. I need a pint."

Harlan watched him head to the bar and talk to Zee, and while he waited he finished eating, his mind racing through their options. They needed help to locate Shadow, but he was reluctant to involve Maggie or Newton. It made him uncomfortable to have the police overlooking their actions, no matter how understanding Maggie was. He hoped she'd been too busy to call Newton.

Within minutes Niel returned, pocketing his phone. "Gabe has found Shadow's horse, but no Shadow. Nahum's gone to wait at the house, and Gabe is coming here to plan our next move."

"Maybe we should ask the witches," Harlan suggested, feeling like they were running out of options and time. "They must have some kind of magic that can help us. Is Alex here?"

"No, he's with Avery." Niel frowned. "I think you need a personal item for one of their finding spells. Shadow told me they've used those spells before with good results."

"I haven't got anything, but you'll have something at the farmhouse, won't you?" Harlan asked, feeling a spark of hope.

"Sure, but that means me running around to find clothing and then witches, and it all takes time!"

A thought struck Harlan. "What about her dressings? Briar was changing them! Her blood will be on them. That would work, right?" He checked his watch. "I know it's late, but she might still be at the shop—it's only a few minutes' walk away!"

"Excellent idea! Monday after work is when they make up new stock," Niel said before draining his glass and slamming it on the table. "I'll call Eli and get them to start preparing the spell."

They rose to their feet, Harlan sweeping the paperwork into his bag, and pulling it over his shoulder. "I'm coming with you."

Twenty-One

S hadow woke up on a cold stone floor, her face pressed against dust and grime. She pulled herself upright, wrestling against her bindings, and cursing all the time at her stupidity.

She could hear Gabe's voice in her head, doing his best I told you so, and even though he was nowhere close, she still wanted to yell at him. She hated that he was right. Her head felt sore, and the room spun, which wasn't helped by trying to sit up. She paused for a moment, breathing deeply in an effort to stop the nausea, and waited for her eyes to focus.

She looked down at her restraints, and found she was wrapped in thick chain that bound her arms to her body. She had very little wiggle room. The room she was imprisoned in was dimly lit and made of thick stone walls, and it smelt damp. She must be in some kind of cellar, and she still had to be in White Haven. The light came from a solitary candle on the floor in the far corner, and as her eyes adjusted to the gloom, she shivered. This was no ordinary cellar. There were markings on the floor, pentagrams and other mystical signs she didn't recognise, and what looked like an altar on the far wall, with an image of the Goddess and Herne the Hunter carved into the stone behind it. Metal lanterns hung overhead, currently unlit, and there was a general air of foreboding.

Her blood chilled. This was a room meant for sacrifice, and as far as she could tell, she was it.

And then a memory hit her that made her feel even worse. Kailen.

Why didn't she listen to Gabe and not go out alone? He would never let her forget this, if she ever got out. She stopped that line of thought straight away. She *would* get out. It was just a matter of when. The good news was that in his effort to catch her, Kian hadn't been able to prepare properly. The chain was not made of iron, and yes she might be trussed up like a chicken, but she could probably escape from it, given time.

She took a few deep breaths and concentrated. Her knife and the Empusa's sword were in the corner of the room, well out of reach, but at least they were here, and she could feel the small tin tucked inside one of the many pockets in her combat trousers. *Good.* She still had the poisonous paste.

Shadow heard footsteps coming down the stone stairs next to her, and booted feet came into view, until finally Kent, or rather Kian, stood in front of her. He was insignificant in appearance, pale with a slim build, his features regular. Nothing to catch your attention normally, but he had her attention now. He wore a long, woollen robe that fell to the floor, covering Kent's ordinary trousers and shirt, and in his hands were a bowl and a knife.

Kian watched her for a moment. "Shadow, I thought it would take more than smacking you on the head to capture you."

"It's your lucky night, then. Do you want to try again without cheating?"

Kian threw back his head and laughed. "It wasn't cheating, it was smart. Why would I fight a fey if I didn't need to?"

"What did you do to my horse?"

His smile was smug. "I inhabited it, of course. I wasn't sure I could, but it turns out that it was easier than I expected."

"If you've killed him, I will kill you, horribly and painfully."

"All chained up? I don't think so." He smiled at her, but she could see the vague expression behind Kent's gaze, the struggle that his real self was experiencing. "I've found that it is quite fun being able to dip in and out of someone.

It makes me incredibly versatile as a ghost. I can leave this unexceptionable body behind, become a horse, or slide through walls to see all sorts of interesting things, and then slip back in again. Poor old Kent doesn't know if he's coming or going. I drugged him earlier and left him sleeping in the wood, ready for when I returned."

She wanted to beg for reassurance that Kailen was all right, but she wouldn't. That would show weakness. And he clearly wasn't going to tell her anything. Bastard. "You'll need more than a chain to defeat me, Kian!"

Kian crouched, his eyes travelling over her body in a way that made Shadow's skin crawl. "I like your arrogance, but I think you'll find that I'm superior to you in every way. For example, I wouldn't have been so stupid as to bring my bones out of the tomb, and have all of my grave goods in one place, especially my staff."

Her eyes narrowed. "You've been in our house."

"You should really have better security, but like I said, I can slip through doors. It was a simple matter to make Kent break in." His face hardened. "But leaving my bones in a messy pile was very disrespectful, Shadow."

"I didn't think you'd need them again! And you're *very disrespectful* to other people's bodies, to be honest!"

"You think you're quite something, don't you, for someone so young?"

"And you have a very high opinion of yourself too, just because you're a necromancer!"

"Never underestimate the dead. They carry all sorts of secrets. They told me about this place!" He spread his hands wide. "This room has known death and sacrifice. There are channels for blood, and there's even a devil's trap! Who do you think this room belongs to?"

Shadow glanced around, looking at the signs and symbols, and realised that the only people she could possibly associate it with were the witches, but they would never use it. Doubt must have entered her eyes, because he laughed.

"Yes, I know about your witches. They have a dark history, for all of their sanctimonious positions now."

She lifted her chin defiantly. "We're not responsible for our ancestors' actions."

"Maybe not, but they benefit from their magic."

She needed to keep him occupied. While he was talking, she wasn't being sliced up. "Where are we?"

His eyes were dark pits, filled with madness and desire. "Old Haven Cemetery—under the Jackson family's mausoleum, actually. It's perfect!"

Shadow was sure that was Reuben's last name, and she tried to keep the shock out of her voice. "How did you find it?"

"Spirits told me. Because I am already one of them, I don't need to raise the dead to hear their secrets. They whisper of this place. And what better place to be for me than surrounded by the dead when I finally resurrect my body."

"You were defeated before, I'll do it again. You're not as superior as you think!"

He reached forward and slapped her, hard. "Watch your tongue, or I'll cut it out!"

Shadow inwardly seethed as her cheek stung and she felt blood trickle down her chin from a cut to the side of her mouth. She wanted to slit his smug throat, but she had to remind herself of the plan. She had to save Kent's body.

She glared at him. "Well done. Feel better now?"

"No. Enough talking. I need your blood, and that is what this bowl and the knife are for. A small incision along your vein should do it." He grinned. "You'll be pleased to know I won't need it all—at least I don't think I will."

"And then what?"

"I complete the ritual to regain my body, and leave this one behind. Although, this man's mind is surprisingly useful." He tapped Kent's head with his finger. "He has all sorts of knowledge tucked inside here."

"You haven't got your own rituals?" Shadow asked, scathingly.

"Of course I have. I'm a necromancer. Death Magic is what I do best. But Kent understands what I need, and he will do my bidding more easily."

They had been right, Shadow thought, *he had needed Kent's abilities.*

Kian edged closer. "Now, don't struggle, or I'll do more than slit your arm open."

He reached for her left arm, pulled it onto his lap, and positioned the bowl under it, before slicing the sharp blade into her skin.

The incision burned as her blood welled, but Shadow gritted her teeth, refusing to shout out. He looked at her, almost challenging her to respond, and then squeezed her arm, increasingly the blood flow. The bowl quickly filled, and when he was satisfied, he placed it carefully to the side, pulled a bandage from his pocket, and swiftly wrapped the wound.

"It wouldn't do to have you bleed all over the floor and die on me before I've finished with you."

"How long does your ritual take?"

"Longer than I'd like, but it will be worth it. Rituals require patience, something you do not have."

He stood, picking up the bowl carefully, and although she wanted to kick his legs out from under him, she didn't want to be stabbed. She knew he'd do it, and right now she had to bide her time. He was right; patience did not come naturally to her.

"Gabe will find me." Even as she said it, she doubted her words.

"That big idiot? He's more brawn than brains. By the time he has, it will just be your body that's left." He headed to the altar, where he placed her blood, and Shadow noticed that he staggered as he did so. He wasn't quite as strong as he made it seem. "I'll bring my bones now so we can begin."

𐂂 𐂂 𐂂

Gabe didn't waste time once he left the wood, driving straight into White Haven.

He was about to head to The Wayward Son when Niel phoned, telling him they were at Charming Balms Apothecary. He drove down the main street, noting how busy it still was, even though most of the shops had closed. Instead, the bars and restaurants were filling up, and this would only make life more difficult.

The one thing he wanted to do was fly—he could cover more ground that way. In daylight that was impossible, but it was dark now. He grimaced. The fortunate thing was that most people never looked up unless they had reason to. And he was as silent as a bird. He could glide above them and they'd never know, especially if he stuck to the outskirts. There was no way Kian would be in town. He'd have had to carry Shadow from the car to the site, and that would raise too many questions.

The more he thought about it, the more he wished he hadn't bothered driving at all. He should be flying right now. As soon as he pulled into a spot close to Briar's shop, he called Nahum. "Is she back yet?"

"No. She's definitely in trouble, Gabe."

"Do me a favour. Head out now. Fly around the outskirts. As long as you're high enough, you won't be spotted."

"Will do. I'll call if I see anything."

The lights were still on in Briar's shop, but they were low, just the lights under the shelves and on window displays. He knocked on the door, and within seconds Eli answered, looking grim. Gabe stepped inside, and Eli secured the door behind him, talking to him quietly.

"We're all in the back room," Eli said, nodding in the general direction. "Briar is starting the spell now, but we're not sure how effective it will be for a fey. Harlan's there, too. I can tell he's suspicious about who we are."

"It was inevitable," Gabe admitted, shaking his head, "and seeing as we're going to be working with him a lot more, he'll end up finding out, anyway. If I'm honest, I get sick of hiding it."

"Me too, but even so..." Eli's voice trailed off.

"Eli, I know that more than any of us, you want to leave our past behind, but we are who we are. You're a Nephilim, and you will always be one. I won't ask you to ever do anything you don't want to do, and," he laughed, "let's face it,

I couldn't. But Harlan will know sooner rather than later, and Maggie will tell him, too. Newton will have no qualms about informing her."

Eli nodded, exhaling heavily. "Yeah, I know you're right. Anyway, come on through."

When they entered Briar's herb room, they found Niel, Harlan, and Briar bent over a map that was spread out on the counter. Gabe had never been here before, and he admired the ordered workspace and large collection of herbs, creams, and soaps.

Harlan looked up. "Any updates?"

"Nothing. Nahum is searching the outskirts of town for anything suspicious. He'll phone me if he does."

Harlan nodded. "Good. With luck, this spell will work."

Briar was holding a piece of blood-stained bandage in her hands, her eyes dark with worry. "I'm going to start the spell now, but the map is small, and I have no idea how effective this will be for finding a non-human. I have to admit, this isn't my speciality, but it should work."

A silver bowl was on the counter in front of her, and what looked like crushed herbs were in the bottom. She placed the small portion of bandage in it, and with a snap of her fingers, the contents burst into flames. She murmured words quietly, and the smoke that rose up stilled suddenly and then started to wind over the map. It swirled above White Haven's town centre and then moved outwards until it eddied lazily above one point.

Briar frowned, confused. "It looks like Old Haven Church."

"The church on the hill?" Eli asked. "Where the Wild Hunt arrived?"

"And where Shadow arrived. It was drenched in blood magic at one point," Niel reminded them.

"But we cleansed it!" Briar said.

Harlan was already picking his bag up. "He's a necromancer; he'll be surrounded by the dead up there. We have to check it out."

"Do you think this is accurate?" Gabe asked, reluctant to run off if they were heading in the wrong direction. It could cost them valuable time.

Briar looked confident. "It didn't deviate, so I think it is."

"It's all we've got," Niel pointed out, "so let's go."

"I'll help," Briar said immediately. "But we should call Alex. He's best with spirits."

Gabe shook his head. "No. This is our mess, we'll handle it."

"But I can help! Shadow is my friend too," Briar said, annoyed.

Gabe could feel her magic rising, a surprising amount from such a petite body, but the last thing he wanted to do was risk anyone else getting hurt. And he had his pride to consider. "I know you can help, Briar, but you've helped us enough, and I thank you for it. This is our fight. And besides," he grinned, "you know we'll be okay."

She fell silent for a moment, considering him, her mouth set in a firm line. "Actually, I don't know that, but you're stubborn, just like she is."

"And just like you are. You can patch us up if things go wrong. Deal?"

"Deal," she said reluctantly.

Harlan glared at him. "I'm coming. I started this."

Gabe had half a mind to leave him behind too, but maybe Harlan should come and learn exactly who they were. "All right. You're in for a treat."

Twenty-Two

As Shadow helplessly looked on, Kian placed his remains in the corner of the room, in the area surrounded by the strange sigils carved into the floor.

He took his time, arranging the bones in careful order, his concentration absolute. When he was satisfied, he picked up the bowl of blood, dipped his fingers in it, and rubbed it into the marks. His staff was propped in the corner.

Shadow wriggled, trying to free her arms as quietly as possible. Every chink of the chain seemed loud to her ears, but Kian ignored her. If she could get a hand free, it would loosen the rest, but she knew there was no way she could get out of them quick enough to get to her weapons before he could stop her.

And then she heard another noise, a sort of groaning, or whispering.

She stopped moving, listening intently, and then felt an icy cold sweep over her. She looked up the steps and gritted her teeth in shock. A man was standing at the top, wearing old-fashioned clothing, his flesh half-rotted off his bones, his empty eye sockets staring down.

What had Kian done?

He stood motionless for a moment before turning away, but she could still see the edge of his feet, as if he was waiting for something.

Or guarding something.

Shadow took deep breaths, willing away her fear and annoyance. She was used to fighting, and wasn't scared of anything—usually—but this... At least she had the Empusa's sword, if she could get to it. She hoped the Nephilim had the other one.

A scrape of metal across stone drew her attention, and she saw Kian place the silver bowl back on the altar, and then pick up his staff. He faced the devil's trap and tapped it on the floor rhythmically as he began to chant, his voice low and guttural, and she felt an ice through her veins that had nothing to do with ghosts.

$$\text{Ϟ} \quad \text{Ϟ} \quad \text{Ϟ}$$

Harlan, Niel, Eli, and Gabe travelled to Old Haven together in Gabe's SUV, and on the way they phoned Nahum to tell him where to meet them.

By the time they pulled up on the car park, gliding in quietly with the lights off and the engine purring, Nahum was already waiting, shirtless.

Harlan blinked, thinking he was seeing things. Why the hell was Nahum shirtless on such a cold night? And where the hell was his car? None of the others looked even remotely surprised, so rather than voice his questions, he shut up.

But there was another car in the parking lot.

"Is that Kent's?" Gabe asked, already opening the door.

"Yep," Harlan confirmed. "I'll get my shotgun out of the back. I think I'm going to need the salt shells." He had insisted on grabbing it from his own car before they left.

Nahum joined them, his voice low. "He's in the mausoleum at the end of the path. I can see a light coming from the entrance, but I haven't got any closer."

Gabe looked shocked. "But that sounds like Reuben's family mausoleum."

"Any particular reason why he'd be in there?" Eli asked.

He groaned. "Reuben found it when he was searching for his family grimoire. He told me about it while we guarded the wood at Samhain. It has an altar and magical signs etched into the floor. It has a devil's trap in there too, and was a place meant for blood sacrifice—from what they could tell, anyway. He was worried the witch would find it."

Harlan's eyes widened with surprise. "Kian is very resourceful, I'll give him that. Any more secrets we should know about?"

"Let's hope not," Gabe said, pulling his shirt off, too. He threw it in the back of the SUV and freed the curved sword from its scabbard. "Can you see Shadow?"

"No, but she has to be with him," Nahum assured him. "He'll keep her close."

"That's what worries me," Gabe answered.

Nahum looked behind him to the dark mass of the church. "We have other problems, too."

"Like what?" Niel asked. He'd left his jacket in the car, and was peeling off his own t-shirt, as was Eli.

Harlan was confused. Was this turning into some bare-knuckle fight? He was pretty proud of his own physique, he kept himself fit with regular gym workouts and boxing, but these guys were enormous.

"He's raised a few bodies," Nahum said, nonchalantly.

"Like actually bodies?" Harlan asked, staring at the church and hoping something wasn't about to attack them. This night was becoming more surprising by the second.

"Yes. The undead have risen."

Harlan shuddered. "Just to be clear, are we talking about zombies here?"

Nahum looked amused. "It's a word I have become familiar with. Yes, I guess that's what they are—zombies."

"A word I have become familiar with." That was an odd thing to say, Harlan mused, but he didn't comment, instead saying, "I'm not sure what's worse, zombies or ghosts. Let's hope that if one bites me, I won't turn into one."

"You fear a zombie apocalypse? I'm familiar with that term too—I've watched the films."

"Well, then you should know that would be a very bad thing," Harlan told him.

Gabe was at the back of his SUV, and he lifted the base of the boot, revealing a collection of weapons, and Gabe, Eli, Nahum, and Niel all armed themselves.

"You wouldn't have something for me, would you?" Harlan asked, thinking a shotgun alone might not be enough.

"Help yourself."

Harlan selected a sharp machete as Gabe asked Nahum, "How many?"

He shrugged. "A small army."

Harlan placed a couple of boxes of shells in his pocket, and loaded the shotgun. "Where are they?"

"Everywhere."

"Can we bypass them?" Eli asked.

"Not really. They're in a tight ring around the tomb."

"They're dead, with decaying bodies," Niel reminded them. "This really shouldn't be a problem."

"We still need a plan," Gabe said. "Shadow is trapped with Kian. We have no idea if she's conscious or not, or even still alive. Our objective is to get in there, quickly."

Nahum glanced at Harlan, and then at Gabe, eyebrows raised. "If we attack from above, we'll have more success."

Gabe didn't hesitate. "Then that's our plan. We circle them, and pick them off one at a time. Whoever gets closest goes into the tomb first. Sound good?"

They all nodded, and then Gabe turned to Harlan. "You're about to see something we don't show to everyone. It's a sign of our business relationship, and the level of trust I have in you, and—" he shrugged, "to be honest, we haven't much choice."

He stepped back, and with a shrug of his broad, muscled shoulders, two enormous wings flexed on either side of him. Eli, Niel, and Nahum all followed suit, and despite his best intentions not to appear shocked by anything, Harlan's mouth fell open. They were, for want of a better word, magnificent.

For a second, Harlan couldn't find his voice, and then he croaked, "What are you?"

Gabe grinned as his wings lifted him off the ground. "We are Nephilim."

"And how the hell did you arrive in White Haven? No, wait, let's keep that for another time."

"You okay on the ground? We'll attack from one direction, if you can mop up the rear."

"Sure," Harlan said, trying to sound more confident than he felt.

With an effortless beat of their wings, they headed to the cemetery, and Harlan ran after them.

Shadow watched, her breath caught in her throat, as a dark figure rose within the devil's trap.

It contorted, twisted, and finally solidified into a crouched, hunched figure with a grotesque face and body. A demon. It scowled at Kian as it rasped, "Who summons me?"

Kian grinned like a petulant child. "Don't you recognise me, old friend?"

"No. You look like a milk maid, a sop with a backbone so weak I could pull it out with my finger nail."

Kian threw his head back, laughing wildly. "I've missed your wit, you old vagabond." He leaned closer to the circle, which was now bounded by a ring of flames and black, acrid smoke. "Look at me properly!"

The being scowled, and its eyes seemed to slip around its face. "Something lurks beneath your skin," it finally said.

Kian smiled. "I once summoned you to flatten a whole village, remember? They refused their king. We set an example that no one else forgot."

The demon wheezed. "Kian. I thought you had entered the shadow realm."

He straightened, his face grim. "I was afforded no such luxury. I have been between realms, trapped within my tomb, until some fool released me."

Shadow ground her teeth. Fool? She was going to enjoy killing him.

"You must need me for something," the creature said. "Revenge, death, mayhem?"

"Possibly, but for now I want my body."

"You have one."

"It's not mine. I want my own back, and you can get it."

"It is dust."

"My bones are at your feet, and you have the power to regenerate me."

"What's wrong with the one you have?" the demon persisted.

Kian was starting to get annoyed, and Shadow continued to wriggle out of her chains while he was preoccupied.

"It is weak! I am fey, and I demand my own flesh."

"It will come at a price."

"Doesn't it always? I am prepared to pay."

"With what?"

"As many sacrifices as you desire."

"You know the rules. A body for a body."

Kian shot Shadow a look of pure malice. "It's lucky I brought one with me. Will a fey do?"

"A fey will be perfect."

Kian marched over to her, put his hand under her arm and hauled her to her feet; Shadow saw her chance. She whipped her other arm free and punched him, hard, satisfied to see him stumble and fall, and then ran awkwardly to the stairs, the chains still draped around her upper body.

With every step her bonds loosened, but Kian was already on his feet, and he threw himself at her, sending them both crashing to the ground.

Kian straddled her chest, pressing his arm to her throat, but he hadn't managed to trap her arm, and she punched him again, in the ribs and the head, finally rolling over him. Kent wasn't a big man, and he wasn't used to fighting, despite Kian's spirit urging him on.

Shadow punched him again, and his head thudded off the stone, leaving him dazed. She staggered to her feet, desperately trying to shimmy out of the chains.

The room was filling with black smoke from the fire around the devil's trap. Inside the circle, Kian's bones were changing, as flesh started to knit across his skull, and the demon cackled.

A groan distracted her, and she looked up to see the corpse lumbering down the steps. With one final twist of her body, the chains fell to the floor and she launched herself at the sword in the corner, grabbing it firmly.

She turned to face the room, sword raised, trying to see through the smoke. It stung her eyes and burned her throat. The bandage that Kian had wrapped around her arm had torn loose, and blood was dripping from the wound. She ignored it; she could bandage it later.

Kent was groaning as he tried to rise to his feet. Surely Kian would leave the body now? Kent was virtually unresponsive. But, where else would he go? He needed a physical form to catch her, and she hoped that meant he wouldn't try to enter hers—after all, she was about to be sacrificed to a demon.

The corpse was now reaching his rotten hands towards her, and without hesitation, she sliced off his head, and it rolled into the corner. But the headless corpse kept coming, and beyond it were another couple of bodies at the top of the steps.

Great, just great. A demon behind her, and reanimated corpses in front.

Just as she was about to swing her sword again, something seemed to move beneath her feet. She thought it was trick of the light, but it looked as if her blood was running down the channel in the centre of the floor towards the altar at the far end. It seemed as if the channel was actually drawing her blood in from where it had pooled on the ground.

She wiped her arm against her body, trying to stop the flow, but the corpse grabbed for her and she dodged out of the way. Whatever was happening with her blood, the threat from the dead and Kian were more pressing. She lifted her sword, and swung again.

Twenty-Three

G abe circled above the graveyard, watching the scene of destruction below.

The ground had cracked open, and the graves were an explosion of earth and rotten wood, as the bodies clambered out of their resting places—because they just kept coming.

Gabe seethed. The dead deserved their rest, not to be used as tools for some mad fey's desire. The corpses were stumbling around the graveyard, and as far as armies went, this one was pretty slow. The group's preference was to avoid them, and they had tried, but as soon as they landed close to the mausoleum, the dead had attacked, clawing and trying to bite the Nephilim. They had been animated by hate and viciousness, and unfortunately when you knocked them down, they kept getting back up again.

Niel and Nahum stood in the centre of them, the swords flashing as they hacked through rotting flesh and bone, body parts flying everywhere. Eli was still flying, swooping down and striking with his blade. Harlan was at the back, and so far he seemed to be holding his own.

Gabe decided it was time to try getting into the mausoleum again and he landed softly, slicing through the corpse immediately in front of him. He picked the others up, throwing them aside. They weighed nothing, unsurprisingly.

He was making decent headway, and barrelled up the steps of the tomb, using his wings to shield himself. The door was shut, and he pushed against it. It didn't budge, but he could see smoke trickling through the gaps around the edges.

He put his shoulder to the door and hit it, hard. It still didn't budge. Gabe glared at it, and steeled himself to try again. If needed, he'd tear the tomb apart, stone by stone.

$$ \text{\textbardbl} \quad \text{\textbardbl} \quad \text{\textbardbl} $$

Harlan had seen enough zombie films in his lifetime to know what to expect, but to be honest, this was way worse.

He was covered in spatters of rotten flesh and shards of bone. And he reeked. Well, the corpses reeked. It was all completely disgusting, and he tried not to heave as he fought his way through the mess.

The good thing was that he barely had time to consider how disgusting it was, because it was all he could do to keep moving. He felt something grip his ankle, and he looked down to see a skeletal hand use him to haul itself out of the earth. He slashed at it, careful not to slice his own foot off, and then stamped down hard.

A thumping sound drew his attention, and he saw Gabe at the entrance to the tomb, his shoulder against it as he tried to break the door down.

He renewed his efforts to get to his side. If it was like this outside the tomb, what the hell was happening inside?

Suddenly, another hand pulled his leg sharply out from beneath him, and he fell flat on his back. A corpse jumped on top of him, drooling on his face, as the earth started to give way.

𝄆 𝄆 𝄆

The second corpse's head went flying across the room and landed with a thump before the altar, and a spray of Shadow's blood went with it.

She was carrying the Empusa's sword and her knife now, and she wished she'd thought to pick up her dragonium blade instead. Too late for that now. Two weapons were still better than one. In fact, now that she was finally free of the chains, she was enjoying herself. It felt good to be pitting herself against something other than the Nephilim. With them she had to hold back, but here, there was no need.

Just as she was about to behead the third corpse, Kian lifted himself out of Kent's insensible body and into the corpse in front of her. As she swung, he ducked and tackled her. They landed inches away from the devil's trap, so close that Shadow could feel the heat burning her skin.

Kian was trying to push her head into the fire with his bony hands, and deep within the empty eye sockets she could see a glowing red light. He was stronger now, much stronger, and she felt herself sliding closer to the flames.

Then she heard a loud thumping above her, and a shout.

Gabe.

With renewed enthusiasm, she angled the sword between her and Kian and thrust upward. He howled with pain and momentarily withdrew, allowing her to raise her knee up and kick him away, scrambling out from beneath him.

The corpse fell to the floor as Kian's shade left it, and now she could see him clearly, confusion on his face.

"How have you done that?" he asked.

Shadow held the sword up. "Do you like it? It's my new toy."

She darted towards him, slashing across his stomach, and saw a tear in his body that didn't bleed, but leaked light.

He staggered back again, his hand again clutching his wound. "I'm a ghost. You shouldn't be able to do that! I command the dead, not you!"

"I don't command anything, but I do have a sword from the Underworld. It's calling to you now. Do you hear it?"

The demon interrupted them, rasping his demand. "I need her now, Kian, if you want your body!"

Kian looked his partially reconstructed remains longingly, and then back at Shadow, a calculating expression crossing his face. He would have been handsome once, she could see it, behind the rage and evil that now consumed him.

She shook her head and darted at him, this time slashing across his arms. "Too late, Kian. You're going where you should have gone years ago."

He held his hands up, imploring her. "No! I am fey, like you! We could make a deal!"

She ignored him, and raising her sword once more, she lopped his spectral head from his shoulders, satisfied to see it rolling across the floor before his whole body disappeared.

Immediately, the still-twitching corpses that surrounded her stopped moving, and with an enormous scraping sound from above, she heard Gabe more clearly.

"Shadow, where are you?"

"I'm here," she yelled back, wondering where that exactly was.

Gabe appeared at the top of the steps, the Empusa's other sword in his hand, and he ran towards her, looking over her shoulder to the where the devil's trap was still encircled with flames. Without hesitation he grabbed her, and pulled her close, backing them both against the wall.

"Where's Kian?"

"Dead."

"I'm presuming he called the demon?"

"It certainly wasn't me," she said impatiently.

"How do we get rid of it?"

The demon answered. He was prowling, testing his boundary, but every time he touched it, the flames flared higher. Kian's remains were at his feet, covered in sinew and muscles. "I was promised a body. Give me flesh, and I will go."

Shadow's arm was really stinging now, and what seemed like a lot of her blood was on the floor. She swayed unsteadily, not sure if it was caused by the blood loss or the smoke. Leaving her leaning against the wall, Gabe picked up body parts, throwing them into the trap until the room was empty, but now the smell of burning flesh was worse than the smoke. He addressed the demon. "Take them, and go."

It lifted his snarling face, defiant. "I was promised the fey."

"I have the Empusa's sword," he growled. "If I throw this at you, do you think it will kill you, too?"

Without another word, the demon vanished, taking the bodies with him. With a deafening crack, the devil's trap closed, and the flames extinguished.

Gabe looked at Shadow. "Is it over?"

"I think so."

And then she noticed her blood still running towards the altar on the far wall, and with an insidious whisper, the wall slid apart, revealing another room behind it.

$$\text{\Large ⚔ ⚔ ⚔}$$

One minute Harlan and the Nephilim were fighting, and the next, the corpses around them collapsed, motionless.

The figure that was pinning Harlan to the ground went limp, and he pushed it off, scrambling away from the churned soil that threatened to swallow him whole. He straightened up, trying to catch his breath, and then joined Niel and Nahum, who were surrounded by a mass of body parts.

"She must have done it," he said. "Kian must be dead."

Nahum surveyed the scene of devastation. "Let's hope so. I'd hate to think this was merely an interlude."

Eli shouted over from where he stood on the steps to the mausoleum. "Gabe's gone in, come on!"

Black smoke drifted through the doorway, and by the time they reached the entrance, Eli was already inside, and Harlan followed him in, hearing Nahum say to Niel. "Stay here, keep watch, and shout if you need us."

The room was full of stone tombs, and Harlan was relieved to see that none of them had opened. Eli had already passed through a door to the side, and was heading down a set of steps towards the sound of Gabe's voice, and Harlan followed, Nahum right behind.

Gabe and Shadow were standing at the back of a creepy chamber, and blood was splattered across the walls and floor. The room was full of occult symbols, and smelled disgusting — the stench of charred flesh and smoke.

"Where did the smoke come from?" Harlan asked, lifting his shirt over his nose.

"A devil's trap," Gabe said, nodding at the corner. "Kian summoned a demon, but I threatened it with the Empusa's sword and it disappeared."

"And where did the blood come from? It's everywhere!"

Shadow was leaning against Gabe, and his arm was cradled around her, holding her up. She held her arm out. "It's mine. Kian cut me. I managed to spread it around while I was fighting."

"Forget the blood! What's with that?" Eli asked, pointing.

On the wall to the rear of the room behind the altar, was an illuminated circle of sigils, and swirling within it was a pool of darkness.

"Shadow's blood has opened something," Gabe said. "Reuben said this place was made for blood sacrifices."

Nahum looked at it warily, clasping his axe. "It's a portal. You must recognise it. It's opening."

"A portal to what?" Harlan asked, alarmed.

"Another realm," Nahum said, glancing at him. "The last time I saw one of those, I ended up here."

"You came out of one?" Harlan's voice rose with surprise. No wonder there wasn't any record of them existing before six months ago.

Eli swore. "No! We cannot let that open. We know the type of things that exist beyond there. What if Kian tries to come back through? We've just got rid of him!"

"Well, I don't know about you, Eli," Gabe said, annoyed, "but I have no idea how to close a bloody portal!"

And then, Harlan felt a cool wind behind him, and hairs lifted on the back of his neck. He whirled around, fearing another corpse was advancing, but he saw nothing. However, Gabe and Shadow obviously did—he could see it on their faces.

"What's happening?" he asked.

"A ghost is here," Gabe said, watching the space in front of him with narrowed eyes.

Immediately, all hands flew to their weapons, but Gabe stopped them. "Wait. I think it's here to help."

The swirling blackness was gaining momentum now, and the signs carved into the wall were bright with a fierce, orange light. It was like gazing into a black hole.

"Someone tell me what's happening!" Harlan said, frustrated.

Gabe thrust the Empusa's sword at him. "See for yourself. I think you'll recognise him."

As soon as the blade was in his hand, Harlan gasped. A man was standing in front of them, of average height and build, with short, dark hair. He had kind eyes, and there was something familiar about him. It took Harlan a few seconds, and then he had it. "He looks like Reuben."

"It's his brother, Gil," Shadow said softly. "He died last year."

"Holy shit."

Gil crossed to the portal, stopping a few feet before it, and drew shapes into the air, and Harlan saw him saying words he couldn't hear. For a few moments, nothing happened, but then the sigils faded, the blackness dissipated, and the wall became just a wall again.

Gil turned towards them, smiled sadly, and then vanished.

Harlan slumped on the steps, exhaustion hitting him like a freight train, but he'd barely sat when a groan disturbed them, and a weak voice said, "Help! Where am I? Harlan, is that you?"

Kent's crumpled body was stirring, his pale face blinking like a mole that had just emerged from his burrow.

He sighed with relief and ran over to help him to his feet. "Kent! Welcome back."

Gabe was looking grim, and dirt and blood were smeared across his face and clothes. "We need to get out of here, and seal this place forever. Come on."

Still supporting Shadow, the Nephilim headed up the steps, Harlan and Kent right behind.

"Harlan, what's going on?" Kent asked, utterly confused.

"I'll tell you later."

Harlan paused at the top of the steps for one final view of the blood-spattered chamber, and then turned his back on it resolutely. Within a few minutes they'd sealed it again, pushing the stone coffin that contained the hidden entrance back into place with a resounding click.

As soon as they were outside the mausoleum, looking at the destroyed cemetery, Harlan felt a wave of guilt wash over him. Body parts were strewn everywhere, and the smell was revolting. "We can't leave it like this. It's horrible!"

Shadow agreed. "Wow! You were busy, boys!"

"We have to put the graves back to how they were," Harlan said, appealing to the others.

"That's not possible," Gabe replied, shaking his head. "The bodies will be all mixed up. But we can at least put them back under the earth. They'll look disturbed, but with luck, nobody will notice for days." He turned to Nahum. "Can you fetch the spades from the house? We'll do it now."

Nahum watched Shadow, who despite her best efforts, was still swaying on her feet, and covered in blood. "You take Shadow home, and we'll handle this. And Harlan, take Kent back to Alex's. He needs a strong drink."

"If I'm honest, I think we all do," Harlan said wearily, still trying to prop Kent up.

Nahum laughed. "Well, ours will have to wait. Get going, Gabe."

"Thanks, Nahum." Gabe passed Harlan his car keys. "Take my car, I'll collect it tomorrow."

He extended his huge wings and picked Shadow up effortlessly. Seconds later, he was soaring over the church, nothing but a patch of darkness on the night sky.

Twenty-Four

H arlan sat across the desk from Mason, sipping his whiskey, and watching Mason's perplexed expression.

It was late afternoon, and Harlan had arrived back in London only an hour or two before. He'd dropped Kent off at his home, updated Maggie, and now all he wanted to do was sleep.

"What do you mean, they're Nephilim?" Mason asked. He still looked pale, even though it was a few days after being possessed by Kian, and although he'd been complaining of headaches, he was focused now. Like a hunter.

"Just what I said. Nephilim, who returned from the dead, last year in White Haven. They have wings. Very big wings."

"How did they get here?"

"Long story, but essentially they came through some type of portal the witches opened. There are seven of them. Shadow lives with them in a farmhouse on the outskirts of the town."

"Do they know you're telling me this?"

"Of course. They're not stupid. And frankly, I wouldn't want to cross them."

Mason downed his whiskey in one gulp and poured himself another. "This changes everything."

Harlan frowned. "It does? Why?"

"I need to contact JD."

"Well, sure, of course he needs to know."

JD was short for J D Mortlake, the head of the Orphic Guild. Harlan had no idea what the initials stood for. Most of the time he lived in his large estate outside of London, but the upper two floors of the Orphic Guild's headquarters were fully furnished for when he wanted to come to town—which was rare. Harlan had only met him a couple of times, because he was also an eccentric recluse.

Mason leaned forward, as serious as Harlan had ever seen him. "Do you know why the Guild was founded?"

"To find occult and arcane items—and to make money from them."

"That's only part of it. JD founded it because he was obsessed with many things, but especially angels—the fallen ones, the Hermetica, and the book of Enoch."

Harlan blinked. "What do you mean, he founded it? It has existed for a hundred years or more!"

"JD is an unusual man."

"I know—I've met him."

"I mean that he's more unusual than you can imagine." Mason looked nervous, and he downed his second shot of whiskey in one go. "I need to call him. He'll want to meet them."

"All of them?" Harlan asked, astonished.

"Just Gabe will do. And Shadow, too. They're valuable assets."

"I'm not sure they'd appreciate being described that way."

But Mason was already picking his phone up, undaunted. "Do me a favour, Harlan. Get them here tomorrow afternoon. They can meet JD then."

Harlan stood, knowing he was dismissed. "How do you know he'll come?'

"I just do. And make sure you come, too."

"What am I supposed to say to them?"

"Tell them it will be worth their time."

Gabe put the phone down and looked at Shadow.

"We've just received another invitation to the Orphic Guild."

She groaned. "Do we have to go?"

"Yes. Give me a chocolate."

Shadow was lying on the sofa wearing pyjamas, her arm bandaged up, and she had a box of chocolates next to her that she was steadily working her way through. The TV was on, and she was watching an old black and white film with the sound on low. She absently picked up a random chocolate and threw it at him. She aimed at his head but he caught it, shooting her an annoyed glance.

She ignored him. "But I really like lying here, and I think I could do it for days." She pointed at the screen. "That's Cary Grant and Katherine Hepburn, and they're trying to raise a lion."

"I think you'll find it's a leopard. They're very different."

"Oh. Never mind. It's funny, sort of. Actually, it's quite ridiculous, but I like it. It's called a screwball comedy."

"That's because it's not supposed to make sense. Like you."

She looked at him, outraged. "I make sense!"

Gabe started laughing, and then found he couldn't stop. "That's what you are. You're a screwball."

"Fuck off!" She threw another chocolate at him.

His hand shot out and caught it again. "That's very fruity language for a screwball!"

"I have more. El and Reuben are very effective teachers! I can throw more than a chocolate, too. You're lucky my knife isn't close by."

Gabe held his hand up in mock surrender. "Well, whether you want to or not, you're coming to London tomorrow, even if I have to carry you there. I smell intrigue."

That grabbed her attention, and she sat up. "What kind of intrigue?"

"I don't know, and neither did Harlan, actually. He said JD Mortlake wants to meet us, and that never happens."

"Who's JD Mortlake, and since when do you call him Harlan? I thought he was Beckett to you."

"I'm calling him Harlan because I've decided I like him."

"So who's JD?"

"The mysterious head of the Orphic Guild, who apparently hardly ever meets people."

"This is because of your giant wings. You've attracted attention."

"Says Little Miss Fey. You're very good at attracting attention, too."

"I know. I can't help it." She stretched luxuriously, revealing a patch of flat stomach and soft skin that gave Gabe ideas he didn't need.

"I don't believe that for one second."

She grinned at him, picked up another chocolate, and threw it so quickly that it smacked off his cheek.

Gabe refused to react. "Happy now?"

"Very. What time do we have to be there?"

"Three. So put on your most polite face, and try not to antagonise him."

The man who sat opposite Shadow looked very distinguished, and was dressed immaculately.

So this is JD Mortlake, Shadow mused, assessing him intently.

His pale grey suit fitted him perfectly, and beneath it was a crisp white shirt. His hair was a thick, luxurious mass of silver, swept back from his temples, and he had a trim white beard sweeping up his cheeks to his sideburns. But it was his eyes that were arresting. They were pale amber, like fine whiskey, and they were fixed on Gabe as if his life depended on it.

Mason, Harlan, Gabe, Shadow, and JD were sitting in leather chairs around the low table in Mason's office. It was cold today, the sky thick with clouds, and squally. Spatters of rain rattled the windows, and the lamps were on to alleviate the gloom.

There was a tray of coffee in the centre of the table, and its rich smell filled the air, but next to it was a bottle of whiskey, and JD already had a glass poured.

JD leaned forward. "You have no idea what it means to me to meet you."

Gabe smiled awkwardly. "Thank you, but I'm not entirely sure why."

"You're a Nephilim. Isn't that enough?"

"I am what I am."

"You are the son of an immortal being. Your history transcends time. You are history."

Gabe laughed. "I should be history. I cheated time."

"And you have a second chance to use your unique skills."

"I guess that's why we're working with Shadow and your Guild."

JD nodded. "Ah yes, there are more of you, I gather?"

"Seven of us," Gabe said warily.

"Astonishing. How are you finding your new world?"

"It's very different, but we've adapted."

Gabe was being polite, Shadow noted, but cagey too, and she didn't blame him. On their way to London, they had debated what JD might want of them, because he had to want something, beyond what they'd already talked about. Harlan looked just as intrigued, which made Shadow think he didn't have much of a clue about what was going on, either.

JD turned to Shadow. "And you are fey. You cloak your Otherness well."

She shrugged. "My life depends on it." He looked at her so intently that she felt uncomfortable, and her patience was waning. "Is there a purpose to this meeting?"

Her abruptness didn't bother him in the slightest, because a slow smile spread across his face, and he eased back in his chair. "Yes, there is. I formed this organisation for more than grabbing trinkets and baubles for money. I established it because I am obsessed with knowledge, and I know there are more things to discover about this world. Look at you two! You are prime examples of that. I have met fey before, but not for many years. I have most definitely never met a Nephilim.

"However, that does not answer your question. There are things I lost long ago that I want back, and I have been trying to track them down for years. I think you can help me."

Gabe shot a look at Shadow. "Do you think you could expand on that? Everything sounds very mysterious right now."

He nodded. "Of course, but I want you to know that what I am about to tell you, I don't tell many people at all, so I would appreciate your discretion."

"As long we have yours," Shadow said.

"You have. Obviously the other collectors in this organisation know about you, but you have my word it will not go further, unless you give our permission." He raised a well-groomed eyebrow. "Frankly, keeping your real nature a secret is an asset."

Shadow wasn't entirely sure she believed that, but she let it go. She could take care of herself, whatever happened, and so could the Nephilim.

Seeing their nods of agreement, JD took a deep breath and continued. "I have been alive for several centuries. Over five hundred years, to be precise. During my natural lifetime, I discovered the secret of immortality. My passion was alchemy, amongst others, and I have dedicated my life to finding other secrets. My name is John Dee. I was royal magician to Queen Elizabeth the first."

The silence was broken by Harlan's cup crashing back onto the table. "Are you kidding me? You are the John Dee?"

JD looked at Harlan with amusement. "I'm glad you've heard of me."

"Heard of you?" Harlan said, his voice strained. "You're one of the most famous men in history!"

"Not to us," Gabe murmured.

"Trust me," Harlan said. "He is." He turned back to JD. "How did you achieve this?"

"My immortality? By endless experimentation. I ensure there are no photographs of me in any era, and I mostly keep to my Mortlake Estate. Mason keeps me updated as needed, as do a few others. He is aware of my many passions, and he knows about my obsession with angels and Enochian language."

Mason nodded, watching their reactions as he sipped his whiskey.

"What's Enochian language?" Gabe asked, confused.

"The language of the angels."

Gabe's face was pinched with suspicion, and he was paler than Shadow had ever seen him. She had a sudden urge to put her hand on his arm for reassurance, but she didn't. He wouldn't appreciate it.

Gabe recovered quickly, and he shook his head. "I've never heard it called that before."

"Likely not. If I'm honest, I coined the phrase. It's an interesting story that I will share with you one day. But my contact, who I won't name right now, allowed me to compile the language of angels, and since then I've been using it to try to work out the history of the world before the Flood. Your history. Why you were made, your purpose. Our purpose. God's purpose. Hermes Trismesgistus found out these ancient truths and documented them in his Hermetica, the most important of which he inscribed on the Emerald Tablet. It is believed that it survived the Flood, and I have been searching for it ever since. I want you to help me find it."

Gabe folded his arms across his chest. "What you seek is both dangerous and foolish."

JD's eyes widened. "You've heard of it?"

"Of course I have. He was renowned in my time as a dangerous madman, but men sought the tablet even then."

"Did you ever see his Hermetica?"

"No. I'm not sure that it even exists."

Mason had been watching their exchange silently, but now he said, "I thought there were many Hermetic texts?"

JD nodded. "There are, but this particular one is supposedly the key to all. I would like you to help me find it. I also have texts you could help interpret."

Despite Gabe's obvious misgivings, Shadow felt excited. This sounded insane, a rabbit hole down which they would all run headlong and never see the sight of day again. It sounded fun.

Gabe grunted, his face impassive. "I shall consider it. I need to discuss it with my brothers."

"Of course." JD nodded. "I also have an easier request. Many years ago, I entrusted my library to my brother-in-law while I travelled. He betrayed me. When I returned, most of it had gone. Sold." He had looked composed, but now his lips were set in a thin line, and it was clear than even five centuries later, this betrayal burned deep. "I was able to recover some of them immediately, but others remained lost. Over the years, some texts have come to light, and others are now in a library for all to access. I have, with much time and effort, rebuilt it over my long life, but other books are elusive. I want you to help me find them."

"Books about what?" Shadow asked.

"Many things. Mathematics, astronomy, cryptography, ancient history, cartography, alchemy, and other subjects. All with my notes inside." JD looked slightly uncomfortable. "It may involve some underhanded methods."

Harlan poured himself a large whiskey and took a healthy gulp. "Of course, the Orphic Guild is an excellent way to find such things." He frowned at JD. "We've already found some texts. I recall a few years ago a transaction with someone overseas. I had no idea they were for you!"

"Indeed, and that's why you're here too, Harlan. You've been helpful before, and can assist Shadow and Gabe now."

Shadow grinned. "I'm in—for the right price, of course."

"You will be paid very well," JD assured her.

"Excellent. Gabe?"

Gabe drained his coffee and stood. "I agree to the search for texts, but the rest I must discuss with my brothers. I'll be in touch. Are you ready, Shadow?"

She looked at him, surprised by his abruptness, but talking about his past always rattled Gabe, so she nodded and stood, too. After some brief goodbyes, they headed for the door. As they left the room, Shadow saw all three men leaning towards each other, their faces animated, but Harlan looked up, meeting her eyes briefly, and he winked before turning away.

That night, Gabe gathered the other six Nephilim, plus Shadow, around a large bonfire in the field next to their house.

Shadow and Gabe had arrived back only an hour or two earlier, and it was close to midnight now. For once, they were all at home. It had been weeks since they'd been together, and the day before, Gabe had arranged cover for Caspian's warehouse.

Gabe's original intention had been to have a party to celebrate Kian's defeat and to burn the remainder of the grave goods, but now it had a second purpose. He wanted to discuss JD's proposal.

He looked around at his brothers and Shadow, grateful for their company. He'd been in a strange mood ever since they'd left London, and he'd brooded on JD's proposal all the way home. Shadow had let him, sensing his reticence to talk. She'd been wrapped in her own thoughts, too. As soon as he'd arrived at the farmhouse, he updated the others on the meeting, and had given them time to think.

"Let's get this over with first," Nahum said. He picked up Kian's rotting leather bag and hurled it into the fire.

Shadow picked up his wooden staff and threw that in, too. The flames turned a dark purple colour and they all stepped back, but moments later they returned to normal, and Shadow breathed a sigh of relief. "Thank Herne for that. I thought he'd left us one final surprise."

"I wouldn't put it past the old bastard," Niel said, as he threw in some of the other items.

They all followed suit, and even the jewellery was thrown in.

"Has anyone commented on the events at Old Haven cemetery yet?" Gabe asked.

"You mean outraged parishioners or the press?" Eli said. "Not yet. Let's hope it's another few days before anyone goes there. The ground should have settled by then."

Barak raised his beer to them. "Well done, guys—and girl, of course!" He nodded at Shadow before downing his drink. "I wish I'd have been there. It sounds like fun."

"I'm fey or woman, thank you," she said archly, and then she grinned at him. "Yes, it was fun. Well, beheading him was. Being trussed up in chains and almost sacrificed to a demon was not."

He grinned back. "I guess not."

Gabe smiled to see them all together, relaxed and teasing each other, but he was too anxious to wait any longer. "What about JD's proposal?"

"I admit, it's intriguing," Zee told him from where he sat in an old wooden chair, nursing his beer. "I'd like to know more about our past. Let's face it—we were pawns, most of the time."

"Most?" Ash scoffed. "More like all! I'm glad to have left it behind."

"But wouldn't you like to know about the reasons behind our making? The events that made us?" Niel asked him. "I'm with Zee. I'm curious. I also think it will be a wild goose chase, but that doesn't mean we shouldn't try."

"Horny fallen angels were the reasons behind our making," Ash said cynically.

Barak looked at Eli, amused. "Something Eli has inherited from his father!"

Eli snorted. "Yeah, like you're a monk!"

Barak threw back his head and laughed, exposing his white teeth, and not denying it, Gabe noted.

"But what if there was more to it?" Nahum suggested, ignoring them both. He poked the fire with a big stick so that the flames roared higher. "We've all heard of Hermes Trismesgistus and his fabled Emerald Tablet. It would be a hell of a search."

"It would be a bloody big tablet, too," Zee pointed out.

Barak had finally stopped laughing and he warmed his hands over the fire. "His history and teachings are layered in mystery. His written works alone—if the rumours are to be believed—are numbered in the thousands. It will be like chasing dreams."

"But who better to chase dreams than us?" Nahum asked, his eyes bright with the thrill of the chase.

"And don't forget there are JD's own lost texts to find," Shadow reminded them. "Hopefully an easier endeavour."

"And of course whatever else comes our way in all of this." Niel grinned, clearly excited by the prospect, and despite Gabe's misgivings, he felt himself warming to the idea.

Ash looked at him. "What about you?"

Gabe considered his words carefully. They were all watching him, and he knew that if he said no, they would honour his decision, but they'd probably resent him for it. Except for Shadow, who'd do what she wanted. She looked amused, but only Nahum really knew how much he'd brooded about their father, and he stood patiently waiting.

"Our past annoys me, as does our fathers' actions and the manner of our passing," he finally said. "There are things I want to know, and this seems to offer us a chance to find out. I'm not sure what good will come of it, but I think we should say yes."

"Yes!" Niel said, punching the air, and with a collective whoop, everyone else chimed in, clinking bottles in celebration.

"For what it's worth," Shadow said, raising her drink to Gabe, "I think you've made the right choice."

"Then let's fly to celebrate!" Gabe said recklessly, eager to shed the trappings of his human body.

Within seconds, the beer had been drained, the empty bottles thrown in the fire, and the Nephilim cast off their shirts and flew into the night, leaving Gabe standing next to Shadow. She looked up at them swooping across the fields, a faint smile on her lips.

"Come here," Gabe said to her softly, not wanting to fly by himself, and sensing that she didn't want to be left alone, either. They were both lonely enough sometimes.

Without hesitation, Shadow stepped into his arms, and he soared into the sky.

$$\text{\Large ⚲ ⚲ ⚲}$$

Thanks for reading *Spirit of the Fallen*. Please make an author happy and leave a review on the retailer of your choice.

Shadow's Edge, White Haven Hunters #2, is on sale now! You can order it here at www.happenstancebookshop.com.

This book is a spin-off of my White Haven Witches series. The first book is called Buried Magic, and you can buy it hereat www.happenstanceboo kshop.com.

Newsletter

If you enjoyed this book and would like to read more of my stories, please subscribe to my newsletter at https://www.subscribepage.com/tjgreensn ewsletter. You will get two free short stories, Excalibur Rises and Jack's Encounter, and will also receive free character sheets for all of the main White Haven witches.

By staying on my mailing list you'll receive free excerpts of my new books, as well as short stories, news of giveaways, and a chance to join my launch team. I'll also be sharing information about other books in this genre you might enjoy.

Ream

I have started my own subscription service called Happenstance Book Club. I know what you're thinking! What is Ream? It's a bit like Patreon, which you may be more familiar with, and it allows you to support me and read my books before anyone else.

There is a monthly fee for this, and a few different tiers, so you can choose what tier suits you. All tiers come with plenty of other bonuses, including merchandise, but the one thing common to all is that you can read my latest books while I'm writing them – so they're a rough draft. I will post a few chapters each week, and you can read them at your leisure, as well as comment in them. You can also choose to be a follower for free.

You can comment on my books, chat about spoilers, and be part of a community. I will also post polls, character art, share rituals and spells, share the background to the myths and legends in my books, and some of my earlier books are available to read for free.

Interested? Head to Happenstance Book Club at https://reamstories.com/happenstancebookclub

Happenstance Book Shop

I also now have a fabulous online shop called Happenstance Books where you can buy eBooks, audiobooks, and paperbacks, many bundled up at great prices, as well as fabulous merchandise. I know that you'll love it! Check it out here: https://happenstancebookshop.com/

Substack

I now write over on Substack, and my page is called Where the Witches Gather. I'd love to see you there. Substack has a wonderful community of witchy writing and seasonal celebrations. You can find me here: https://substack.com/@wherethewitchesgather

YouTube

If you love audiobooks, you can listen for free on YouTube, as I have uploaded all of my audiobooks there. Please subscribe if you do. Thank you. https://www.youtube.com/@tjgreenauthor

Read on for a list of my other books.

Author's Note

Thanks for reading *Spirit of the Fallen*, the first book in the White Haven Hunters series. I love Shadow, my stranded fey, and the seven Nephilim, and couldn't wait to write their stories. I'm also very fond of Harlan and the Orphic Guild. I know that together there'll be many opportunities for fun!

Shadow comes from the Otherworld of my series Rise of the King, about King Arthur. I thought that seeing as I had another fully realised Otherworld, it made sense to link her to that one. And I love crossovers and connected universes.

I'm intrigued by alchemy. It's such a huge, diverse, and ancient subject that it seemed to fit perfectly with the Nephilim. I'm not entirely sure where we'll end up going, but I'm looking forward to finding out. I am planning on a few short story prequels coming soon—for Shadow certainly, and hopefully Harlan and Gabe, too.

Thanks to my fabulous cover designer, Fiona Jayde Media, and to Missed Period Editing.

I owe a big thanks to Jason, my partner, who has been incredibly supportive throughout my career, and is a beta reader. Thanks also to Terri and my mother, my other two beta readers. You're all awesome.

Finally, thank you to my launch team, who give valuable feedback on typos and are happy to review on release. It's lovely to hear from them—you know who you are! You're amazing! I also love hearing from all of my readers, so I welcome you to get in touch.

If you'd like to read a bit more background on my stories, please head to my website – https://happenstancebookshop.com/- where I blog about the books I've read and the research I've done. I have another series set in Cornwall about witches, called White Haven Witches, so if you love myths and magic, you'll love that, too. It's an adult series, not YA.

If you'd like to read more of my writing, please join my mailing list at http s://www.subscribepage.com/tjgreensnewsletter. You can get a free short story called Jack's Encounter, describing how Jack met Fahey—a longer version of the prologue in the Call of the King—by subscribing to my newsletter. You'll also get a FREE copy, of Excalibur Rises a short story prequel. Additionally, you will receive free character sheets on all of my main characters in White Haven Witches—exclusive to my email list!

By staying on my mailing list, you'll receive free excerpts of my new books, as well as short stories and news of giveaways. I'll also be sharing information about other books in this genre you might enjoy. Finally, I welcome you to join my readers' group for even more great content, called TJ's Inner Circle, on Facebook. Please answer the questions to join! https://www.facebook.com/gr oups/tjsinnercircle

About the Author

I was born in England, in the Black Country, but moved to New Zealand in 2006. I lived near Wellington with my partner Jase, and my cats Sacha and Leia. However, in April 2022 we moved again! Yes, I like making my life complicated... I'm now living in the Algarve in Portugal, and loving the fabulous weather and people. When I'm not busy writing I read lots, indulge in gardening and shopping, and I love yoga.

Confession time! I'm a Star Trek geek—old and new—and love urban fantasy and detective shows. My secret passion is Columbo! My favourite Star Trek film is The Wrath of Khan, the original! Other top films for me are Predator, the original, and Aliens.

In a previous life, I was a singer in a band, and used to do some acting with a theatre company. On occasion, a few friends and I like to make short films, which begs the question, where are the book trailers? I'm thinking on it...

For more on me, check out a couple of my blog posts. I'm an old grunge queen, so you can read about that on my website.

Why magic and mystery?

I've always loved the weird, the wonderful, and the inexplicable. My favourite stories are those of magic and mystery, set on the edges of the known, particularly tales of folklore, faerie, and legend—all the narratives that try to explain our reality.

The King Arthur stories are fascinating because they sit between reality and myth. They encompass real life concerns, but also cross boundaries with the world of faerie—or the Otherworld, as I call it. There are green knights, witches, wizards, and dragons, and that's what I find particularly fascinating. They're stories that have intrigued people for generations, and like many others, I'm adding my own interpretation.

I also love witches and magic, hence my additional series set in beautiful Cornwall. There are witches, missing grimoires, supernatural threats, and ghosts, and as the series progresses, even weirder stuff happens.

Have a poke around in my blog posts, and you'll find all sorts of articles about my series and my characters.

If you'd like to follow me on social media, you'll find me here:

f facebook.com/tjgreenauthor/

P pinterest.pt/tjgreenauthor/

♪ tiktok.com/@tjgreenauthor

▶ youtube.com/@tjgreenauthor

g goodreads.com/author/show/15099365.T_J_Green

O instagram.com/tjgreenauthor/

BB bookbub.com/authors/tj-green

|● https://reamstories.com/happenstancebookclub

Other Books by TJ Green

Undying Magic #5
Crossroads Magic #6
Crown of Magic #7
Vengeful Magic #8
Chaos Magic #9
Stormcrossed Magic #10
Wyrd Magic #11
Midwinter Magic #12
Sacred Magic #13
White Haven and the Lord of Misrule Yuletide Novella

* * *

White Haven Hunters
The action-packed spin-off featuring Shadow and the Nephilim.
Spirit of the Fallen #1
Shadow's Edge #2
Dark Star #3
Hunter's Dawn #4
Midnight Fire #5
Immortal Dusk #6
Brotherhood of the Fallen #7

* * *

Storm Moon Shifters
Paranormal Mysteries set around the wolf shifter pack, Storm Moon.
Storm Moon Rising #1
Dark Heart #2

Moonfell Witches
The First Yule Novella
Triple Moon: Honey Gold and Wild #1

Printed in Great Britain
by Amazon